THE HARPY 2: EVOLUTION

JULIE HUTCHINGS

inked entertainment

Vampires of Fate

Running Home (Book 1)

Running Away (Book 2)

Crawling Back (Book 3, coming 2021)

The Harpy Series

The Harpy (Book 1)

The Harpy: Evolution (Book 2)

Book 3 (coming 2022)

Five Poisons

The Wind Between Worlds (Book 1, coming 2021)

This one is for Timmy
I believe in evolution

*W*hiskey and flashbacks were my chicken and egg scenario: I didn't know which came first. I did know which one I liked better.

Robbie found me on the kitchen floor this time. Ginormous vulture-clawed feet scratching the hell out of the cabinets while I flailed in that waking-up-from-a-falling-dream state. My body morphed in and out of the Harpy second to second: dirty white wings bursting out of the back of my arms, making minced hamburger meat of the skin and healing haphazardly over and over, splattering blood across the doomed cabinets. Feathers forced themselves out of my thighs, jabbed through my shorts, ripping the seams as the lower half of my body became the bird; my calves scaled over, went back to normal in rapid shifts. I screamed and screamed—more from the 3D images of the man who abused me, Carl Painter, than from the agony of the quick-change. He'd dismembered me deeper than any Harpy seizure could.

I know all this because Robbie couldn't get anywhere near me to help. So he caught it all on his phone. Even over the noise of my screaming, the smashing of the cabinets, I could hear him crying and begging me to remember where I was. Who I was.

The change shuddered to a halt, caught in the act, when the three loud bangs on our apartment door forced the Harpy to crawl back inside me. The morphing stopped.

"Shhhhit," Robbie said.

I tried to clamber up, waiting for the door to open, mere feet away from me in our cookie-cutter apartment. *I can't hide this,* I thought, smeared in blood, beer bottle smashed on the floor, cabinets trashed, stray feathers the size of broom handles scattered everywhere like a dirty white turkey exploded.

Robbie looked at me helplessly and I scrambled around, grabbing all the feathers. More banging on the door.

"Open up! Police!"

Fuck.

"One second!" Robbie called out. But I couldn't clean this up fast enough. Gulping, Robbie opened the door a crack. Two cops stood there, shoved the door open wider. And there I was.

Me. A half-dressed disaster of blood, rat's nest platinum hair, panting like I'd run from a murder scene.

Not this time, I joked to myself.

"Rob, hey," the rookie officer in the back said.

"Hey, Officer Sampson," Robbie said, defeated already. Not me, though.

"We haven't been on this call together before," Officer Tremblay said to the rookie, nodding at Robbie.

"No sir," Sampson said. "But Robbie works at the boarding house. Went there to pick up that kid for robbery about a month ago, remember?"

Tremblay grunted. "We got the call again, son," he said in this warm, Lipton Cup-a-Soup voice—soothing enough to calm the nerves but thin enough to show the comfort would be over soon. Warming us up. Well, warm Robbie up. He knew me too well to get warm.

"Um…" Robbie cleared his throat, spoke up. "My girl-friend suffers PTSD, sir, and she's…well, she's been drinking, and it…" he trailed off. The shame in his voice, the way his shoulders slumped, his hands in his pockets, told me more than I wanted to know.

He'd given up on me.

Tremblay craned his neck over Robbie's head, pushing the door open more, and saw me. "Oh, Jesus. Blake, what the hell."

I laughed a little, trying to charm him in that Harley Quinn way that didn't work on normals. "Officer Tremblay, what a surprise. Yeah, rough night," I said, nodding at the broken beer bottle on the floor, the puddle mixing with blood, "but I'm keeping it inside, you know?"

"See that you do," he grumbled. "I don't want to hear another complaint about this apartment. Get yourself cleaned up, Charity, and keep it down. You sure you're all right? I see blood." He tilted his head to talk into his radio, but I blurted out a string of *don'ts* before he said anything. He rolled his eyes, giving in to his kinder side. "You shouldn't be drinking with that mental condition of yours."

The Harley Quinn laugh again. "Well, what kind of mental patient would I be if I didn't do the wrong thing, am I right?"

Nobody laughed but me. Robbie's head hung lower, if that was possible, but my canary chirped at me from the other room in solidarity.

The cops left, and I took a desperately-needed shower. Robbie threw out my shredded clothes again and cleaned up the floor while I was in there.

"I would have done that, Rob. I just needed to get clean, you know?"

"Yeah, me too, so I did it."

He was making me nervous—a sucky feeling I was unaccustomed to because one has to actually give a shit about what a person thinks or feels in order to be uncomfortable about it. Left me out of the running. Until Robbie.

Leaning on the wall, happy to feel the solid fake wood against my bare arm in the tanktop, I eased into my fortieth apology that week. "I don't mean to have...episodes...like that. I'm sorry about the cops, and I fucked up your cabinets..."

His face poured out offense as he turned to me from the couch. "I don't care about *our* cabinets, Charity. You're not having these episodes *at* me, you're not doing anything except suffering. I'm sorry. I shouldn't be angry about you going through this, it doesn't make sense." He dropped his head into his hands and I went to him, welcoming the feeling of comforting him instead of the other way around.

"You're pissed off because I'm still the Harpy. It's not like it used to be, it's not every night. You know where I go when I disappear now. I'm trying to be finished with it, but it's...it's a drug. You get that. You wanted to be enough to take the Harpy away, and I'm sorry that you... I have a reason to be *me* as the Harpy, you know? I mean, obviously you don't but I can't just like, live for someone else, not even you. I need a reason. This, me as just me, I've got no *reason.* It's not your fault."

He raised his head, that goddamn beautifully expressive face telling me everything. He may have been Communicator Extraordinaire but his face always told me more. "I didn't think you needed *fixing*, Charity, never did. And I don't blame myself for you still being the Harpy." There it was. The resentment. Expected that sooner rather than later.

"No, you *blame* me."

"I don't need to blame anyone! You are who you are, I just wish—"

"I get it. You wish I wasn't who I am."

"Oh, cut it out, Charity."

"No, *you* cut it out! Stop being such a martyr, with the 'loving me for who I am' crap, because that's all it is—crap. I'm not one of your boarding house fixer upper kids, I'm not your project, I'm my own. I'm working on myself when I have the fucking patience, but my patience runs real thin when I've got you motivationally speaking at me all the goddamn time."

Then I saw what part of me had been looking for all along, really--for him to just prove that he was like everyone else, because then I'd have been right to never completely trust him or anyone.

The breaking point. The moment when he gave up, like everyone did. Then I'd be right. Nobody sticks around and everyone wants to hurt someone.

Robbie jumped to his feet, eyes burning with fury, teeth gritted, hands in his hair the cute way he usually did when he was nervous, this time minus the cute. "I need to get out of here," he hissed. And he slammed out the door. The sight of the back of his hair, the bottoms of his jeans sloppily hiked up over his combat boots, flannel shirt trailing, seeing him walk away, gave that beast inside the final nudge to come out.

It wasn't an easy transformation anymore. Bodily proof of my fractured mind, I guess. Where I'd once thrown my head back in triumph when the scaly skin tore over mine, replacing my nicely-shaven legs with gross bird ones, now I buckled in pain. I grunted when the talons slowly, torturously, eased out of my toenails, shredding them in half. It blotted out the agony when it happened to my hands.

Second by second, more and more changes replaced me

with the Harpy, until the big show: Enormous white feathers sliced their way through the backs of my arms, filthy from the second they erupted, every time. Dirt just came from within me.

They crashed into both walls, knocking down some signed Star Wars thing of Robbie's, the ultimate show of disrespect. I winced. As fucked up as I was, guilt only made me *more* eager to ruin everything. Careful not to screech, lest my cop buddies were summoned again, I gnashed my teeth, threw my head back, and forced the final spray of feathers from my skull—a new addition since my not-so-long-awaited return to Harpydom. The plume split my wild platinum crimpy hair-splosion down the center in a pretty unflattering way. Not that my victim would care about my hair anyway, with my tits free as a bird themselves, and me, you know, being a humongous half-vulture waiting to eviscerate them.

"I don't give a shit how ugly he thinks I am," I said to myself. But it wasn't true. I gave plenty of shits, and he wouldn't ever find me ugly. He'd seen me at my worst and my best; they weren't so different.

I tore out of the apartment, long since versed in the ways of getting out unseen faster rather than quieter. Hell, life's too short and hard to go through it quietly. Being quiet never got me anywhere.

It never got Carl Painter off me. Being quiet couldn't save his daughter from him either. Can't afford to be quiet when you're the small one; it was always the youngest girls I freed from the clutches of their abusers, rapists, narcissistic bastards who tore them down, that I remembered longest. That I made a point to remember.

Rose.

Her name came to me like the whistling of wind through the trees as I soared just above everyone, seen by no one—a trick granted by the Queen in her dying moments, trying to bargain with me like some rancid fairy godmother. She said, "Remember that Charity Blake is invisible. But the Harpy is not. You need guidance, child, let me do that for you."

I didn't have to say no. Death was her answer.

I mostly forgot I could make myself invisible—like when I rushed out of Robbie's—my—apartment. Flying close to the muggles wandering around outside was a new habit, and sometimes I forgot to put the effort into going invisible then, too.

Still felt like nobody saw me, even when they freaked out to their friend or husband or dog walking with them. I'd be long gone. Disappearing and being invisible were not the same thing; one feels better than the other.

I was suddenly transfixed by the glow of red that meant I'd found my mark. I landed with a *thud* in the dark in front of an even darker concrete place. The grass was up to my thighs, no cars or lights outside. No lights at all, actually. No windows this side. "I do love an abandoned building. But what the fuck am I here for?" I muttered.

I'd flown until the buildings became sparse, the streets basically made of potholes, no cop cars, more trash than people. Nothing to offer here, not even the trifecta of liquor store, 7-11, and Western Union. In this part of the city, where weeds were the vegetation and factories were ghost towns, where the bridges crumbled into murky rivers, one more concrete building didn't raise a flag. Whether or not anyone cared to find it.

A chill ran up my spine and ruffled my feathers.

Rose. She's here.

Like puppet strings attached to my heart, a tug on my chest yanked the organ toward the building, dragging me with it. I grimaced at the nausea it caused.

Who the fuck is Rose *anyway?* The name had invaded my brain, and worse, my *heart,* forcing itself in.

I crept closer, intrigued, looking for a door, pissed at the number of ticks I was definitely picking up. Halfway around the building I found it, a rectangle with no handle blended right into the wall. To the left of the door I spotted a glint that turned out to be the world's smallest plaque with gold writing that said FACILITY. Red button beside it. Holy shit did I want to press that button but I was certain they'd know I wasn't a singing telegram.

They who? There're no cars anywhere around. And still no windows.

My stomach flopped over and over with this invasive *need,* some knowledge working through me that I had to get into that building, that it wasn't as abandoned as I thought, that *she* was in there. I'd never been here before, I would have remembered.

Right?

The Facility wasn't a place people visited. Everyone in there was hidden away. And for a reason. My heart knew it, my *bones* told me. As if I'd been taken apart inside and replaced with a need for her.

Try as I might to not care that this Rose was in there? I did.

She'd been stashed here, pocketed, gotten rid of. Someone would rather have an empty spot where Rose was rather than Rose herself.

Why?

Anyone worth hiding was powerful. The kind of powerful I wanted on my side. In this fuckshow of a life, I always wanted the strong on my side if anyone was ever on my side. Sometimes it felt like the air itself was out to get me, and I always knew, every minute, that a fight was coming.

I started to walk away, knowing that if I'd really intended

to leave, I would just fly off into the night. There was no death glow here now that I'd landed, and some girl, some woman somewhere was being destroyed from the inside out *right now*, and I could help her *right now*.

But a knowing had been placed inside my mind. Like building blocks taken down and built into something else, new information formed in my brain that hadn't been there before. Somehow, I knew that girl inside the anonymous block of dull concrete was being destroyed too, slowly. And something about her made her a threat.

A threat who could be turned into a weapon against those who needed destroying. If I hadn't known better, if it weren't impossible, I knew just who'd be on the hunt for a fresh-faced weapon.

ROSE

$\mathcal{M}$y mother told me over and over how she should have named me Hope. That "Rose" turned out to be too ordinary for me.

It wasn't until later that I stopped smiling when she said it. I was a *Rose*. Beautiful for a short time. Then dead.

That's all I ever really was for her. A rosy smile, a rosy disposition. When I was six, seven, eight years old, I was only the little forest fairy with freckles and just-wild-enough honey-colored hair. My careless way of flopping into the grass, giggling like it was telling me jokes, made even the stiffest adult loosen up to see. They'd fawn from the kitchen window, enjoying a cup of coffee with my mother while I was lying in the grass in a homemade sundress. My mother never bothered to ask me not to ruin them—I wouldn't. I'd climb trees in them, play in the dirt in them, and my sweet pink personality covered up the mud spots. A mini Mother Nature. A princess in a princess-free world.

The adults never knew that I was constantly feeling for every blade beneath my fingertips, feeling for the seed, for how it grew, how it came to be. While they thought I mindlessly watched the clouds, blowing bubbles of Fruit Stripe gum, I was letting the ants race over my fingers as they worked, feeling the sequence, noting how they avoided the same mole on my index finger, how there was never any part of their chain out of order. I'd carefully roll to the side and watch them gather food, build the ant hill, *seeing* every second. Never a moment passed that I wasn't learning, reading the world, watching, pulling the layers apart to understand more clearly than the surface. Nothing got past me.

"The sun followed you in," my mother said, a smile lighting up her eyes more than the glow from the kitchen window. Every dust mote glittered in her presence, the old flowered curtains reached for her while they blew in the breeze. The dishes didn't *clank* so much as make tinkling music for her as she washed them. Strawberry-blonde hair framed her face, wisps tickling her nose. Her eyes were cornflower blue. I'll never forget that: cornflower blue, just like the Crayola crayon.

But when she looked at me, all that shabby chic beauty surrounding her went unnoticed. The only light in the room was me.

Drying her hands, she came to kneel in front of me so our eyes were level. I loved how she made me her equal when I forever felt as though the whole world was bigger than me.

Maybe that's why I started to take it apart.

She put her damp hands on my shoulders, smile reaching those cornflower eyes. "Soup for lunch, then we go down to the Point. See if any seals are hanging around. How's that sound?" Her teeth glinted. Smooth enamel, a hard layer under that like the crust of the earth, veins like waterways, miniature tree roots, bone…

"Rosie?"

"That sounds nice, Mommy," I blurted. Our cottage was a

short walk away from White Horse Beach, and Manomet Point was a quick drive in the old Buick. The world fell off a cliff there to the ocean, the tiniest fence warning folks off. But we'd stand, teetering as close as we dared, the cold sea air spraying our faces, to watch the seals bob up and down or lounge on the rocks below, the sun setting over the water.

People bustled in and out of the fish shop behind us, getting their fresh-off-the-boat lobster and haddock and clams to bring home for dinner. And Mommy would hold my hand, feeling it all with me. I didn't know then that she couldn't see the layers that I did: the slight differences in wavelength from crest to crest. The grains of sand and plant and rock rolling underneath and within. The miniscule feet of the sea stars. The orbs of gases inside the salt. It never ended. I felt how it never ended.

I'd been seven. And I saw everything.

"What do you see down there?" my mother asked, as if reading my mind. She always could see inside my heart. It wasn't until later that she saw inside my mind, too. That I was constantly *dissecting*.

"I see the world," I said. "How big it is and how much is inside it."

She dropped to her knees again. Always on her knees with me. This time she was so serious that it frightened me— I knew nothing of fear back then.

"That's right, Rosie," she said hurriedly. "The world is *so* big, and there's so much more in it than you'll ever know. *Keep looking.* There's always more to see, baby. Always. Don't ever let anyone tell you there's an end in sight."

I searched her eyes, and it was the one time that I didn't understand what was behind them.

"I'm not quite sure *what* is distracting Rose, Mrs—"

"Miss. Miss Preston."

"Miss Preston," the teacher said slowly, apologetically. My mother hated being mistaken for a married woman. She was a totem of independence and nothing less.

"She understands the work. I don't understand why that isn't enough for you, *Mrs.* Waters."

I watched from a red plastic chair in the big empty classroom as my mother and my second-grade teacher argued in the hallway. The room both bored and overstimulated me. So many colors, all so clear and with hard edges. The alphabet painted over the blackboard in bright red. *Oil, water, four different colors made of three different colors held together with a different substance—*

"—not backward!"

"I never said the child was backward, ma'am."

I could feel my mother's teeth grinding from yards away.

"Not only is Rose not backward, she's a damn sight smarter than her teacher. It's hardly a child's problem if you can't hold her attention." My mother's pink sundress shook against her calves in her anger. Such a soft thing to wear for a woman who could be so fierce. She gathered herself together, stood straighter, sensing my attention to her in the void of space and moments. In a lowered voice, she said, "Rose is an exceptional child. If you claim she's—what was the word, vacant?—in class, then it should be all the more impressive that she understands the work so well. Wouldn't you agree, Mrs. Waters?"

Totem of independence.

My teacher cast down her eyes, a submissive movement masked by turning her heel to check her shoe for something that wasn't there. She lifted her head again, and took a deep breath. "I would agree, Miss Preston. I would.

Perhaps I should have thought this meeting through a bit more. It's just…it's just that I wish I could relate to Rose more. She feels so far away in class, I fear that we'll lose her before she can take her education seriously. I hope you understand."

My mother smiled and relaxed her shoulders. She put a hand on the older shoulder in the cheap cotton blouse. Mrs. Waters pushed her glasses up by the nosepiece. She was about to cry; her jaw clenched, the muscles in her throat tensed, her stomach caved just a little as she tried to hold the discomfort in. But my mother's reassuring side was as powerful as her ferocious side, and the gray-haired teacher let out a sigh before she knew what happened.

"Thank you for caring about her, Mrs. Waters. The love of one teacher can do such powerful things." My mother spoke low, soothingly. Clearly victorious and closed to any challenges.

"Thank you for your time, Miss Preston," Mrs. Waters murmured. She stood in the hallway and didn't move until my mother and I were walking through the bright blue door.

⁓

"Where's your dad?"

The impish blonde girl in my class, Amelia, kept her eyes on the dirt as we dug in with sticks. She twisted her head, found a different angle to come at the hole with. We didn't know what we were digging for, we were just digging.

"I don't have one."

She pursed her lips and pushed harder at a particularly hard patch. "Of course you have one. Everyone has one."

"Not me."

She gripped the stick with both hands and stabbed the

dirt fast. "Maybe he ran away. Some daddies run away because they don't like kids."

"Maybe," I said quietly.

Finally she looked up, piercing blue eyes on mine in a way that only children could exhibit. A heartless sort of gaze. "Maybe your daddy didn't like you so he ran away."

I dropped my chin to my chest, blinked at the dry, hard-packed dirt, the pebbles in it, the sediment, the layers below the surface, the worms far below where it was cooler, softer, the heat as the earth grew deeper, the organisms harder to recognize but all made of the same bouncing bubbles of life under their skin, rushing blood…

"Where do you think your daddy is?"

I focused on the surface of her, the dirt-streaked, pale cheeks, the lines in her lips, the pink flesh in the corners of her eyes, the frayed ends of her white-blonde hair, dry at the scalp like the dirt in my hands. I shrugged.

I wished, many years later, that I'd said so many things, but I couldn't think of them then. I can barely think of them now.

~

*M*anomet was a town where the biggest thing was the ocean, with little sandy, cracked-pavement roads leading to the beach, and cottages meant only for stumbling to bed, exhausted from swimming, barbecuing, fireworks displays and the heat of the sun. But for some of us the patchy lawns separated only by berry bushes or decorative white fences, chipped and weathered by the salt air, was home. In a world where I could see every miniscule detail of every single living or inanimate thing, down to their very molecules, our little cottage and the single-entity neighborhood of sea grass and brush pines punctuated with the *shush shush shush* sound of the ocean, gave me some simplicity.

I grew more aware every day that my mind was too big for such a place.

It wasn't only the kids at the bus stop that wondered where my father was. Their parents did, too. And Max, the owner of the arcade down the street where I'd buy my Fruit Stripe gum and play Asteroids. And the waitress at the diner across the street from that. And my teachers. And the principal. Everyone wondered where he was. Everyone but me.

"Rose never asks questions?" I overheard the elderly neighbor, Annie, say to my mother one sunny afternoon. She could speak safely from her joining back yard, separated from us only by a single tree surrounded in pansies. My mother smiled at her from the chicken-wire enclosed garden where she picked pea pods. I, of course, was in the grass. But I could hear them.

"She doesn't. And I don't know that I'd answer them if she did, really," my mother said.

"And you—" Annie tentatively began.

"I don't ask questions either," my mother said gently.

That was enough for me to know.

~

"You're staring, Mommy."

"What? Oh! I guess I was, huh?" She breathed in deeply, somehow freshening the air for both of us, and sat back in the tattered armchair. It didn't even creak under her weight, though it had been with us for as long as I remembered. I could see the springs, rusted and crooked. The cushion stuffing congealed in spots, thin and threadbare in others. The seams tearing in dozens of places.

"Who's staring now?" Mommy said softly and laughed that tinkling laugh of hers.

"Me!" I ran and jumped onto her and tickled her sides, our hair wrapping around us both until the afternoon light was hidden, the smell of tea and the ocean momentarily taken away.

When we'd both tired out, she sat me up on her lap, and looked deeply into my eyes. That never stopped. While I watched the other kids wave their parents goodbye at the bus stop, or run away from the calls to slow down and wait, my mother and I were always side-by-side. Present together.

This time was different.

She stroked my long hair, pushed it behind my ear. "What are you thinking when you stare like that, baby?"

"I don't know." Now *that* was what a child would say. I surprised myself.

The brightness left her eyes, and her lips turned down a little. It was the first time I'd ever seen her look at me with anything but joy. I began to put my head down, saddened by whatever I'd done to make her feel this way... But I stopped myself. Peered deep into her eyes.

At the thin film that covered them.

The different parts on the outside, but more so the connecting parts on the inside.

The vessels, pumping blood through.

The great nerve in the back that ran the whole show, kept the other parts moving.

It went further.

Into the brain.

"Right there. Right there, what are you doing, Rose?" my mother snapped.

"I... I..."

She took my chin in her hand. "Rose, you just...*leave*, you just check out and you're somewhere else. Somewhere...

stronger. What are you thinking? What were you thinking just now?"

The tears came without my permission. Crying didn't come easily to me, it never had. I couldn't understand why tears connected to feelings, why the body would produce such a thing when the heart ached. And I didn't understand them then.

I told her what I saw in her eyes, and in the grass, and under the dirt. I told her about how buildings are put together, how I saw the ingredients in her baking working together to build something new. I told her I could see how everything was made, how it survived. And when she asked me the only question she could—"*How?*"—I told her the only answer there was.

"Because I know how to take it all apart."

~

The TV never stopped flickering.

In the eighties, TVs did that. I sat on the brown flowered sofa, morning light warming my toes, eating my Lucky Charms, and the TV flickered, ruining *The Smurfs* for me.

I loved quiet Saturday mornings. Mommy always slept later on Saturday. I loved her being home for me all the time: hot breakfasts before school; meeting me at the bus stop every day, rain or shine; every school event; the park on warm days, the beach whether it was cold or warm. But I relished the silence of Saturday morning when I could hear every little thing everywhere.

The TV was ruining it.

Slamming my cereal bowl on the coffee table, I stomped to the TV, unplugged it, took a deep breath, and *looked*. I looked the way only I could, mentally unwiring it, envisioning every circuit, every spark, every connection that made it what it was. My own brain buzzed, buzzed, filling the space that the flickering had taken up, and then it stopped. When I'd seen every layer, it went quiet.

Then I went to work. First, I took the TV apart, laying out the switchboard with its wires and dials so I could put my hands on what I'd seen.

When Mommy got up it was all back together. She was so happy the TV never flickered again.

After that I searched for things to fix, to build. Bigger and bigger things, more complex things. Once I'd fixed the toaster, my mother went to the basement to find some other old broken things to entertain me. Going through a cassette player, walkie talkies, and an old lamp. Mommy and I went to the thrift store to find more things for me to take apart. My favorite was a Tomy robot that could actually play cassette tapes and carry my crayons to me at night when I was too tired from building all day. It wasn't long before I started picking out spare parts to build new things with. Building is another way of taking things apart, after all, but it *feels* different. All those layers working together, so complex, can fall to pieces so easily.

I worked best outside. There, in the chill ocean air, I gave old things a fresh start. They arose like springtime amidst the birds and the pansies, the eggs in the nests above, the butter-flies growing from cocoons. They became something new. But I preferred taking things apart.

I itched for things that needed *help.*

One afternoon, when my mother was having tea with Annie and I'd finished all my ginger snaps that the old woman had an endless supply of, I asked her if there was anything I could fix.

She thought for a moment, Mommy's eyes watching her as she sipped from the china cup. Annie mumbled about how her grandson fixed everything that needed fixing, and she didn't need much anyway. But when I sighed, she smiled, gazing at me. She knew I needed this.

"Well…"

She excused herself and went to the basement, coming back with an old radio that she dusted as she walked. "This belonged to my husband before he passed away," she said, handing it to me. "He'd listen to it in that armchair right over there while I made dinner right over there," she told me, pointing at the spots in the house as if seeing it all again like watching a movie. "I've kept it, but it hasn't worked since he got sick. After he was gone, it just… Well, it didn't seem important, now did it?" She patted my hand, then my cheek, and I began.

Time passed. I don't know how much. But I'd taken the radio apart and rebuilt it time and again, and it never worked.

When I growled in irritation, fingers digging into Annie's braided rug of rusty warm colors, my mother came over and offered me a piece of purple-striped gum.

"Having a hard time with it, honey?" The kindness in her voice betrayed something else—that she was beginning to see it; that I needed more than what she could give me.

"Yes," I muttered, and dug hard at it again. She sat on the rug beside me and pulled my chin up, tearing my eyes from the machine and back to humanity for a moment.

"You understand what's wrong with the radio. Don't you?" she asked me.

"Yes, but I—"

"But you can't fix it. Right?"

Teeth gritted, I shook my head. It was a simple fix, and yet it eluded me.

"Maybe, just maybe, this little gadget needs not just understanding, but some care. You know what I mean?"

I shook my head, puzzled. "What do you mean, Mommy?"

"Well…" She took the skeleton of the radio from my hands, and I reluctantly let go of it. "This particular thing has a history. Just like people with history, the working parts fade. They don't always work the way they should, but they work in their own way. Ways that don't make a whole lot of sense. I think if you try a little *less* hard and look at this radio as Annie's husband's, as a thing with its own history, you'll see a different way. There's always a different way, baby, you just have to give it a chance."

Her words lulled me into a peaceful bedtime-story-like state, calming me. But there was a quiet sadness in her eyes, and if I'd really looked, I would have seen that she was talking about herself. About her and I. How we worked in our own way as a family. And something *more* than that. Something I wouldn't see until it was too late.

I took the radio back and my mother went to the table for yet another cup of tea with Annie, who'd watched the whole scene inquisitively. I popped the gum in my mouth. The murmur of their voices made my heart beat more smoothly, made my brain move slower, made my eyes less keen and more dreamlike.

I felt the radio. I gave it a chance to show me its story.

"My goodness," I heard Annie say admiringly. "Her hands are moving so fast, I can't even see them!"

"No," my mother replied in a trembling, hushed voice. "That's because they aren't moving at all."

I didn't—couldn't—tear my eyes away, but I saw my mother tiptoe over to me, slowly drop to her knees in my peripheral vision, her features a blur at my side. Her breath caught. *She's afraid,* I thought.

The realization made me take a sharp, choking breath and sit up straight from my hunched-over position with the radio. My head buzzed, my arms tingled, my eyes unclouded.

Mommy took the radio off the rug, dropping it once from her shaking hands, gasping with a quick fear of ruining it.

But she couldn't ruin it.

I'd fixed it. And it would work now.

My mother got to her feet in a trance, brought the radio to Annie with captive breath. Annie took the radio from her hands, her eyes wide. Lingering on me, she turned the radio on.

And like all the lamps I'd rewired, her eyes lit up.

⁓

"I've never seen anything like it," my mother whispered on the phone. It always amazed me how she knew I could do things no one else could, but thought I was too oblivious watching TV to listen to her on the phone. "She did it with her *mind.*"

I ate my soup and I watched *The Facts of Life* as my mother spoke more and more urgently in muted tones to Annie, curling the phone cord around her hand as she paced the kitchen floor. "I won't speak of it, not to anyone but you. It stays *between us,*" she hissed into the receiver. When the episode was over, her eyes met mine. Hers were wide, fearful. Layers of fear formed her expression. She held the phone away and said I could play outside for a while before bedtime. Meaning I was to go outside and play for a while to give her some privacy.

It was dark when I came in from climbing the neighbor's tree. Mommy kissed my forehead and said it was time for bed. It was too early, but I didn't argue. It gave me a stomachache.

She wanted to be without me for a while.

⁓

*A*melia sniffled and sneezed one afternoon as we made a lawn chair fort in the yard. Dark circles ringed her eyes, a gray pallor hazed over her skin. She'd stayed home from school the day before because of her cold but then she got "stir crazy," she said, and asked to go today.

"You should have gone home after school, Amelia. You feel very badly."

"I do, but I like playing with you," she said. She could say things like that, really straightforward, and I liked it. I liked it even when she asked questions I didn't want to answer.

I *looked* at her. "It's just a cold," I told her.

"How do you know that?" she said offhandedly.

I didn't answer. I couldn't think of words to explain how I could see the layers of the virus in her, where it traveled, what it was made of, how it moved.

"You're staring," I heard her say faintly, but didn't *really* hear her.

I didn't hear her—but I did see her. The pressure behind her eyes, pushing outward. I saw the swollen tissue of her nose, the redness of her throat, the little bumps in there, aggravated. I saw the ache in her arms and legs and it troubled me. I *saw* the cold, balled up in her chest and spitting out little bits of itself to run all over her body. Heat grew in my chest at it.

"Mommy?" Amelia called faintly. She moaned, was blinking a lot, and wouldn't take her eyes off me, leaned away from me. My friend who I thought was so brave, was scared of me. I wanted to do something nice for her so she wouldn't be. I didn't want any living thing afraid of me, not ever.

Then her eyes narrowed, and she breathed in deep through her nose. She blinked lazily. Her eyebrows went up when she worked it out—that she no longer had an ache in her features where fluid had gathered. She rolled her shoulders like I'd seen my mother do after a long day.

"I feel better," she whispered. "You did it, didn't you?"

I nodded.

"I won't tell," she said, and smiled. I smiled back, the angry heat in my chest simmering to a warmth because my friend was no longer sick, because I had been the one to make it go away. And she wasn't scared of me anymore. My smile reached all the way to my heart. I saw it there, filling it up even more. I'd done a very, very good thing.

I didn't question why Amelia wasn't going to tell anyone about this good thing. It was our secret. I liked having a secret with my friend. It was special, a small and inexplicable thing between two people connected by nothing tangible, and it was mine. Ours.

I'd soon learn that being able to do good things wasn't always good.

Amelia and I never spoke of it again.

~

The sun burned so brightly that it left spots in front of my eyes, and the flowers drank it up like water. The warmth on my legs in the grass, the sweet floral air, the buzz of the bees, and seeing the growth inside it all, underneath it all, made me blossom in the start of summer.

There was nothing to fix here. Nothing to take apart.

So young, and it was a momentary sigh of relief. A chance to just *be* without the compulsion to *change*. The more I understood what I could do, the more I wanted to do it.

Except for the times I didn't want to. The times when the thoughts of what would happen if I *didn't* disassemble took over. The invading thoughts of terrible ends if I just *stopped* sometimes tore me out of bed and made me work when I needed so desperately to sleep.

The darkness was settling in, even then.

The *need* pulsed like a fresh bruise that I wanted to hide.

My mother told me never to apologize for being myself. For the first time, I questioned if she *really* meant it. After all, she was hiding what happened with the radio. Because of that, I kept my first secret from her: that I made Amelia better.

The next secret was easier.

As the heat of the days swelled at the approach of summer, a boy named Sean Singh, one of those who always made fun of me, became more cruel, as if his restraint had burned up with the sun. He'd gone from throwing wood chips at me during recess when I sat alone in the grass, to throwing stones, taking jabs at my homemade dresses, saying I talked to the animals, and calling me a freak tree-hugger. One time on the bus he put a wad of gum in my hair from the pack he'd stolen from me the day before. My mother cried when she saw it. I flinched when he was near, when the distinct smell of dried sweat invaded my space merely to make me uncomfortable. He enjoyed it.

I would not treat a person badly who wanted to be alone. I would never hurt any person like he hurt me. I wouldn't hurt anything at all. That's why I became a target for him. I could see how to help; he could see who and how to hurt.

It was a Tuesday when I was leaving the girls' bathroom that I bumped into him. I was still adjusting my skirt, not paying attention.

"I thought you peed outside, Nature Girl," he spat at me. Actual spittle hit my face. He smiled when he saw it but I wouldn't wipe it off. I was afraid. Afraid of what he'd do if he knew it bothered me.

I made a little noise, an unformed word that I couldn't get

out and watched my feet in embarrassment. That was his chance to understand how scared I was.

"I don't like you," he growled, too close to my face.

I don't like you either, I wished I'd said. *You are piles upon piles of ugliness inside. Your heart is full of holes, stuffed with dirty, dirty things.* He didn't have layers of growth inside him —he had sheets of scabs all over his heart. He'd been hurt so much he didn't know anything else.

Then he ripped my skirt down.

Right there in the school hallway, he pulled it down around my ankles, my pink Hello Kitty underwear with it. That never left me, how stupid that Hello Kitty face made me feel, my naked pink skin showing. How everyone would know about the babyish underthings and talk about my girl parts. Sean Singh laughed as I struggled to pull my clothes back up, moaning at the nightmare of being naked in the hallway, shaking, head spinning, terrified of someone seeing me, coming out of a classroom and finding another reason to heckle me. He reached over and pulled them down again, his ragged fingernails scraping down my thighs. I cried out, stumbled over, fell to the tile floor in my haste and he laughed harder. And then he kicked me in the stomach.

I retched, and he stepped back, realizing he'd gone too far. I saw then that his whole life would be about going too far now. He couldn't feel true happiness unless he was hurting someone.

He ran off, leaving me on the ground to catch my breath, dry heaving, sobbing, too frozen to get up. I couldn't breathe, blood in my ears pounding as I waited for the bell to ring, for more of them to come out and laugh at me, take their shots.

A new urge swelled in me, taking my breath away again.

I wanted to take him apart inside and insert something deadly where it didn't belong.

It seems *not* getting sick isn't a good thing.

The doctor hit my knee with a tiny rubber tomahawk, and he shined a light down my throat while I choked on a stick. He took my temperature and my blood pressure, and listened to my heart, and he checked off all the things on his paper, but he still wasn't happy.

"She's not sick, Mrs. Preston."

"Miss."

"Oh," the doctor said. Heat rose to his cheeks and his heart quickened. He struggled not to smile too widely. I saw it all, every layer. "Well. There's nothing wrong that I can find. And nothing in her history showing any illness, not so much as coming in for a cough or a bump. You say she's *never* been sick?"

"No, never. She's got an iron core. But you agree, her color is off, right? She's so gray." Mommy's voice was getting high-pitched, anxious.

"Yes," the doctor said, pushing his glasses up. "And her eyes are dilated. Does she complain of headaches?"

"No. But she doesn't complain of anything."

This whole conversation happened while I sat there under their scrutinizing eyes, feeling just afraid. I felt nothing but afraid.

"Is she having trouble at school?"

Don't make me talk about it. I put my palms flat over the scratches on my thighs that they'd assumed were from my constant tree-climbing.

I watched the hard swallow in my mother's throat. "It's difficult to say," she said in a whisper, her eyes not leaving mine. She knew of every teacher's inability to "relate" to me, of my inability to make friends, of the way I didn't smile around other kids. I didn't tell her about Sean Singh.

The doctor turned to my mother then, shifting away from me for the first time in this entire conversation about me. "Why is it difficult to say if she's having a hard time in school?"

My mother shifted, shuffled her feet. "Well, she's not much of a talker, my Rose. She keeps to herself."

"Is that right, Rose?" the doctor asked me. I nodded. He had a kind but disturbed wrinkle to the corners of his mouth. I liked him. I liked his glasses and his sandy blond hair. He was soft but strong. "You don't get along with the kids at school?"

"I…I'm not like them." My head kept telling me, *Don't mention Sean Singh, don't mention Sean Singh, don't mention Sean Singh…*

"No, I suspect you're not," he said with a kindly smile. "Your stomach hurts before you go to school sometimes?" I shook my head. "You'd rather be alone than with other people?" I looked at Mommy, because she was the only one I always wanted to be with.

"I like to be with Amelia."

"Good," he said, and patted me on the knee. He cleared his throat, tightened his lips. "Does she ever have thoughts of… Do you ever think of hurting yourself, Rose?"

"Whoa, whoa, what is this?" my mother said, brows knit together. "Rose is not suicidal! You think I wouldn't know if my daughter wanted to hurt herself?"

Not myself. But maybe someone else.

The doctor smiled, but he didn't mean it. "I'm sure you're a very good mother, but it's important to see beneath the surface, isn't it? Have there been any changes at home, anything upsetting?"

My mother took on the demeanor parents got when they came into school for a talk with the principal about trouble their kids were in. The same generic parent stance, where it was more important to defend themselves than it was to get to the bottom of the issue. A defense mechanism.

I wondered what Sean Singh's defense mechanisms were.

When my mother didn't answer, just swallowed hard in my direction, the doctor turned my way.

"Rose?" he said very quietly, head level with mine, as if that would eliminate the knowledge that my mother was in the room. "Has anything happened at home?"

I can fix things with my mind now, I could have said. The secret was hard to keep from him. He so much wanted to help.

It was a danger I hadn't known before. To be assaulted with the prospect of saying too much. Humiliating myself that way scared me almost as much as Sean Singh. Which must have shown on my face because the doctor said, "You can tell me."

My mother coughed, and the color drained from her face.

"I'm feeling better," I said, unable to omit the robotic tone from my voice.

The doctor wiped a hand over his face. "Of course, of course. Well, I think we should perform some blood tests, just to be safe. And Miss Preston? If anything comes up, anything you wish to discuss, be certain to call."

With a pat on my head and a deep sigh, he left the room.

∼

I got the blood tests done. And I went back to school the next day.

My mother muttered to herself about the doctor. "How dare he? Like you're the only child who gets scared about school, like I'm the only single mother in the world, always thinking I'm doing something I shouldn't, as if I'd do something to my little girl…" Catching herself, she turned her attention back to me. "He thinks something is wrong here, at home. So I shouldn't keep you out of school because you just don't feel good, baby. If you're *sick*, you're sick. But if you just don't feel good—"

"I understand, Mommy," I said, smiling my biggest and brightest. "You're afraid to give him anything more to worry about."

Her tension melted into an adoring warmth so luminous that it could blot out the sun, and she took my hand. "You magical little thing. Yes, that's pretty much it."

"That *is* it," I said.

She laughed. She always thought it was funny how literally I took everything. Why say anything except exactly what needs to be said? "Yes. Yes, it is."

I went to school for the last three days of that week. Even though my stomach hurt to think of Sean Singh and what he had done and would do, and what *I* might do if he did. The fear of him and myself only made the other things that were usually just a little uncomfortable about school much more uncomfortable. The teachers watched me more warily. The other kids seemed to wonder why I never asked questions, too. I only talked to Amelia, and she only talked to me most of the time, but even she was quieter than usual.

"Sean Singh pulled my skirt down," I said to her at recess when he ran by the stacking tires we sat upon. I left out the part about the underwear. "And he kicked me in the stomach."

Amelia acted different with me. She blinked a lot, fear in her voice—fear for me. "You have to tell," she blurted.

"Why?"

"Because he has to get punished! He can't hurt you like that, Rose."

I'd never heard her speak with so much feeling before. And it was for *me*. I threw my arms around her and squeezed her so tightly that my shoulders hurt for a second. She hugged me back. A couple of the kids made fun of us but we ignored them.

"Let's go tell," Amelia said when I let go.

"I don't think so," I muttered.

"Rose, he's so mean to you—"

"You shut up," I heard behind me, and then a sharp push on my back. Not enough to send me to the ground, not this time, but enough to warn me.

"Leave her alone!" Amelia shouted at Sean.

"You shut up, too. If I get in trouble because of stupid girls, I swear—"

Then I did it.

I'd never hurt anything in my life. I could see where pain came from in the smallest of creatures, and the thought of causing such a thing ripped at my heart. And so when I hurt Sean Singh it was tentative, fearful, a pulled punch. I *saw* his intestines—we'd just learned all about the human body in science, and so I had words for all these parts now—and I wanted to unroll them, completely take them apart. I wanted to see the blood.

The thought of blood didn't bother me. Blood made beautiful things.

I wanted to see his blood, but I knew it would only feel good for a minute, to hurt him. It would feel wrong, it *was* wrong. My anger, fear, embarrassment, could be locked away inside me. Doing a terrible thing could not.

Past the surface, the heart and lungs and veins and cells, it was the easiest thing in the world for me to find his empti-ness—a place to put something that didn't belong. The boy was filled with nothing. I think if someone survives too much pain it becomes part of their body; runs through just like blood. I strained not to see his pain, to think only of mine.

And just like I'd taken the ugliness out of Amelia, I put something ugly inside Sean Singh.

He winced; it didn't bother me like his jeering cruel pinched face—and he put his hands on his belly. He retched. Just like I had on the floor outside the bathroom, naked from the waist down. And he threw up on the same wood chips he'd once loved to throw at me. He threw up again and again, too fast to recover in between, and kids gathered around, covering their mouths and running for the teacher.

Amelia's eyes were as wide as the tire swings. She knew. Of course she did. I'd made her better, and now I was making him worse.

I shrugged at her. And I smiled, just a little. She smiled a lot.

~

The doctor called that night. It was Friday night, and I thought that was funny. Like doctors never went home. I half-listened to them, hearing the words "tests" and "abnormal." My mother made an appointment for the next morning to get my head checked out.

"It's not good that the doctor wants to see my brain. On a Saturday."

Mommy put a bowl of spaghetti in front of me on the old kitchen table, and continued bustling over the stove. "He's just making sure," she said.

"You're scared."

She stopped stirring the saucepan. "Yes. A little," she said. "It's no use trying to tell you I'm not, Rose, you'd see right through me." Back to stirring. "Your brain is the most perfect thing in the whole wide world, baby. And I want to make sure it's safe."

That was true. That *was* what she wanted. I didn't understand why she was worried about my brain. Here I was, a girl that could see the blank spots between the coiled intestines in Sean Singh's abdomen, and yet I couldn't see why my brain's health would worry my mother. So oblivious I was.

We went to the hospital and I got put into a machine to check my brain. I saw how the machine worked; fascinating. Beams of energy and metal and pictures all together.

"A tumor," the doctor—a different doctor—told my mother. "A strange tumor that has grown incredibly quickly, too quickly even for itself, unable to attack predictably. It's quite unique, and quite…well, quite unreal, if we're speaking plainly. The tumor appears like a virus, but it is of course, a mass. And yet the symptoms, the brain's reactions, are like that of a stroke victim—"

"Stop! Stop being fucking fascinated by it and tell me how we fix it!" my mother yelled at him. He was so nice, he understood, and answered her.

He sat down on the edge of his desk, not on the chair side where he'd be comfortable, and he said, "We don't know how. To fix it. We're researching every possible case that could be related to Rose's very singular condition, and consulting with Boston on experimental…"

I didn't hear much more after that. I tuned it all out and tried to look inside my brain as much as I could, to try and find this new monster I harbored. But I couldn't see, not in there, not with people around.

I'd never looked so deeply inside myself. With so much to see in the world, why would I try?

My mother talked to the doctors for hours, and it sounded like I would be at the hospital more than I'd be at home. The hospital. With its blank walls and concrete floor and bad lighting. And so many sick people. I wasn't one of them.

I was allowed to eat anything I wanted for dinner that

first night. (Pizza and vanilla ice cream.) My mother wouldn't stop staring at me from across the table with such sadness I felt the blood vessels in my heart expand and contract, threatening to burst with the quickened flow through them.

"I won't die," I told her.

She choked on her pizza, scrambled for a napkin to spit it out. "Of course you won't, Rose! Of course you won't!" And she ran to her bedroom in a flurry of tears, slamming the door behind her.

I didn't want to be alone at the table with the pizza. I hated that she was scared. I didn't want her to be afraid ever. Staring out the kitchen window into the dark trees, I took an absent-minded bite of pizza in the quiet.

My chewing was the sound of bowling balls dropping, my mouth opening like boulders moving.

I was alone.

Alone.

I put the slice down.

This was my chance.

Breathe. In. Out. In. Out. In...

I stared now at the refrigerator, heard its hum.

Breathed in—delicious pizza—out.

The magnets on the fridge went hazy—it wasn't them I needed to see.

Felt my eyes glaze over.

I *looked.*

Deeply, I looked for the thing that was killing me. *I don't feel different,* I thought. I could do different things now with my brain, but it felt like I was...

Growing.

No, not me. The *tumor.* It was growing, taking over.

The worker bees don't take over the queen.

The seeds don't take over the grass.

The fetus doesn't take over the womb.

And the brain doesn't take over the heart.

Further into my mind I sank, finding all the strata of my being in quick succession.

Inside me, normal body stuff like everyone else. But I couldn't find anything more. Nothing that would hurt me in there.

I turned my sight inside further, gripping the table, I looked, looked, looked…

"Rose! *Rose!*"

Mommy shook me hard, making the metal legs of the kitchen chair dance on the ground, muttering prayers for me to wake up, to be okay, and swearing.

"Mommy."

Blinking so fast I can't believe she could see, she said, "Rose? Rose?"

"I'm here, Mommy."

She collapsed to the ground, sobbing, lying on the kitchen floor while the refrigerator hummed and the pizza got cold.

Things would never be the same.

~

I went to school every day. Sometimes I was tired. Sometimes I had to leave to go to the hospital. Every time the kids treated me like I was a puppy in an alley or like I was a disease they shouldn't breathe near.

Sean Singh didn't talk, didn't breathe, didn't come near me at all.

"Why do you go to the hospital so much if they don't think they can fix you?" Amelia asked me. I shrugged.

The whole school knew somehow that I was dying. They'd whisper that I was the same as always, or that they always knew something was wrong with me. The adults wanted to hold my hand in the hallways and would pat my head as I walked by, even pull me into a hug. As if thinking I was "off" before was erased because I would die soon.

Everything dies. The end of the story, it's right there in the layers under the skin. I'd never been afraid of it, it was only one more layer.

"You ready to go, baby?"

My mother still kept up that smile in public, even though at home she cried a lot and kept her distance from me without knowing it. Her fear, not only of my dying, but of *losing* me—two different things, she felt—brought up a terror in her heart that I saw, of losing someone again. I didn't know what it meant, who she'd lost. Seeing feelings, watching thoughts emerge from the colors and shapes of them was new to me. As the tumor grew, so did my strength.

The brain taking over the heart.

I turned my attention to the cars going by on the way to the hospital, to avoid my mother's constant glances at me. She noticed the tiny bird-like bones that were my wrists now because I'd stopped eating most of the time; the idea of it seemed silly. I didn't do much at all, really. The days ran together, the moments became one, and all of it was leading to the end.

No school for a week or two. I'd lost count of the days while the other kids counted them until summer vacation. We didn't go anywhere except the hospital anymore. My weight loss terrified Mommy, but I just understood it—this is how the end begins. I usually just wore a t-shirt around the house now because they were all big enough to be night-gowns. The pallor of my skin in the mirror combined with the darkness behind my eyes turned me into a ghost. No more pink cheeks, red lips. And yet...

I felt *better*.

The tests always said my tumor was more horrible than the last time—but my heart didn't agree.

I think it was gearing up for something big.

Mommy woke up one morning to find me outside in the yard, climbing a tree, singing with gum in my mouth. She screamed for me to come down. "That's too much for you, Rose, you're going to get hurt! You aren't strong enough to do this!" But I could see the bruise-green of her feelings, and the thing she didn't say. That I'd done something *away* from her, and she was scared. Angry. There was a selfishness there, a darkness there to match my own.

"I know my body, Mom," I said. When I said that, a light turned on in my head.

I need to know more.

The doctors didn't know what the tumor was. My mother didn't know what they were doing to treat it. My school didn't know much of anything except that I was weird, and they'd probably forgotten all about me by then. It was up to me to move forward if I wanted to grow faster than the tumor. It was the first real choice I'd ever made.

I reached up high in the tree, stretched as far as I could, and pulled down a thing that didn't belong, though it was so natural. A monstrous black feather. I smiled.

~

Once I came down from the tree, my ashy pink sticklegs red with bloody scrapes, my mother took over. After cleaning me up, letting her hover over me, she was thrilled to hear that I was hungry. Her face glowed like sunshine again, making me long for the days when our cottage felt more golden than gray. I voraciously ate all my breakfast for lunch (pancakes and sausages), went outside again for an hour, *and* came in for a sandwich (peanut butter and fluff, plus six cookies). My mother couldn't stop smiling. I danced in the living room when *The Facts of Life* theme song came on. Mommy danced with me. We watched *Jaws 3-D* when we weren't ready to stop sitting together on the couch, and then we watched *Valley Girl* which was really inappropriate for me in parts.

"Let's walk to the beach," Mommy said, taking both my hands in hers, eyes wide, voice giddy. "Let's go to the beach one last—"

She choked on her words.

"It won't be the last time, Mommy," I said soothingly.

She pulled me close roughly, kissed my hair, and rocked me back and forth. I never wanted it to end. I would make sure it did not.

"Goddammit, I fucking knew it! You're too much of an asshole to die, you couldn't make it that easy, could you?"

"You weren't ready to let me go yet, were you?" she purred.

I found myself slowly shaking my head instead of spitting out a comeback. "It doesn't matter." Nothing mattered. It didn't matter that I'd tried to do right and get rid of her, it didn't matter that I'd saved Robbie, it didn't matter that I was trying to get rid of the Harpy in myself—I never could. Because I didn't really want it to go away. And I hadn't really wanted her to go away either. Not completely. The other Harpies cried out to me from the trees, the moans of the suicides entangled in them muffled. *I'm one of you,* I thought, *and I'll never be anything better.*

"You're messing with me, my head. I'm not here to chat. Tell me what's in the Facility."

The Queen was very goth CoverGirl for someone who I'd thought was fucking *dead.* I couldn't bother to ask how she was still alive, only be annoyed that she wasn't more zombie-like.

"You ask too many questions, Hazel," she said dismissively.

Fucking hell with the *Hazel*. She insisted on calling me that—my birth name and the official title of the shitstorm that was my "childhood."

"Who's Rose? What's she doing in there?"

I knew when her face was extra smug, and this was it. She was trapping me. The bitch had all kinds of super-intricate schemes that she loved to execute. It made me kill her once, this shit she pulled. But this time, I knew I was falling into it, and I still stepped off.

"You've been visiting the past, haven't you?"

"Come again?"

She smiled condescendingly. "I knew it would happen before long. You can't move forward figuratively. And now you can go back—literally."

"What the *fuck*?" Just when I'd started getting clean of Harpy life, trying to just say no, the Harpy game leveled up with a fancy new feature. Stood to reason if I could travel in and out of Hell and halfway around the world like fucking Santa Claus in a single night to find prey, next step would be time travel.

"Rose is in the Facility, yes. But in the 1980s. Your powers are growing, Hazel. You're becoming a stronger, more capable Harpy."

It rang true. It made a sort of weird sense. That was part of the Queen's bitchery, was that a lot of the time, she was *right*, but it was always about stuff I didn't want to talk about. "Let me get this straight. I can't get over years of rape, so now I'm a Time Bandit," I said, winking at a staring eyeball lodged between the branches of her nest.

She laughed, and I fucking hated that it made me happy.

She was my Regina George. I hated her but I still wanted her to like me. "Your way with words," she said, shaking her head. "Time will never change you. You're a Harpy now, in flesh and soul, and you will forever be exactly as you are now."

"Wait. So I'll be hot forever?"

"That's not what I mean," she spat.

"But it's true, right? Like, I'll never get old and I'll always be a Christina Aguilera-knockoff from the *Burlesque* days? I'm into that. Totally into that."

"That's not all that time is!" She shook with anger. "Time isn't about age, you fool! Time is a state of mind. Time is growth and change—something you'll never know. As long as you are this," she motioned at all of me in my bare-ass nakedness, "you will never be more. The world, that boy of yours, everything will change, and you will never be more than this. Because you. Can't. Move. On."

It drilled into my heart with a finality I wanted to run from. She made it sound like a death sentence worse than what the souls of the Wood endured.

"I can go invisible and time travel as a Harpy, yeah? But that means my actual life suffers even more. Because I can't go forward. No best-of-both-worlds shit for me. Man, you suck."

"I'm not sorry, Hazel. I want you here. *You* want to be here." She leaned forward, sincere and smug, and cooed, "You prefer this power. This purpose. Simplicity and complexity in perfect balance."

"Cut the crap, I'm already on the team, I'm just an alternate. Tell me about Rose. Why her, why did I go to that place in the eighties when there's plenty of people for me to help right here, right now?"

"You're needed where you're needed. You can be everywhere and nowhere."

I rolled my eyes, focusing on the red sky. *Don't listen to her bullshit.* "I'm not listening to your bullshit. I don't want a kid sister, Queenie baby. This ain't the kind of job you take an apprentice in, no padawans needed. And I'm only part time bird bitch these days anyway, one foot out the door."

The other Harpies howled from the trees, like I'd hurt their feelings. "Oh, boo hoo! Go back to eating the entrail appetizer, would ya?" I turned back to the Queen, sighing, but would not be defeated.

"You *will* help her," the Queen said in her hypnotic voice.

I grabbed her by the collar of her ridiculous black gown and yanked her up. She yelped, which made me proud. "Listen to me," I growled. "I get you. You think this kid will spark some pity in me, make me step right back into the thick of my memories. Don't you?" I nodded my head waiting for her to do the same but she only stared at me, eyes glistening. "Put me back a few steps, put me right where you want me, right here before I ever thought I could have a life up there. Well, you're fucking wrong. You'll see. I *can* move on. I'll get better and I'll leave you here in Hell where you belong."

I dropped her back to the blood-stained ground and shot up into the dead sky, opening a portal without a second to spare.

ROSE

"*I*t's disappearing."

"Disapp… You said it would only get bigger and more invasive."

"We…I'm flabbergasted by the progress. There's no precedent for it, no precedent for the tumor itself. What's happening in Rose's brain is…it defies explanation. It defies reason."

Dr. Trask and my mother stared at me in my paper gown on the examining table. My eyes went back and forth between them. They talked about how I never got sick, how my immune system was a medical phenomenon.

"Could I speak privately with you, Miss Preston?" the doctor asked.

My mother tore her eyes from me to look at him stonily. "No, actually. Rose is a child but she's not *just* a child. She should hear all of it."

With a reluctant smile, the doctor told her what was really disturbing him. "I said, Miss Preston, that the tumor was disappearing—and that's exactly what I meant."

"I don't understand."

"The mass isn't getting smaller, it's not shrinking like a tumor would if it were, in fact, *able* to be cured. It's *disappearing*. As if parts are being removed. And not at random; the most advanced and deteriorating parts of the mass are being—"

"Dissected," my mother finished breathlessly.

"Yes!" the doctor exclaimed, as though he'd been trying to think of the proper word. "Yes, ma'am, *dissected*. It's quite impossible."

My mother's eyes welled with tears when she turned back to me. "Yes. Quite impossible," she whispered.

~

My mother asked me to tell her over and over again what I'd done to my brain, but I couldn't explain it very well. I was only a child, after all.

"I took it apart, Mommy. That's all."

I couldn't make her understand any more than the doctor would have understood. Amelia would have understood. Amelia always took my oddness in stride. I missed her. My mother wouldn't have approved of how I'd turned my brain inside out without fear of something terrible happening, but taking that chance meant I found the tumor. Adults never wanted to take chances unless they knew the outcome, which wasn't a chance at all. I found the tumor's strongest spots, where it was spreading like an empire across the world. My world. I removed the heart of the tumor and was left with just the dumb, murderous bubble; that was the hardest part. The target was so big, so pink and gelatinous and just *nothing* that I couldn't focus, and it took longer to make it go away.

But I did it. If I couldn't control my own brain, what chance did I have?

I saw a lot of doctors after that, but nobody even thought

of asking if *I* had been the one to make the tumor go away. My mother sure wasn't telling our secret. There was another man, though.

A man in a white coat different from the doctor coats. It was more worn, used like a tool. The man who wore this coat became The Scientist when he put it on. When he looked at me, he saw science. And what he said made sense.

"What I've surmised is that the tumor pressed upon parts of the brain that generally lie dormant. You've of course heard that people only use ten percent of the brain at once—though I believe that's an underestimation." He waved his hand, grinning, as if afraid he'd go off on a tangent. "I believe Rose's tumor, for lack of a better term, pressed the buttons on other parts of her brain, allowing her to use forty percent of her brain or more at one time. I believe that without even realizing it, Rose healed herself."

"Imagine that," my mother said with a sidelong glance toward me. "Without even realizing it."

"Indeed," The Scientist agreed. "I'd like to keep seeing Rose, if you wouldn't mind."

The alarm on my mother's face spoke for her. "To do what? What could you want from her when your *doctors* were useless? She healed *herself*. What else is there to say?" Her face flushed hot pink, and her hair was getting frizzy on top where her scalp was sweating.

The Scientist breathed like a dragon through his nose, but his smile was warm. "Rose can teach us plenty! Imagine, would you," he said, standing up from his rolling chair, "if we can find out more about this tumor, how the tissue could possibly be used, the things it could heal—"

"But the tumor is gone."

"Yes. It is gone. For now."

"F-for now?" Her voice rose higher and higher. Her hands shook as she fiddled with her bracelet.

"I apologize, but I suspect the tumor will return. This young lady has evolved to access remote parts of her brain," he said, incredulous, eyes glittering. "I don't believe she will stop there, Miss Preston. Do you?"

My mother's voice became lava in her fury. "You'd love that. Wouldn't you? You'd just love for this child, *my child* to be a lab rat so you could make a big name for yourself while she dies. To use her *tissues*? You spoke of using her brain tissue like she's a piece of meat."

Coldly, he said, "I would *like* no such thing, Miss Preston. I look at this child and see *life.* The saving of it, the evolution of it, the majesty of it! Certainly you can't think we'd choose science over—"

"*WE?* Who's *we?* And as a matter of goddamn fact, Mr. Cleary, I think you would. I can hear it now: 'One child's life is the price we've paid for the lives of the millions this knowledge could help us cure.' Well, I'm not buying it." She pushed him out of the way and lifted me to my feet by the arm. "Leave my baby *alone,*" she spat, inches from his face before we strode out the door.

This Mr. Cleary—a name I would come to know well—wasn't about to let us off that easily. "Miss Preston," he called after us. "Miss Preston, I think you'll find that our resources are inconceivable, and cooperation is inevitable."

My mother spun on him with a gleam of pure hatred in her eyes. "Don't you dare, threaten me with your petty resources. You know nothing of what I would do to protect my child." With a lingering stare at him, she turned and punched the door open, slamming it into the wall.

"Mommy, I'm scared," I said. I remember that because it was so uncharacteristic of me to be afraid. Probably another part of my brain that opened up because of a malignant tumor, or one that was eliminated.

She tugged me across the parking lot, her icy hand

squeezing my fingers painfully together. "Nothing to be scared of, Rosie," she said without a smile, without pausing her head spinning, waiting for someone to come at us and steal me away.

"I don't believe that," I whispered.

~

*A*fter the tumor, things were different. I was different. My ability to see the machinations of anything I focused on, amplified, becoming a sort of x-ray vision that never let me rest. I'd obsessed with the novelty of taking things apart before; now it's who I was. My brain scanned everything in my path, nothing untouched, right to their cores in a glance. Plants, fingernails, buses, batteries, corn flakes, rocks, dogs, pencil lead, anything you can think of, their mechanics and composition visible to me like a training manual, their intricacies overpowering the whole picture. Every living thing, from bushes to birds to butterflies, we all had the singular function of ensuring survival by any means necessary. And I was no different.

I had evolved. The simplicity in my childhood I'd always longed for and was never able to have was now even more beyond reach.

But what came with it—aside from very early bedtimes and numbing migraines—was an ever-growing search from inside me for the secrets of my past. The secrets my mother hid from me.

I resented my mother for her silence, and I clung to her as well. She was the only one who could indulge my fantasy of simplicity. It was an illusion. There was nothing simple in the world for me, and even those stolen moments of baking cookies with her while we danced to MTV were fraught with seeing too much and fear of being snatched away from each other. She would have destroyed everything in her path to keep me with her, under her thumb and in her heart. The duty changed my glistening pearl of a mother, so like nature itself, into a warrior beast that burned brightly and fast. Her sunshine was gone—only blazing, scorching fight or flight instinct remained. No dust motes flitted around her face in the daylight of our kitchen—only layers of dust that she no longer paid attention to, so exhausted she was by her vigilance. She was deteriorating in every way from the effort to keep me safe.

We didn't see Mr. Cleary for months. We crept to our necessary doctor's checkups on the "healing process" so as to stay out of trouble, but Cleary knew everything. We knew it. My mother lived in constant fear—around every corner was a lurking man in a suit waiting to snatch me up, to take apart our little family. Her life became about me in a different way than before; no longer just happy to be with me, no longer nurturing, but overlording.

For nurturing, I had Annie next door.

The little old woman with her snow drift hair made me feel like the child I was again. Annie would build block towers with me, only to watch me disassemble them a different way each time, not even pausing to discern the weak and strong points. With her, I could almost bury the graph-paper-world I now lived in. She'd make me tea in a real china cup older than she was, a hill of ginger snaps on the saucer, and we'd talk over the round table overlaid with doilies about her long life and my short one. It gave me hope, that if I worked hard enough, like with the tumor, that I could erase this unending *seeing*.

I didn't go to school any longer. My mother said I was too ill, which turned into saying I was homeschooled. She couldn't really teach me—that would take away from her mania, her harried paranoia, her bouts of self-pity and flip-flop of neglect and smothering me. She'd coo over how special I was, that everyone would use me if I didn't hide it, take me away from her. And when I wasn't able to be just Regular Rose for her, when I couldn't hide how much I *saw* for a second anymore, she'd hole up in her bedroom and leave me to myself, as if I'd betrayed her.

Death hadn't concerned me until then. But what had become of my mother and I was like a death in and of itself. And I wanted to see more.

I paid attention to where death showed itself. The way the plants and trees and flowers reacted to their own decay, the way life kept its distance from the odors of a dying animal, the emptiness of an unfertilized robin egg.

All I had known was light and life until the tumor. Now the darkness shined as brightly.

A squirrel got hit by a car on our street. One morning when my mother was in her neglectful phase, hiding from me, claiming that the prospect of being without me was too much for her to bear, I had the opportunity to run outside, scoop the squirrel up and bring it into my lawn chair fort with the orange afghan over the top. The goo and blood on my hands didn't bother me—the squirrel was hurting. He *hurt* and I could see why. The sticky fur on my pink corduroys was not in the realm of my vision—his half-crushed heart was.

Squeezing in through the hole between the two up-ended lawn chairs, I put the creature on the grass under the dappled dark of the overhead blanket. The squirrel made not a sound. The black eyes didn't meet mine, the limbs didn't move. They weren't broken, I could see that. His rib cage was, and the heart… Well, his heart was a half-thing now, but he still had life. There was life there.

"I look at this child and see life," Mr. Cleary had said. I took a deep breath.

Leaning close, the smell of his insides wafting over me, I pulled a piece of gum out of my pocket and I whispered, "I can fix you. Just listen to the birds and I'll work."

I hope he did. I hope he listened to the birds and the soft shush of the grass as I moved. I hope it didn't hurt too much when I pushed on the place where his heart had been whole. I don't know if I did any of it with my hands or my thoughts —I don't remember the *how*, I only remember feeling so deeply that I could make him better, seeing the diagram of his body like a map. I twisted his ribs in my fingers, like rolling Play-Doh into a tube, *making* something. I took out the broken pieces—he didn't need those anymore. When that was done I looked hard into his chest, hard, hard, until his tiny button heart beat in time again like a clock.

"I don't know how to fix your cuts," I said, irritated, chewing my gum faster.

Things on the outside rarely need fixing. They're used to being abused.

I gasped. The thought came from both outside and inside my head. A woman's voice, not my own, silk-smooth. My brain had opened up a space where someone could get in.

And the words the voice said infuriated me.

Abused.

All my gentleness, the fresh pinkness of my little girl persona fled me for a split second, and an image of myself in a red hellish landscape invaded, erasing my x-ray vision for a moment, showing me only this horror. This horror that didn't frighten me in the least.

I remember grunting, not with effort but with some other feeling. Something I didn't recognize and didn't want to know.

Before I could snap out of it and figure out how to mend the squirrel's little heaving chest with the giant gash in it, he jumped up, chattering, and darted out of the fort, leaving a puddle of blood the size of a silver dollar pancake. I smiled, and leaned back against the lawn chair wall, listening to the birds and imagining Hell.

~

*W*hen I came inside, my mother didn't ask where the blood on my pants came from.

I turned on the TV and sat on the couch, putting my feet up on the old coffee table. I wasn't ready to get changed. I didn't want to wash my hands. I wanted to feel near that squirrel and its tiny, simple life, the wet redness stuck to me like battle scars. I wondered how many of those my mother kept hidden from me. I sensed that I had more.

There was no denying by now that I had a gift. My abrupt extraction from the world by my mother once the tumor disappeared made it painfully obvious. I was her Rapunzel, trapped away in her tower to preserve a gift that could help so many.

So sitting on the cracked leather sofa with bits of squirrel and spots of blood and dirt all over me, I raised my chin triumphantly. A warrior back from a particularly draining battle, fueled with adrenaline and a vision of the universe that would melt most minds. Inserting myself into my little-girl-world summer seaside cottage, covered in blood, reeking of wounds, was like waving a rebel flag. A flower budding in the dark. A butterfly emerging in the dead of winter.

I rubbed the crimson blood into my pink corduroys to make it stick forever.

~

That Monday, I went back to school. I came out of my room, dressed and ready, with my Hello Kitty backpack—I winced picking it up, remembering the underwear that I'd thrown away after Sean Singh saw them.

I wore that backpack like battle armor.

My mother poked her head around the corner of the kitchen, singing, "Scrambled eggs, scrambled eggs—" and instantly stopped. Eyes narrowed, her top lip curled up with revulsion, as if this were the blood-covered outfit and not a vibrant red dress she'd made me herself. I knew she'd feel betrayed that I'd made this choice without her, that I was deserting her this way. "You want to go to *school?*" she spat. I nodded slowly. She forced a smile. "Good idea, honey," she said. "I was thinking it might be nice for you to—"

I asked her to stop talking about it.

Seeing Amelia again felt like coming home—the way my home had been once. An effortless comfort. She didn't say she'd missed me or act like anything was different. We just ate lunch together and had quiet reading time together as usual. The other kids made fun of me as always. It didn't make me feel bad anymore; I had a secret and all they had was unfounded revulsion.

I started raising my hand in class. It wasn't a surrender to finally trying to fit in—it was a rebellion. Back then, I would have said I rebelled against the school that thought I was "off," that wouldn't accept me even when I was near death. Now I would disagree.

I would say it was against my mother.

Being away showed me that school, friends, not fitting in, being ridiculed, having secrets, even what happened with Sean Singh, all of it was part of *my* layers. Like the rings of a tree denoting a new year. Every part of my life was part of the bigger machine, the workings of the whole, and to shut out any one piece was to not utilize its entirety.

I was nothing if not a girl who used everything at her disposal.

Being back at school let me feel light again and it showed. I talked to more kids, played with them sometimes. The bullying dwindled now that I got up from the grass and joined in a game of kickball without being asked—even though the sound of the ball bouncing made me wince, an inexplicable sledgehammer to my heart. I missed the ball every time, but I tried again and again until the cheers for me matched the ones for the great players. I answered questions in class even though I knew the subjects more thoroughly than the teachers ever could. Sean Singh taunted me every time I got an answer right—which was every time—and other kids would roll their eyes when I raised my hand, but I ignored them because I *saw* their layers all too well. But now…it bothered me to see the new targets receive that cruel treatment. Sometimes an angry heat flared deep in my belly that could burn down a house and made me sink back into the aloneness where I was safe, though I ached to help them.

My emotional capacity was growing.

The layers of the world were always there, an x-ray in my every moment, but in this simpler structure, I didn't lose myself in the workings of the world. Because I wasn't alone. I took part in the simple result of the complicated construction. I had *fun*—a thing that hadn't interested me much when the tumor was my closest friend.

The joy followed me home. I played with *toys*. Block towers—albeit extremely complex ones—popped up all around the house. Board games got dusted off and restored broken family time with my mom. Stuffed animals got names. Dusty Barbie dolls were pulled out of the closet, removed from their original boxes, tottered around the living room to shop, kiss their Kens, drive in their hot pink cars.

Hot pink…a color so manufactured, a layer of dirt on a natural blush that rattled me before, was now part of me. It was simple. An easier childhood that I deserved after all I'd been through. Outside was too big, too *thick.*

"Baby, why don't you go outside for a while?" my mother asked one sunny afternoon as I bounced a superball off the floor as hard as I could to hit the ceiling.

"I don't want to," I said simply.

"You've been playing inside all weekend, Rose. You need sun."

"I don't want sun right now. Let's play Candy Land!"

Clenching her fists, she spat, "I cannot play one more board game…" She took a deep breath. "Rose, let's go outside, we can work in the garden." I bounced the ball harder, harder, picturing smashing the board games underneath it each time, pieces and dice and cards flying everywhere. "Rose. I'm sorry, I didn't mean to snap. *Rose!*" She plucked the superball out of the air as it sped by. "You need to go outside, you used to love going outside! I could hardly get you in for dinner. Now…" She wanted to ask me what caused the sudden change of heart, but she didn't want to know the answer. She'd been doing such a good job ignoring my brain, pretending I was Regular Rose. I suppose I'd been doing the same.

Well, I was tired of being ignored.

I turned fully toward her, hands on my hips. "Which is it, Mommy? You want me to hide in here, or do you want me to stay away from you?"

She swallowed hard, stepping back.

Very quietly, "Rose, you were sick and…special. I didn't trust them. But now, I think you seem more like the rest of us. It feels safer, baby. We can go back to the way things were."

Every fiber of my being felt that she only wanted my safety, that she loved me more than her own life. I *was* her whole life. I couldn't see the layers of her love, how confused she was—only how manipulative she'd been, how subtle her cruelty. "Am I Regular Rose now, Mom? It must be a relief that I can hide myself in plain sight these days so you don't have to. Maybe I can be a little fairy for you to show off again! I'll go outside when you want me to, hide inside when you want me to, play with you when you're in the mood, be nothing for you when you're not." I swallowed back tears, making my voice thick. "Maybe I should have stayed sick."

"Don't say that," she breathed.

I withered quickly, this volatility toward my mother warring with that child I once was, with the family we'd once been. The flame in my gut burned hotter and more viciously than ever. "We both know that I'm still not like the rest of you, Mommy," I said, counting the lines in the wooden floor. "I'm tired now." She didn't say a word as I climbed into my bed and sluggishly pulled up the covers.

~

"**W**ould like her to come over for tea."

Annie's voice. I hadn't been able to smile for the weekend, but that warm, slightly scratchy voice that had become synonymous with comfort pushed the corners of my mouth up. I poked my head out from my blanket cave.

My mother's whispering voice came next, faraway and helpless. An exasperated, isolated kind of helplessness that permeated the walls.

"The girl has had a tumultuous time of it, Sarah. She's

always been so lighthearted, and that's not true anymore. I can see how sad she is, can't you?"

"Great, now you think she's a mental case, too. You want to ask if she's suicidal next?"

Annie's voice hardened and my breath quickened. "Half the reason you came here is because she—" Her voice cut off. *What did she mean?* "Sarah, the child survived a brain tumor, you've stashed her away, shaming her for being a…a *prodigy.* Because of *your* fears, you denied her a life. Did it ever occur to you that she probably *wants* to talk to these doctors, scientists, just to be able to speak! She's been in and out of school more times than—"

"That's not my fault!" my mother cried.

"The child has more inside her than either one of us, it stands to reason that depression would be part of the package. And…" She hesitated, but it was unlike Annie to keep anything to herself. "And it's only natural that her mother would suffer emotionally from it as well," she finished softly.

My mother didn't answer. She knew she'd been seen.

I could envision Annie wrapping one arm around my mother as her voice lowered to a cooing. The snuffling associated with tears came next and I wondered briefly when the last time I'd cried was. I couldn't remember.

~

"*I* don't want to talk about not feeling well, Annie," I said over a cup of tea in her house, my legs swinging, feet *scuff scuff*ing the floor.

She reached across the table, the lace runner catching on her sleeve. She grasped my wrist, as if she knew that I didn't like holding hands. "I want you to listen to me, Rose. I know it's not a habit of yours, to listen, because you just know things other people don't. But I'm hoping you'll listen to me now."

I nodded once, eyes trained on hers, glassy with age but sharp.

"I won't always be here, Rose. I'm an old lady. But having lived a long time doesn't mean I always know what to do, especially when it comes to you." Her eyes got glassier and she blinked it away. "You are many, many wonderful things, young lady," she continued in a hoarser voice. "I suspect you know that. There are those that will want to keep you, protect you forever, keep you a little girl." She leaned forward, steel in her spine, iron in her voice. I wanted to be as strong. "You are not merely a little girl, Rose Preston. You *are* a child, but there is nothing little about you. You're something in between little and grown, and something far more than both. Stay strong, Rose. I suspect you'll have many reasons to."

My mouth hung open. Embarrassed by it, I filled it with tea and kept watching my old friend as she watched me. Another ten-year-old would have been unnerved, terrified even, by the old woman's prophetic and obscure words, but not me. Not me.

I knew they were true.

Increasingly, Annie's talks with my mother became more heated. Annie often walked me to the bus stop while my mother watched sadly from the big window. I didn't understand what was happening exactly—Annie said that must be a first for me, not understanding—but Annie thought I needed help. And my mother didn't want to get it for me.

I didn't know if I needed help or not.

Since Annie said those prophetic things to me, I'd thought more and more about her dying. The way I saw death was constantly changing. The disassembling of life was nothing new to me, but feeling so bitter about it that it seeped into every pore...it made me desperate. Sleep was a thing of the past, as I relentlessly racked my brain for a way to stop the inevitable while lying in the dark. I couldn't lose Annie. The way she cared for me, it was a growing love, something that changed and had life. My mother would always be the center of my universe and I would be hers—but it was a stifling love. Dark. Secretive.

I never told my mother about what I did for the squirrel, about Amelia's cold. Certainly she'd kept many more secrets from me. Secrets that riddled my brain, pushing their way in while memories pushed their way out, meeting in the middle and pulling me apart.

After school one afternoon, Annie waited with the buses for me in her old Lincoln Town Car.

"Why are you here?" I asked, opening the car door.

"Hello to you, too," she said with a smile, and patted the seat. A pack of Fruit Stripe gum waited for me on the dashboard, getting warmer and softer. I took it down and unwrapped a piece—I liked to be the one to make it soft and warm. "I'm taking you somewhere to talk about how you're feeling, Rose," Annie said.

"I talk to you," I said, the red-hot power blasting through my chest. Even though I *wanted* this, it wasn't me exactly who wanted it. My head roiled with needs: my mother's, my brain's, my heart's, my childhood's, my sight.

Her hands on the wheel, eyes on the road, she said, "You don't say enough, honey. And I fear that you never can, not to anyone who knows you." She glanced over at me, sizing me up, wondering if I could handle what she was about to say. I knew she would say it anyway. "For all you see, you see yourself the least, kiddo. But you're falling apart more each day. Closing off. Staying inside, your bedroom lights off too early, the way you stop eating, the weight you're losing that you can't afford to. What you're going through in that brilliant heart and head of yours is *feelings*, kid." She laughed mirthlessly. "I don't think you know what to do with them."

That was my first visit to the psychiatrist's office.

"Caught ya lookin', Psychiatrist," I said, walking into his office and flopping onto the sofa.

He chuckled. "Yes, yes I suppose I was. It's a new fashion statement for you, Charity, isn't it? I've not seen you in so little makeup, and in sneakers? I didn't know you owned a pair."

"I like it when you're cheeky. Yeah, I'm just…turning over a new leaf, I guess? I mean, I have been for a while, been Harpin' it up a lot less."

"You don't seem especially happy about it. You still enjoy that lifestyle?"

I was long over the I-didn't-choose-the-Harpy-the-Harpy-chose-me speech, so I did something that I took as a step in the right direction—I was honest. "You know I do. But I'm trying to remember that just because you like some-thing doesn't make it good for you. Not whiskey, I don't care if that's good for me or not."

"How are you feeling about the change, Charity?" He adjusted the buttons on his sweater vest. Maybe I'd try that ensemble next.

"I feel…I feel pointless." Actual honesty. "The Harpy does something. Me? I do things but none of them are smart."

"This is your chance! It's exciting to me, at least, that you're giving yourself a chance to be whatever you choose. This is a big step, Charity."

"Yeah, well I might disagree, Psychiatrist," I huffed, anger building. "You know, I've got this boyfriend who's like, perfect, to an annoying degree now, and I've got my bird, who, who, loves me all damn day and I'm just like *why*? What the hell does he see in me except a hand that feeds him?" I growled, furious suddenly, full of guilt and venom. "I'm the one in the fucking cage, can't you see that, Psychiatrist? With your goddamn degrees and your sweater vest? I'm here to *get better*, what a fucking riot that is. I'm getting better, yay, getting better than I was. So much for loving me as I am, that's a joke. I'm better and what am I? What the fuck am I?" Poor Dr. Mortimer's face was a mix of pity and pleasure because he was doing his job right. "I'm a caged bird, Psychiatrist," I said as normally as I could, but with grinding teeth. "I've got the wings but I can't use them."

Dr. Mortimer steepled his hands under his chin, pushed his glasses up. "Charity—"

"Psychiatrist." Had to keep the names in perspective or he'd forget.

He didn't smile this time. "You're at a crossroads greater than any you've been brought to before. The fact that you're so angry about it, that's good, Charity, really good. Change is painful, it shouldn't always be done with a smile. You've got work to do, Charity. You always do, you're a work in progress. I know you think you're only doing it for Robbie. I don't think that's true, though. I think you're doing it for you, but you don't know who that person is. She'll fly again. You'll fly again."

I nodded. "I'll fly again," I repeated. I just had to stretch my wings a different way.

ROSE

My mother started smoking.

The pack of cigarettes lay on the spotless table defiantly, daring me to question them, flouncing their filth in my face.

This was her answer to Annie bringing me to the psychiatrist.

We ate dinner in silence, me pulling apart a piece of over-cooked steak with my fork and knife as if it had insulted me as much as the cigarettes.

"Why are you doing that, baby? Just eat," she said.

Aren't we mad at each other? I thought. *Is she apologizing? What for?*

"I'm not really hungry, Mom."

She dropped her fork, the ringing church bell sound against the plate making me gasp and stare.

"You used to call me 'Mommy,'" she whispered, smiling so strangely that I wanted to run from the table. The weight of it smothered me.

"Sorry," I whispered back, "Mommy."

It reminded me of a movie I'd found by accident on TV late one night when thoughts of death kept me up, *Mommy Dearest*. My mother's smile scared me more than the crippling scene with the wire hanger. This I couldn't turn off, and I couldn't possibly see how it would end well.

Her face crumpled, but no tears fell. Her hands shook until she put them down firmly on the table as if holding it there.

"I don't know what I'm doing anymore, Rosie. I'm trying to be a good mom but I've just *failed* you, you don't even know how much." One dry sob and she raised her head, met my eyes. "They say parenting doesn't come with a manual, but I'm pretty sure you could write one," she said with a wet, hiccupping laugh. "How can I take care of you, baby? How can *I* take care of *you*?"

Red-hot anger pulsed in my gut, throbbed a line up through my chest. Anger that I was being asked such a thing. *"You are not merely a little girl, Rose Preston. You are a child, but there is nothing little about you."* Just like Annie would do, I reached across the table and I held my mother's hand. "You're doing great, Mom," I said.

She smiled sadly, shoulders dropping. She'd been waiting for me to take away her failure.

There's a cocoon in your mind, Rose, I heard in my head in that silky voice. *Force it open.* The intrusive thought connected to the heat in my stomach, two halves of the same thing somehow. My mind was threatening to unleash some secret monster into my life. No tumor…something *else*.

I let go of my mother's hand and went back to poking my steak, but the thought of eating it sickened me. "Sorry, Mom, it's cooked too much for me. I…want to see blood."

I pushed back from the table and ran outside into the falling dark, my needs so much darker.

~

aking things apart was an obsession I'd literally hidden from under my covers for weeks. The lattice of x-ray grids that swarmed my vision only disappeared in the darkness. That's what I wanted, inside and out —all-consuming darkness.

But even the darkness couldn't hide the secrets festering in my brain, *itching* at my scalp to wiggle out, until I couldn't take it for another second. I burst out of my bed, ran out the door, the screen slamming behind me.

Night brilliance. Thick ebony, muffled movement, hushed life. Fresh air to stifled lungs, smooth black to an aching mind. The cold grass caressed my bare feet, the air colder from the beach breeze. I fell to the ground, stared into the bruise-dark sky. I tuned out the ants and worms, roots and earth, my vision overwhelming after such little use, unfocused, racing, pushing. I looked as hard at the clouds as I could, thin, wispy tendrils, almost nothing. But I knew better, to look past the surface. A month ago, I wouldn't have even had to try—my vision had been shoved away, just as I was. But there's a difference between hiding something and ignoring it.

It's fear.

I won't be afraid of my own memories, no matter what they are.

Gritting my teeth, I pushed to see the ice within those clouds, a weave like Annie's fence, molecules like bubbles inside that, almost alive in their movement but not quite.

Almost alive, but not quite.

An unbidden image of the squirrel, its blood on my hands, my pink pants, its wounds unstitched, its eyes vacant. Almost dead, it was almost dead, but not.

Annie would be dead.

Stop!

My hand shot out and grasped a wriggling thing, a creature that squeaked at its sudden capture. A mole. I squeezed it, eyes still scanning the clouds, the ice within, the movement, but my hand felt veins, twig bones, organs the size of M&Ms, a heart beating so viciously it seemed to attack life rather than live it.

"Attack."

Moaning at the silky voice in my head, adding to the pressure in there, I had to *do* something to make the bloody images stop, make something happen to replace the thought before it even happened, before death proved to me how quickly it worked.

"Violently attacked. Rose, remember."

"Noooooooooo," I moaned, clutching my head, pushing it back into the grass, the blades taunting me with their very makeup. *No, not grass—feathers.* The whirring of the world stopped in its tracks, my breathing the universe's heartbeat, and I reached to the side of my head with one hand, the other still clutching the wriggling mole, to pluck away an ebony feather. I kept reaching, discovering a halo, a cushion of black feathers around my head. My heartbeat-breathing hitched. And I thought I saw a pair of black jewels glittering in the matte black sky between tree leaves, a presence that defied being taken apart.

I squeezed my eyes shut against it.

It took more willpower than I'd ever used in my life, more than when I fixed the radio, or made Amelia feel better, more than when I repaired the squirrel, more than destroying my tumor. But I opened my hand and let the mole go.

I let it go, but that's not what I wanted to do with it.

Growling, sobbing, still on my back, I dug my fingers into the grass forcefully enough to feel soft soil underneath. I dug and dug up to my elbows, aching for death, and found the miniscule bones of some small creature there, ran my fingers over and over them, arms anchoring me to the ground until I couldn't bear myself another second.

I curled onto my side in the grass and wished sleep would take me away from the world I saw too well.

"What the—"

Traveling backward was a bitch of a sensation. A combo of being too huge to exist in a tiny Polaroid picture found in some closet, and of being invisible, substance-less in a world more real than me.

So it was even weirder to be flying along, minding my own business in the past and having that glow, the one that told me where the Big Bads were, drive me down into a yard. A really quiet little yard with tall trees ringing it. Plopping myself between these trees, I watched where the red glow came from.

A kid. Not just any kid.

The little girl was laying on the mushy ground with her goddamn arms buried in it up to the elbows.

"Rose," I said to myself.

Holy hell, did someone do *this to her? Some sick punishment?* Not my usual calling, but Rose wasn't a usual kid obviously. We had a connection.

I stepped out from the cover of trees with one claw, sinking into the ground a little, but that was when she popped up like it was nothing, arms covered in black dirt. And like some mangy dog, she started digging. Kid was growling, wildly digging, crouched inhumanly, soil spraying the air behind her, falling onto her dirty hair. "That's not dirt," I muttered, and squinted, inching closer.

Feathers. Black feathers. *Sonofabitch!*

Then out of nowhere the kid stopped digging, rubbing something between her fingers. I inched forward more, remembered I could be fucking invisible and handled that, got close and saw she was fiddling with *bones.* Really small bones. I wondered if she'd buried some pet there—but I had the feeling she just sort of knew where random bones were. Creep. She held the bones to her nose as she crouched there, sniffed them deeply. Double creep. Then her shoulders fell. She shuddered, snapped her head side to side, making me flinch, a little nervous that she *would* see me, because shit— weird kid. As if snapping out of one of Psychiatrist's hypnosis sessions, she woke up to reality, and didn't like what she saw. Her body racked with sobs, and she fell to her side, curled up, and just lay there still.

I had no clue what I was doing there. I hunted dirtbag dudes, relieved them of their shitty lives. I didn't hang out with weird kids. Or I hadn't until now.

I found myself rooted to the spot, maybe a foot away from her. I couldn't reach out to her, no matter how much I wanted to, wasn't sure I wanted to at all.

The kid *scared* me.

Not just creepy digging scary, but the real kind of scary. Real scary, like I knew she meant something to me. We had a connection—even if it was Queen-created, Queen-approved, stamped with the seal of black feathers. I could walk away from the kid right now. She'd never seen me, didn't know me.

Rose, eyes squeezed shut, murmuring to herself, shivering

on the soft, wet ground. She unwrapped her little arms from herself, covered in goosebumps and blotchy with cold, and stretched out a shaking hand, hot pink fingers spread wide.

She knows I'm here. I'm invisible but she sees me.

In my own fucking time and place, I was a beacon of LOOK AT ME and still, nobody saw. Nobody ever fucking saw me.

I reached out my own shaking fingers, touched her tiny ones, and she grasped them, flooding me with inner warmth.

I was free.

The ambulance lights woke me before the siren did.

I sat bolt upright in bed. *I'm in bed?* I was clean, fresh pajamas. My memory was…wrong. I'd been dreaming of the mole biting my hand until it was nothing but a raw stump, but the nightmare I awoke to was worse.

My mother held me close as they wheeled Annie into the back of the ambulance. Nobody could answer questions in their haste, we could only stand there in the cold night in our pajamas and wonder.

"Mom, can we go?" I pleaded, voice scratchy with too little sleep.

"Yes, baby, of course."

We followed the ambulance to the hospital, and after a while a doctor told us what had happened to her. She'd collapsed when it was still light out, which is all Annie remembered. It had been hours that she laid there, slipping in and out of consciousness, until she finally crawled to the phone and dialed the operator.

"I never saw anything wrong," I said as my mother talked

in a quiet hospital voice to the doctor, but they weren't listening to me.

We stayed with Annie all night. My mother was good in the way that she didn't make a fuss about me needing my sleep, and nobody bothered her about getting shoes on my bare feet. She always exuded a feeling that there was no law above a mother's, and it became true. I was sure Annie could feel the love in the room, even as she lay in fitful sleep.

When my mother drifted off in the stiff bedside chair, I tried to think of what had happened between the mole in my hand and this moment, but everything was a blur, like trying to see through a window in the pouring rain… My arms should have been dirty, I remembered my arms in the dirt… different pajamas. My mother hadn't been the one to find me, that was clear.

I remembered the black feathers. The mysterious eyes.

Shaking off the gap in my mind, I focused on relishing the moment of independence to roam the dark hospital hallway in my nightgown and bare feet in search of a vending machine. The beeping of monitors, the *hush-hush-hush* of nurses' uniforms as they hurried in and out of rooms, the quiet conversations, it all made an odd melody that I soaked in. *I like this place,* I thought.

I was digging through the coins in my mother's change purse at the vending machine, contemplating trying coffee on the sly, when I heard, "Rose?"

I spun around, instantly guilty about having left Annie's side *and* having taken my mother's change purse, and came face to face with…

"Hi," I squeaked.

He was kind and pleasant, and I didn't know his name.

"Doctor Trask," he said with a crooked smile and a soothing voice. "I took care of you here, remember?"

"I remember," I said quietly.

"Are you sick again, Rose?" he asked with such intense concern that it instantly warmed me to him. His gentleness was like a sweater. He'd tried to fix my brain but couldn't.

"I'm not sick," I said a little more loudly this time. "The tumor is gone."

His gaze drifted around me, as if he were hoping to see a halo or maybe wings. "It most certainly is, sweetie. Extraordinary. Unprecedented."

Unprecedented. That word again. It was better than "cunning" anyway. "The Scientist sent you for me," I said.

"Mr. Cleary? No. He didn't send me. Scientists have to find unexplainable phenomena and try to explain it. He was looking for you all along, wasn't he? For someone who offered something new. But I didn't come here for him."

I trusted Doctor Trask. I liked his sandy hair and simple, poetic way of speaking. He was handsome and young. He was honest. And he didn't see ugliness the way a lot of people do.

"I don't want to show that scientist anything," I said, unwrapping my Mr. Goodbar. "He wants to use me, make me a guinea pig."

Doctor Trask edged past me to the vending machine, digging in his own pocket under the white coat. "I imagine he does." He shrugged. "You *could* just help him. See what he might be able to tell *you*, right?" He turned around with a Zero bar, took a bite, and leaned back against the machine. "I bet you could use some answers yourself." Another bite.

"I don't ask questions." My mother had said that so many times about me, it became part of who I was. *Rose doesn't ask questions; she raises them.*

"Then how do you find out more about the stuff you don't know?" He took a bite of the white candy bar, as white as his coat.

"I know everything I need to," I snapped. "I see things—" I

stopped myself, filled my mouth with candy. Secrets were not meant for people in white coats.

It wasn't fast enough. A flicker of interest crossed his face—concern that something was wrong with me. He wrapped the rest of his candy bar in the silver paper. With narrowed eyes he said, "Rose, you had something show up in your brain then disappear. *Poof.*" He made a little hand explosion next to his head. "That's a wonder beyond anything I've ever seen—and it shows me there's a whole lot more going on in your head than anyone else's in the whole *world,* probably. Don't be afraid to let someone look harder, okay? Give Mr. Cleary a chance. Who knows what might be uncovered? Those questions you don't ask...they might all be stuck," he delicately tapped my temple, the Zero bar wrapper brushing my cheek, "inside."

He smiled at me warmly, put his hand on my shoulder as he walked by, going off to do his job and make a bunch of little miracles occur for someone else. I turned to watch him go. Over his shoulder he said with a smile, "You know where to find me."

~

*A*nnie came home a couple of days later. We picked her up in her own car so she'd be comfortable, and I helped her up the stairs as my mother opened doors and babbled about "anything you need," and "check on you," and "casserole."

When she was settled on the couch, I asked Mom to put on some tea and I sat beside Annie, holding her hand.

I was holding her hand.

My eyebrows furrowed. I remember the feeling of them knitting together at this little change in my demeanor, the strange feeling of giving in that I wasn't certain I disliked. Simply holding hands with her.

"You'll be okay, Annie," I said for both our benefits.

"Oh, I know, honey," Annie said breezily, waving a hand for emphasis. "I'm always okay."

"Me too."

As my mother bustled about in the kitchen, mumbling, Annie told me to keep going to the psychiatrist so that I *would* be okay. I told her I would try. I nearly didn't, but I decided to tell her about meeting Doctor Trask in the hallway, and the odd things he said to me. She wasn't surprised, but she was alarmed. And the worry deepened the pain in her head and her chest. I could feel it, the ache was so vivid. My eyes stung, my throat hurt. She was so much closer to dying than she'd been before the hospital.

I could do something about it if I tried hard enough. Death was a question. And I was the girl with answers.

~

For the millionth night in a row, I found myself dying for sleep, but standing in the yard sucking in the chilly beach air instead. I screamed into the night as loudly as I could, letting out all the hurt and confusion and irrational, scorching child's anger that knew no bounds and only sought blame. I wasn't *enough*. I was just a kid who had a tumor once, and it left my head just a little better than it had been. That didn't mean I could cure death.

My mother's feet pounded into the living room as she called out for me frantically. "Rose? Rose! Rose!" When she spotted me through the screen door, she ran out and threw her arms around me, and she sobbed, rocking me. We didn't have to say a word—our fears and frenzy spoke for itself.

Neither of us knew what to do next about anything in our lives.

"Go back to bed, Mom," I said, drying her tears with my nightgown sleeve.

"What about you?" she said, our roles reversing before my eyes.

"I can't sleep."

"Let me make you cocoa. It will help."

The cottage was silent in the night, the sound of the water boiling the most comforting thing I could remember. I was making a habit of taking comfort in the night when the world was quiet—but I always seemed to find someone to complicate things.

I closed my eyes at the *clunk* of the mug on the kitchen table, my mother's fingers trailing across mine as she pulled her hand back and sat across from me. She was still making little sleepy sounds, sniffling here and there, rubbing her forehead when she plopped her elbow on the table.

"What demons have you up at night, Rosie? When did you change from my baby to a little girl who can't sleep?"

I just chuckled—a thing I thought only old men did, and now me.

Mom wasn't looking at me, but into her mug, the steam enveloping her face. A lovely thing, all sweetness and delight, but hidden. In a haze that wasn't quite real.

The realization sent a hot, dull butterknife into my psyche. *Not real. Hiding. Lying.*

"Not. Real." The itch in my brain, that voice that wasn't mine, it jumped in. I wanted to disassemble the thought, figure out what wasn't real, what the hiding and lying was, what this smokescreen was that my mind held the key to.

I battered my brain, shaking my head until the thought was knocked out and I had to squeeze my eyes shut. When I opened them, my mother was still intent on her mug. She'd seen nothing. I was on my own, trying to find something that wasn't there, some secret, some unknown intruder in my mind. Something I knew but didn't know. My head bobbed in exhaustion.

"Good night, Mom," I said, and left my mug still steaming on the table, my mother squeezing my hand as I dragged myself by.

~

Toys, dolls, magazines and children's books lay scattered all over my bedroom floor. I couldn't possibly recall why I'd used them, what fascination they held for me.

I had something new to hold my attention.

I checked on Annie first thing in the morning, knocking on her white metal door and waiting with bated breath until she came into view, yellow terry bathrobe swishing. Happy to see she was up and moving, I let her be. We were friends, but no old woman wants to be constantly hounded by a little kid.

My short, but deep sleep had allowed me to dream. I didn't remember any of it, but when I woke up to the blazing sun streaming in my window, I knew what the dream had taught me—that I had to find the right tools. Find the right tools. *Find the right tools.*

My endgame was to ensure Annie stayed healthy and alive for as long as I possibly could. And I had the ability to do it. I'd fixed, *changed* that squirrel, I could do something like that for her. The body is a universe of interworking mechanics, and yet they're all independent, any one able to malfunction.

It would be challenging, but nobody else would take this chance, not one other person in the world could even try.

Taking death apart from a living being—it would be excruciating, make her pray for death if she lived through it at all.

It would take practice.

Bringing her pansies from around the tree was a gut punch that everything beautiful died. The smell of ginger snaps made me question what smell would replace it when she was gone. Leaving her reminded me that it could be the last time.

My brain was getting stronger, gearing up for something big, I'd known it since the voice in my head appeared, known it since the tumor showed itself, giving me flickers of knowledge, of memory, pathways into the construct of my mind. I wanted to open these doors in my head more than anything in the world because behind one of them was the answer, all the answers.

Dr. Trask's words came back to me: *Give Mr. Cleary a chance.* He could help me find the answers I needed, help me open all those secret doors. The answer to helping Annie lurked behind one—but what would I find behind the others?

Mom had slipped into the treating me like a ghost phase, so I was getting out more and more. I'd walk to the arcade or to the beach without her knowing, returning to fewer and fewer questions all the time. It was one of my excursions to White Horse Beach on a rainy day, no tourists, that I found the tool I needed.

An injured seagull—that wasn't uncommon—but this one was old. I could *see* how he'd given up, unable to bounce back from its withered, mangled leg. The poor thing was mangy. Some gulls went close to it, as if to comfort him, while others avoided it like a disease. I went right over to him, straight through the bird mob—the birds sure weren't afraid of me. My mother called them beach raccoons.

"Hey there," I said, squatting beside him. "You want to come home with me, maybe?" I furrowed my brows, trying not to cry for the creature, hopeless, motionless in the rain. I took off my slicker to wrap him in it. He scarcely moved.

"You're sicker than I thought. Aren't you, buddy?" I cooed to him as I walked back home. The rain was really coming down now, and I was shivering more than the bird. "I think I can fix you."

I went to the bulkhead around the back of the house, the doors screeching as I pulled them open. I couldn't let my mother see what I was carrying—she'd long since discouraged me from bringing home wounded animals.

In the basement, I emptied a cardboard box of Christmas lights and filled it with old t-shirts and clothes I'd outgrown that my mother couldn't bear to throw away. She had at least five plastic bins full of everything from onesies to old sneakers. I smiled about it—how she'd needed me with her so much that every little thing made her feel closer. I was sad for her. Afraid for her. Afraid that I would leave her behind.

"I won't leave you behind," I said to the bird, which was closing its eyes now and letting me run a finger across its head. I don't think it trusted me as much as it just didn't have the strength anymore. I hadn't even heard it make a noise yet.

I fell back on my butt, exhausted myself. The beach tended to take everything out of me since recovering from the tumor, and carrying the bird in the rain made it doubly hard. The gull nestled down into the makeshift nest, going puffy in its comfort. I saw him: his rapidly beating heart slowed down. He felt safe. Content.

I reminded myself that there was every chance I would kill this creature.

Drained, I stretched out on the concrete floor beside the bird, wishing I was as comfortable as he was. And I cried.

～

The rain still pelted and I was still bone-weary, but I went back to the beach the next day and found some crab pieces that had washed ashore to bring home to the gull. My mother sat at the table once I'd returned, chain-smoking. She hadn't noticed I'd left.

"Little nature girl, what are you doing out in the rain? I thought you were still in bed."

I dropped my slicker on the floor, the crab shells making a tiny *crunch*. "Mom, you said good morning to me and kissed me on the cheek."

"Was that this morning…" she mumbled.

More and more she covered up her exhaustion of me by creating itty bitty alternate realities. Like not "remembering" that she'd seen me, when I knew she had. If she wasn't questioning where I was walking, what I was thinking, or talking to me so much as I read a book that I couldn't complete a thought, she was completely non-present, ignoring me as if I were an alien she hoped wouldn't notice her. It was harrowing.

Cold-shouldering her, I slipped out of my wet clothes at the door, leaving them where I dropped them, and headed for my bedroom to get dry pajamas. Rainy days were never spent out of pajamas if we were home. I missed that. I missed the mom, right there in the kitchen. She'd envelop me with a hug and a blanket when I snuggled up beside her, and our rainy day TV-watching and board game-playing would commence.

That part of our family had been taken away by the tumor.

I shut the basement door softly so as not to remind her that I existed, the bundle of crab pieces in the pouch I'd made with the bottom of my pink PJ shirt. I'd put on enough weight that they fit again.

Old t-shirts still wrapped around it loosely, the gull sat where I'd left it and seemed even older than it had the day before. He squawked when he saw me, or smelled the crab more likely. "Shhhh, birdie, save your strength. I'll feed you." I unwrapped a yellow striped piece of gum for myself, and got to work with him.

It pecked at me, made me yelp, not gentle at all as it went for the crab. I dropped the pieces in the nest and watched him eat, wanting to pet him, but I absolutely could not grow attached to the creature.

"You're not a pet," I said softly to him. *I said I wouldn't abandon you just yesterday.* "I'll help you, but you aren't my pet." It turned its black eye toward me. "We're friends though, aren't we?" I said, smiling so wide I felt it in my ears.

The rain pitter-pattered on the cottage, the silence and cold wrapping around me, the pecking of the hungry gull sweet and soothing to watch.

Watch.

I pushed the x-ray vision aside that showed me too much, that clouded my sight with minutiae, and looked with my heart, with my brain.

The skin on his neck shows between the feathers.

Dirt mars his back that he should have preened off.

The leg is completely immobile now.

Rain sings pit-pat-pat-pat.

His heart beats slowly, bump. Bump. Bump. Bumpbump-bump. *Irregular.*

His liver is mottled.

His blood isn't moving well.

His throat is constricted.

He's cold despite the warm nest.

The cold floor makes me shift in my cross-legged spot.

His pancreas is overworked.

His bowels are weak.

My teeth hurt from grinding them so hard. I took a breath that swelled my stomach, my shoulders dropped from beside my ears. So much was wrong with the old bird, it was difficult to know what to do, where to go. I was helpless.

Frustrated, angry, heated in the belly, I growled—and yet the dying bird was perfectly content nibbling away, sitting in long-term aching and discomfort. If that was what being old was like, I wanted no part of it.

Instantly I was disgusted with myself for thinking that. Annie was the most wonderful person I knew, I loved everything about her.

Bitterness whirled in my belly to think how much I loved Annie when my own mom was right upstairs, alone, hating me for being different. I was angry at myself for what she would surely see as a betrayal.

The guilt threw me into a swell of anger, heating my stomach until a faint glow showed through the pink shirt.

I had to act. No wallowing in bad feelings and fears. I focused on the bird.

At first, I sought a place to help, looking deep inside him for where I could make a difference to the creature—but it was just everywhere. Quickly exasperated, tears welling, heart pounding, eyes feeling like they were bleeding, I looked...

Muscles, thin, stretched...

Past the gizzard, larger than the organ that matters...

Kidneys. No bacteria there, nothing invasive;

same in the lungs, the bladder. All just functioning poorly. Slowly.

Flustered, I got up, legs buckling from the mental exertion, and went to the bulkhead door with an old plastic *Star Wars* cup. I filled it with rain for the bird, who was dehydrated. But that wouldn't prolong its life.

Nothing natural would prolong its life. But I was as unnatural as they came.

I gave the bird his water, but couldn't bring myself to sit with him again. He drank what might be his last sips of water alone.

~

No matter where I went in our little cottage, the bird's beating heart thundered within me as it waited. Waited for…death, for me, for the next minute. The ticking clock was there all the time, reminding me more and more of Annie.

"I want to buy it," my mom said. I blinked hard.

"You don't have enough money, Mom."

"Just because you're the banker doesn't mean you can tell me how to manage my money, young lady," she teased through a grin as she handed me the ends of her Monopoly cash. I handed her Park Place.

We'd been playing Monopoly at the kitchen table ever since I came up from the basement, the rain making muffled sounds against the window screens and the roof shingles. We ordered a pizza, and Mom tipped the guy extra for coming out in the rain. He thanked her profusely, and for the first time ever, I bothered to ask,

"Where do we get money from, Mom?"

She put the pizza down on the counter. "Oh baby, you're ten. Stick to worrying about Monopoly money, huh?"

"Mom, I had a brain—"

"Don't! Don't tell me you had a brain tumor so you can handle anything. You're still my baby and what you don't know won't hurt you."

Slamming my hands on the table, our game pieces toppling, pink money falling to the floor, I yelled, "What I don't know *gave* me the tumor to begin with, Mom! Burrowed into my brain! Your lies are finding their way out. My secrets," I tapped my temple so hard it hurt, "are digging their way out. I can see *everything.* You won't see what's right in front of you."

My mother didn't get angry, didn't yell back, didn't deny it. She gave me a slice of pizza instead of an answer. Perhaps I'd always known not to bother asking questions because I'd be met with the same answers.

Falling back into my chair, I bit into the soft, red, gushing pizza slice and gulped in time with the bird's heartbeat below ground.

～

I didn't see Annie the next day. I couldn't. The rain was the kindest excuse, but the real reason was that I'd thrown away being my mother's baby because of one stupid question, and that I heard the old woman's heartbeat in the dying bird in my basement.

I'd summoned every bit of willpower I had to get out of bed when the sleeplessness became too much, and the heartbeat turned into angry spiders crawling through my skin. I couldn't bear the numb darkness seeping in through the cracks in my x-ray vision.

"I'm going to play in the basement for a while," I told my mom, answered only with silence and listless eyes. She was a mirror of my sadness.

Silence and listlessness found me again in the basement. The gull had barely touched the water. An odor emanated from him.

"Here you go, buddy. Try this." I held a pizza crust to his face but he made no effort toward it. *He's not a pet; he's a mission.*

84

When I planted myself in front of him, it wasn't with hopefulness. It was with determination, despite knowing I would fail. Experiments have to fail, theories have to evolve, chances have to be taken and squandered, but one time, *one time* is all it takes to succeed.

He nosed at the pizza, poking it, and I concentrated. I had nowhere to start, nowhere to focus, so I dove in with my mind. Threw every bit of my energy into it.

I moved something inside him.

He twitched.

My heart jumped as his did.

The bird cocked his head, pecked at nothing with sudden, useless urgency.

Deep breath. I pushed the x-ray vision away, looked hard inside him to find the weakest part of his liver. My fingers flexing in front of me through the air, I took apart the softest, thinnest part of the organ.

He twitched again, but this time there was a hot stab of pain through us both. I gasped, but recovered fast. It meant something was *working*.

I went at him again, removing the hurtful parts just like with my tumor. I didn't notice at first that I was mumbling, "I'll fix you, I'll fix you, I'll fix you…"

The bird squawked, its head twisting oddly.

I took it as a good sign, or I wanted to. Maybe—definitely —it was an excuse to *look* deeper, harder, to pluck out the offenders. My head shook on my shoulders, I gritted my teeth, I dug my fingertips into the cement floor. "I'll fix you."

He pecked at the pizza crust, needing to *do* something with the energy coursing through him.

Energy coursed through me.

The gull let out a pitiful cry, and I heard, felt, a squelching squeeze in him—the wrong part.

Panicked, I pushed harder, not removing but rearranging,

trying to refit him back together in a way that would work, desperately taking him apart, rebuilding but failing, failing just a little every time.

I'll fail if I do this to Annie.

It became her organs that I ripped apart with my mind.

I screamed, my stomach flipped.

I'd kill Annie. My mother would lock me away again, far, far worse this time. I'd deserve it, and she'd tell me she was protecting me from evil men who would make me an experiment.

Just like I was doing to this bird.

But I couldn't stop now. Couldn't stop wanting to fix so much more than a bird, even more than Annie. Deeper than that, I knew that there was something very wrong between my mother and me. Something I couldn't fix.

I poured all my desperation into taking the creature apart, all the failing pieces of him, so I could put him back together.

He stopped moving, staring into my eyes. And he fell over in a boneless heap.

"No! No no no no!"

I picked him up too roughly, the broken leg flapping across his sunken chest. Its head hung back, throat muscles vibrating as he tried to breathe.

But he couldn't. It was over.

"Right to the core, all the way in. Taken apart."

I said the words as if they'd been said through me, incredulous, disturbed, pained, but expectant in a way. That something had to happen next. That the destruction couldn't stop now.

It feels too good to stop now.

The scream erupted like molten lava from my throat, anguish overflowing from a black hole of memories with no bottom, surging through me, taking me apart.

Vision blurred by tears, I put the unmoving gull on the cement floor. Then I picked it up again and put a red, threadbare towel under it, as if that were somehow respectful, as if it changed anything. As if I hadn't undone the animal.

Undo you from the inside out.

The words boiled in my belly. I felt the maliciousness of them—and it wasn't my own.

A memory.

I choked, vision shifting, blurry to black, then back again. I held my stomach, retched, but had to yank my hands away like I'd touched a hot stove.

The red heat of my anger showed through my skin again.

The bird was dead. I'd never found the thing that made it what it was, that made its life so frail.

I put my finger on his chest, not looking for the heartbeat; that wasn't why I did it. I pushed aside the dirty white feathers, touched the pinkness of his chest. I rubbed the fragile bones, to understand how such a breakable being ever survived to begin with.

You have no right to be alive.

I screamed again at the unbidden memory of gut-twisting words, at the sudden clench of my bowels that made my forehead sweat and my stomach yowl. I wanted to curl up in a ball, but I didn't.

I pushed harder on the bird's lifeless chest.

Small but strong, I thought. Annie said that about me.

The miniscule bones popped softly, a tiny *crunch* that satisfied me more than the leftover pizza. The thick, red sauce.

Hungry.

I kept going. Scratched at the soft pink skin until it wore thin, pulled it apart until I could see inside.

That was when the taking apart became easy.

Because if I couldn't get this one right, I would learn from it.

I should gather up the bones, feathers, the tiny heart I'd torn free, wrap them in the plastic we seal the windows with in winter, hide it in the workbench we never used. My mother wouldn't come down here, but if she did…

Well, what was one more secret between us?

I trudged up the stairs, exhaustion rippling through my limbs, bumbling confusion and mania in my mind, exhilaration rumbling in my heart. A red-hot hunger for more pushing out through my own soft pink skin, stripping the fragile me away.

Sharing my patented Harpy adventures with Robbie was never date night material, and even less so after our most recent run-in with the illustrious Plymouth PD. But he did come home after he'd cooled off, and things were…back to our withering sense of normal.

So a basic shit show.

We ate spaghetti at our two-person kitchen table in silence, me with one foot up on my chair, the scales having left marks all down one shin that itched like a bastard. Robbie's eyes kept darting to them but I refused to scratch them. I got more annoyed every second.

"New girl," I said through a face full of pasta. "Not sure what to do with her."

"What do you mean?" He jumped on the conversation like he'd been waiting for it for days.

"Meh, don't wanna talk about it. Tell me what you've been doing. Your day job is better dinner talk than mine."

He sighed hard at my contradictory bitchiness, but didn't object. "New kid for me, too."

"Oh, that's cool, right? Getting the help he needs."

"Yeah. Yeah, I guess."

"You *guess?* Nobody could get better help than hanging out with you."

That smile would put me straight into a cold shower. "I hope so. He scares me. Not like, I'm *scared* of him, but I'm afraid he doesn't think he can be helped. The stuff he says…"

"He wants to kill himself, doesn't he?" I stabbed my spaghetti. Robbie leaned back in his chair, ran both hands through his hair. "I get it. You didn't want to tell me because I work at the place he'd end up."

"This isn't about you."

"Everything is about me."

He glared at me…but then he smiled. "Well, of course I don't want to talk about it with you! You…you *like* the Wood of Suicides. The Wood of *Suicides*, Charity. I mean, if you were making them feel *better* there, if you were helping them instead of…" His grimace and hard swallow at the thought of the words said volumes.

"Instead of eating them? Hey, it's a fucked-up food chain, but I'm in the middle of it."

"Cold."

"Listen, I'm doing better. I have…hope now. I'm not clear of the Wood but I, I… I can't fix everyone's problems, and the people down there, they made their choices. I can't change their pasts—" I gasped, cutting myself short, trying to hide it from Robbie.

But I can go back in time.

He took my hand across the table, pulled it closer, leaned in to kiss it, tousled hair falling across my wrist. "I love you," he murmured. "I could never—can't imagine not going insane from what you're going through. You're *so* strong, Charity, I know that you can break free of that place, of the Harpies."

"I love you, too," I choked out. God, it was always hard to

just *say* it, no matter how much I felt it. "I put you through a lot of shit—as if it isn't bad enough I have fucking Harpy seizures all over the place, you still let me have a unicorn collection in our room and that's just wrong. But you've got to let me work through this life of mine. You're not encouraging me, you're shaming me." He started to object but I pleaded with my eyes for him to just listen. "I'm not an addict, Robbie. I don't become the Harpy because I can't stop—"

"You're wrong," he said quietly.

That gutted me. I pulled my hand back, cracked my neck, ran my fingers down the torn-up length of my shin where scaly legs had been. "With all your high and mighty work at the boarding house, I thought you'd know that healing isn't a straight goddamn line. Psychiatrist tells me all the time." *Get it under control, girl. You're getting pissed off. He loves you, he's the only one.* It showed in the softness of his brown eyes as he listened to me get more and more worked up, being defensive. "Baby. I'm finding my way through. I'm good at clawing my way out of a disaster, I work best under pressure. You—you have the boarding house, you're the new home that all those kids find when there's nothing left, and they couldn't be luckier to see that face, those eyes when they're at their worst. But I'm not school guidance counselor material, I'm no Big Sister, you won't find me playing b-ball with the foster kids in a *The More You Know* commercial, and Robbie—it's not a contest! You help your way. Me, I gotta go where the real dirt is, dig out the real monsters. I can stop the bad shit in its tracks. *I'm* the knight in shining armor for once. It's a fucked-up mantle to wear, but it's got some honor to it. *I do.* I want another way to be good, to have some fucking reason in life, but in the meantime? It's my job to make the fuckers pay."

Robbie's shoulders drooped, but he smiled, laughed a little. "Jesus, you are some motivational speaker, Char."

"Thanks," I said, shit-eating grin alive and proud on my face. But I didn't want to tell him about Rose anymore. The kid needed something from me, and I wasn't getting to her in human form. I didn't want him to ruin it for me, and that ruined *him* for me a little.

All *Lady and the Tramp*-like, we ate our spaghetti together until I had to get up for raw hamburger to sprinkle on top.

Some habits don't need breaking.

~

"You're the best birdie, aren't you, baby?"

Keegan huddled down in the palm of my hand. You know, I don't think canaries are supposed to be real cuddly, but screw the fools who said that. They never saw me and my bird. The thing about Keegan was how he treated freedom. That little orange guy could have flown out the open window—or into the screen that he thought was an open window—but he never tried. He came right to me when his cage door was open, which was pretty much always. Always when I was home, anyway. Don't want your bird flying into mirrors and shit when you're out grocery shopping or whatever.

Freedom was knowing what your purpose was. His was to be my bird. Mine was TBD. But I was getting there.

We crapped out on the couch while I thought about my silent revelation when I'd been arguing with Robbie: I *could* go back in time.

I could go back in fucking *time.*

"Time travel ain't just for Michael J. Fox anymore, Keegs," I said, running my finger down his back as he cocked his little head at me. "The question is, what the hell do I do with it?"

What does one do if they can go back in time? Obvs, they right all their wrongs. Fix the regrets, right?

Evan.

My *relationship* with Evan destroyed both him and Jen. Evan, forever tortured in the Wood of Suicides; Jen, a Harpy and glad to be one. The Happy Harpy. If I'd made a different choice, would Evan not have pushed Jen too far, would he still be alive? Would Jen have snapped out of that abusive cycle she was in? I mean shit, I couldn't fix everybody's bad ideas.

I gasped, made Keegan flutter in surprise. Moans issued from my throat, my vision blurred, Keegan becoming a tiny sunset-colored blob. My head pounded in time with my heart, the pain of both doubling me over, trying so hard not to clutch the bird too tight or drop him while I drowned in the moment, in that one, single, horrifying and over-whelming and miraculous thought.

What if I *could* fix everybody's choices?

What if, instead of destroying those sons of bitches that would victimize, torture, ruin the women and girls I saved, I could save them too? Would I give them the chance?

What, are you gonna talk a fucking psychopath out of being a psychopath, Charity? You've spent too much time with Psychiatrist.

Those weren't the thoughts that numbed me, though. It was this one:

What if I can stop Carl Painter before he hurt me?

Short breaths became pained long ones, long blinks became clearer eyesight. I put Keegan back in his cage, fell back onto the couch, and rubbed my hands over my face a million times.

I had the power to move through time like I moved through the air. If I changed something about that first time

Carl touched me, if I made him never even meet my mother… What if I had the chance to kill him before he ever did anything wrong? Knowing that he would one day?

But if I killed him, would he have his daughter? Would she be alive? Or would she be better than she'd ever imagined? If I killed him, would someone else take his place in destroying who I was? If I killed him, or convinced him to not do the terrible things he would do—if I could even do something like that—who would *I* become? The Harpy could disappear in that moment, no need for her to ever exist, but who would I, Hazel Harrington, be if I didn't have *that* past?

I sighed at the next question in my endless string of insane questions.

Would I have chosen to be the Harpy if I could?

Think of all the people you've freed from the worst possible situations. Would you risk not being able to help them?

No way. It couldn't be that easy, that I got stronger and now I could change the past.

But Rose is in the past. And the Queen wants me to help her.

The Queen hadn't said anything about rules to time travel. Not that I'd given her a chance. But she would have, she would have told me, she was never unclear about shit like that, ultimatums and rules. They were fun for her, and made it seem like she was being fair. No, I knew this bitch.

"Your powers are growing, Hazel. You're becoming a stronger, more capable Harpy."

Building me up so I'd play right back into her hands. Then she'd let me back myself into a corner, get myself in trouble so she could offer me some kind of devil's pact and make it go away. No, she was giving me just a long enough rope to hang myself, letting me wonder if I could make my disastrous life into something better.

Or maybe she knew that I wouldn't change a thing. That

I'd live through it all over again because I liked being a monster too much.

"Gah, what the fuck." I stormed to the kitchen, popped open a beer, and sat on the floor with the chicken wings I'd been planning to cook for Robbie for dinner. I did stuff like that sometimes—cooked for him. Because it was nice. Because I could do nice things sometimes if I tried, when someone deserved it. The raw meat satisfied more than one craving in me when I needed to think, though. And I talked to myself. "I could help people like Robbie, do something that isn't ripping people's throats out." Tore off a piece of thigh with a head twist. "I could be okay. Never raped or beaten or anything. I could...run away sooner." *What about all the women you've saved since then? The little girls who won't ever see the Harpy destroy their abusers?*

"Yeah, but what about *me*?" I said out loud, throwing the bones back into the bowl, fingers greasy and cold. "I deserve a normal life, too."

I picked up the beer can with my nasty fingers, muttering to myself, wondering how much time had passed as I philosophized over the possibility of time travel.

And I stopped. I didn't drink it.

With an eye roll that hurt my brain, I put the beer can down on the floor again. Because Robbie said I should drink more water.

If I couldn't do that one stupid thing to make sure my own life was better, did I deserve to change my past? Who the hell was I to judge who deserved what?

Said the bird bitch who judges and executes people all the time.

Fact remained that it was kinda my job to decide who deserved to live. A responsibility everyone else might be afraid to take on, but not me. Not me. I could be accused of a lot of things, but turning down a good challenge or a burger wasn't on the list.

In my own apartment I would have left the beer can and bowl on the floor until I cared about picking it up, but in *our* apartment, I put the bowl in the sink and poured the beer down the drain. "Goodbye, old friend." Slugging down a glass of water and wincing like it was bad vodka, I came up with a hard and fast idea on how to test out this shit of time traveling and saving the world. I wished I'd been drunk to do it.

*S*ummer days were spent alone, or visiting with Annie. Watching over her. She seemed to heal just seeing me, and I felt like a lead brick was lifted from me to see her. I felt *real* with her, more than my mother's daughter, more than a prodigy, more than this new hunger for death. Not more real than the intrusive memories and the voice in my head, but real enough to ask questions.

"Annie, where does my mother's money come from?"

A touch of fear lit up her droopy eyes. "Well, I don't think that's anything you need to worry about, Rose."

My teacup *clinked* roughly into its saucer. "She said the same thing. You know I can understand a family budget."

Annie smirked into her teacup. "It's nothing *I* should be worried about either," she said. I didn't move, didn't blink. "You are a rare creature, aren't you, Rose Preston?" she muttered. She pursed her thin lips even thinner and let out a breath that she must have been holding in for as long as she knew this secret of my mother's. I don't know if the breath relieved her or aged her even more.

I stole the moment to push her to my side a little harder.

"I *am* a rare kid, Annie. I can handle more than the average ten-year-old." Tears sprang to my eyes as flashes of the tumor, the squirrel, Sean Singh, the aloneness, my mother, the memories, the voice, other vicious things I couldn't quite place raced through my head and heart. "This simple thing barely matters when you've seen what I've seen," I choked out, tears coursing now, "and she'll never tell me. If it's nothing, why won't she tell me?"

With a sharp glance at the door, Annie took on a renewed vigor. "Baby," she said, just like my mother would, "do you remember anything of your father?"

"I don't ask questions," I whispered. Jolt of fiery nausea.

"That's not what I asked." She leaned over the table and tapped my forehead lightly, pushing me as much as I'd pushed her, and I regretted ever asking, ever sitting down at this table, ever coming over here, ever leaving my bed where I never got pushed. "Do you *remember*? Remembering doesn't depend on anyone else, Rose. You're a child, and you shouldn't have to rely on yourself, but at the end of the day…"

She trailed off but I was still ready to throw up at the mention of the word *father*. I couldn't stomach the thought of *my* father. I didn't have one of those. I refused to add that non-mystery to the mix now.

"I don't want to talk about this anymore."

"I'll tell you what you want to know."

"I figured it out, okay? He pays for us to live."

"In a way, yes. But do you know why?"

I threw myself back from the table and launched to my feet, the chair tipping over behind me. "I don't care! He isn't real! I don't need whoever he is, I don't want to hear anything else, nothing!"

But Annie had fire to match my own, and she wasn't going halfway.

"Your mother never wanted you to know, but God help me, if the *knot* of memories in your brain didn't cause that goddamn tumor, I don't know what did. That thing was no regular tumor, that was *made*. It was in your head, trying to tell you what happened to you—"

That was when my mother came slowly into the house without knocking, an expression of disgusted fury and horror mingling on her face.

"Rose Preston, what have you done?" she wailed.

~

*T*he bird lay in pieces on the basement floor.

My mother walked slowly, soundlessly through the laid-out parts. And they were—laid out. In a wide circle. Bare skin caked with blood, crisp white bones, an array of feathers in meticulously placed size patterns. Claws removed from feet, feet still loosely attached to skinny legs in a separate place. His head, with the same black, vacant eyes—but the top removed like a cookie jar lid. The heart and brain beside each other, partners in this horror.

"What did you do, Rose?" Mom's voice sounded nothing like her.

I spun on her. "I didn't do this!" I yelped. I never wanted to hurt any living thing. It occurred to me… "*You* did this! To teach me a lesson about keeping things from you."

"Rose, how could you think—"

"How could *I* think? How could *you*? I helped him, he was dying! Are you the only one who can keep secrets?"

"Rose," Annie warned.

"Not you, too," I moaned. *Betrayal, betrayal, over and over again.*

"Rose," Annie said again, eyes imploring. She raised her hand, and she pointed.

In the center of the circle, touching my mother's foot, was a pile of crab legs. And a Fruit Stripe gum wrapper. And space for just one small girl.

My brain screeched, a high, piercing whistle at the memory of chewing gum, feeding the bird the crab legs—or trying to. He never ate much. He wasn't going to live, and no matter how hard I *looked*, I couldn't see how to help him.

And if I couldn't do it for him, I couldn't do it for Annie.

Grieving already, my knees weakened, and it was Annie I went to for help. Not my mother. "I'm sorry," I whispered.

Annie crossed the floor in two steps and gathered me into her arms while I could all but feel my mother stiffen in the circle behind us.

"You did this," Annie whispered into my hair. "Why?"

"I don't remember," I whispered back.

She pulled away, looked hard at me, hard the way I looked at the bird. "Why did you do it?"

"No, no, it's not that." A calm passed over me, settled on me like a blanket of mud and lead.

"Not what? Rose Preston, you cannot tell me you don't remember why you ripped apart a bird like this." She gripped my upper arms hard enough to bruise.

"No." My voice, like a thing I could hear through space. Not mine, far away, unfamiliar and scary. "I don't remember doing it at all."

Real fear clouded Annie's face. She looked over my shoulder at my mother, and there were no more words that any one of us could say.

～

I'd only seen the psychiatrist that one time. My mother had been terrified that someone important would find out that I was crazy and take me away. She refused to bring me again after I came home with Annie and I wouldn't talk for two days. After that first visit to the "shrink," my mother evolved from overprotective and paranoid into a gruesome spy. Her constant scrutiny and suspicion made my x-ray vision flare into a warning beacon, unable to ignore her motives. Her determination to discover what I'd learned, what had come to the forefront in my mind, what I'd told a stranger, made her cruel, restless. How could I talk to someone who'd turn on me like that?

It never occurred to her that I couldn't.

The words that came from the psychiatrist's mouth rattled around in my brain, my memory only showing me his lips forming them, one tooth slightly overlapping the other.

Hiding

Not real

Trauma

Prodigy

No space in my head for anything but those words that disassembled me, trying to piece them together, make sense of them, trying to hear in my head the other things he'd said around them to find some truth in it, a start and an end, anything but the endless repetition. I tried to build them together over and over, a word tower with no bottom to hold it up, and I was the one coming apart.

How was I supposed to speak about that? Speak through it, when the words took up my everything?

Hiding

Not real

Trauma

Prodigy

Hiding, not real, trauma, prodigy hiding not real trauma prodigyhidingnotrealtraumaprodigy...

After the bird, my mother's fear of me overruled her fear of whatever secrets I'd reveal. Annie made the appointment, handing my mother the time and date on a scrap of paper, her mouth a firm line, refusing to take no for an answer. Not because of what I'd done to the creature, but because I couldn't remember doing it, she'd said.

This was a different psychiatrist. "Someone worth the girl's time," Annie said. The new psychiatrist's office was far. We drove for a long time on the highway, away from where there was more ocean than road, past where there was more road than people, through where there was more traffic than roads, and into the city where there were more buildings than sky. Once we'd parked in a lot packed with cars of all shapes and sizes, I opened the car door.

The noise hit me like an airplane flying right over my head. So many *noises,* a hundred pitches, a thousand sources, not an ounce of silence, from the smoggy sky to the rivulets running into the sewer, to the pipes below, to the rats in the water, to their hearts as they ran, to the bones in their—

I fell to the ground, huddled in the shadow of our car, cowering from the relentless sound that wouldn't stop coming at me, through me, into me from every angle.

"Rosie! It's okay! It's okay, baby!" My mother held me tight, I breathed in the fresh cotton scent of her sweater, opened my eyes a little to see the warm camel color of it, the color of the beach. I tried not to see the thread, where it came from, who made it, the scent of the creature it came from, to instead picture the sea grass, the shoddy picket fence around the dunes, anything but this bedlam of sound.

"This was a mistake," my mother groaned, ready to cry herself.

I focused on her voice, the vibrations of it in my hair. "What was?" I managed to say, muffling my sobs, tired of them and the way they stole the air from my lungs and collapsed my chest.

She kissed my hair over and over. "What was I *thinking*, bringing you back to the city?"

Just like that, all the noise stopped. The air stopped flowing, I stopped breathing in the fresh cotton scent. I heard nothing, saw only the tiny threads of her sweater, every fiber, every piece of miniscule lint.

And I remembered.

My fingers, soft, whitish-pink, young. Twirling a blade of grass, the sounds of cars distant but still near. No beach noises. No salt air. No wild beach grass or overgrown woods. Tended copse of trees between tall, plain buildings.

And my heart was running. But I didn't get away.

My stomach roiled, my bowels threatened to release, I couldn't care, couldn't drag myself away from the memories and the noise.

The noise rushed in through the window.

White walls, white carpet. Nothing comfortably worn, not our cottage now. Everything new and crisp, no personality. No natural sound, just a killing quiet, too loud in my own little head.

Climbing up onto a red-painted wooden stool. Barefoot, the grain underneath sanded smooth.

The city noise rushing in with a spring breeze as the window, already cracked an inch, went up higher.

My pink-white fingers running along the edge of the screen, feeling its perfect fit into the window, as if the entire thing had come out of a machine in the sky, dropping this apartment and moving on to make another.

I was a flea inside it. Unseen, but still a blemish on the white carpet. I had no right to be there. No right at all. I was just wrong.

The noise outside was quieter than the noise inside. The noise in my head. The always-there noise in my head.

Inside was killing me. Crushing me, that flea on the carpet. I didn't stand a chance. I had to get out.

The screen popped out as easily as the window went up.

Out on the ledge, the noise in my head was silent. My brain stopped pulling me apart, trying to find whatever I'd done wrong to be punished like this. The layers of the loud city outside would keep me, like a piece of the machine, if I jumped in.

I gasped so hard that I jerked myself out of the memory, coughing. I fell back against the car with a *thud.*

But there was *more.* I remembered something else, something else, something else, something I didn't want to remember.

My mother stared at me, eyes as wide as that apartment window, the cars all coming into focus around us, the noise returning. It didn't hurt my head, my ears this time.

For the first time since that moment on the ledge, I *liked* the noise.

The noise was like light. Everything became clearer inside; everything that I chose to look at. I'd never considered that I didn't have to *see* anything I didn't want to.

"Let's go inside," I said gravely to my mother.

"What? We have to go home, baby, what just happened—"

"I'm *fine*," I barked. She wanted to protect me, but this wasn't protection; this was hiding. I turned my anger on her quickly, not entirely certain why. "I won't curl up in a ball under the covers *every* time something hurts, Mom." I shrugged her hands off my arms and stood up so fast that I stumbled back into the car. Now I was determined to see this new psychiatrist, not caring if he was a "shrink," or if I'd be made fun of for the rest of my life. The rest of my life might end with the next memory, the next hole in my brain. The haze I'd been in after discovering the dismembered bird evolved into a reckless desire to move forward and see what crazy thing would happen next. An utter lack of control consumed me like the fire in my belly, raging to find out the truth.

"It's lovely to meet you, Rose," the man in the sweater vest said as I rushed past him to the leather couch awaiting me.

"Your office is nice," I said, my voice robotic.

He didn't have a chance to respond before my mother grasped his hands and said in a messy, frightened whisper, "You're supposed to be the best young psychiatrist in Boston, Dr. Mortimer."

His laugh was a rich, warm being. "That's what they tell me."

I saw them glance at me out of the corner of my eye, my mother's lips moving fast as she gripped the stranger's hands. I pretended not to notice how unfocused her pleading was as I opened a piece of gum and took apart everything in the office in my brain. The desk, the blinds, the globe, the dark carpet, the glasses on Dr. Mortimer's nose, the lack of picture frames, the heart pounding in my mother's chest, the filaments making up the paper inside the file cabinets, everything that made this place what it was.

A place to find what was wrong with me.

Hiding, not real, trauma, prodigy.

"I want you to stop talking now," I said in that same robot voice to my mother. Her breath arrested, as if she couldn't believe I would speak at a time like this, as if I were a prop in her disaster story of a troubled child that had meant the world to her.

"I'll be right outside, Rose," she said, and cleared her throat. "If you want to go—"

"I want you to stop talking now," I repeated, staring at the empty chair across from me. I wanted it filled with the man that I could *tell*.

She burst into tears and hurried into the waiting room.

Dr. Mortimer wasn't thrown by my gritted teeth, the goosebumps all over my body, my clenched fists. He smiled kindly as he sat down and pulled his armchair closer.

"You came closer," I said before I could stop myself.

He leaned forward, elbows on his knees, hands hanging between his legs as if he were watching a football game.

He watched football.

I gasped at the kind man who was waiting to talk to me, really waiting to hear what I had to say.

"My father watched football," was the first thing that came out.

"**S**he was very clear, Mrs. Preston."

My mother didn't speak. Didn't object to "Mrs."

"Rose recounted several very vivid memories."

Hiding

Not real

Trauma

Prodigy

I still sat on the leather couch. It was dark outside now. I'd been talking for hours, I was sure of it. Taking it all apart, from the bottom up. All those words, they meant things, things that had happened to me.

Fire burned in my chest.

My mother didn't speak. Dr. Mortimer did.

"I'd like Rose to stay at the hospital where we can keep an eye on her and I can see her again tomorrow after she rests. She's very distraught. In her current state of mind, she cannot return home. With you."

My mother didn't speak.

Dr. Mortimer had been shocked by my anger at my

mother. It was not what he'd been after. He was expecting to hear about why I killed a bird.

My mother's mouth opened and closed as little sounds came out that weren't words, but feelings. "I…I want to bring her home. Where she's safe. She shouldn't be here, I should never have brought her back to Boston—"

"Please, Mrs. Preston, stay calm. Rose has been acting strangely, you said. What happened with the bird in the basement has obviously struck a chord with you, you realized that it implied a deeper disturbance in your daughter. It's—unusual—for therapy to extract such memories so quickly. It's unsafe for her to experience these traumatic memories in an unsecured environment without professional supervision, even more so considering her reaction to them when she was only five. Mrs. Preston, the child is ready to be helped."

Steel formed her words. "I. *do*. help her."

Hiding

"We've been hiding," I muttered. "You hid me. You hid it all *from me*. Those memories are mine! Did you think they wouldn't find me?" Then darkly, from down where the heat grew, darkly, voice sinister, my eyes burning, "Did you think I wouldn't find them?"

I was standing now, facing the two horrified adults. Their chests caved in, puffed out, caved in, puffed out as they breathed heavily, eyes bulging.

"R—ro—rose," my mother said, lifting a hand as she approached me, like I was a rabid dog she needed to trap.

"NO!"

My stomach heated up like lightning struck it. My hands leaped to it, and with a yelp, I pulled them away.

The tender pink palms were the red of the Lobster Hut sign at Manomet Point. Little bubbles appeared in the creases. I looked down at my belly to see the angry heat burning brightly through my rose-colored t-shirt. Shocked, I gaped at my mother, whose mouth was working up and down in her terror. She didn't come to my side.

She backed away into the door.

"Were you ever not afraid of me, Mom?" I whispered, the questions bubbling out finally.

She swallowed hard, brows knitted together in confused pain. "Fear and love live together, Rosie," she said, tears in her sparkling eyes. "What choice did I have?"

"The truth."

"You're just a little girl."

"I am *not!*" The heat burning my belly rolled up through my body, scorching my throat, and with my words came the faintest shimmer in front of my mouth, like the sizzling waves over hot pavement.

"Incredible," Dr. Mortimer whispered reverently.

His praise made my mother stiffen. "Incredible?" she snarled. "That's my little girl burning up over there!"

"What is this, Mom?" I asked, voice trembling, chin puckered up. My hands throbbed, numb in spots, sweat trickled down my back.

She pushed off the door and came toward me, tentatively. "You see now," she said, "why I have to hide you. You're not normal, Rose, and the world isn't kind to kids who are different."

"I don't need kindness. I need the truth. You *hurt* me with your lies. This thing in my head," I tapped my temple hard, as if I could knock the memory of the tumor out of it, "came from my memories, Mom!"

"You can't know that," she said, but she knew it as well as I did.

"I know it. Hiding is *lying,* and your lies almost killed me!" I cried out again, and this time the roll of heat became a tidal wave bowling through my organs, my skin, overflowing into my mouth. A lick of flame burst forth with my words, blistering my lips and tongue, sending Dr. Mortimer and my mother stumbling into each other, against the door, and into a bookshelf.

I let out a sob, terrified as a Salem witch, needing my mommy to hold me and tell me I was okay. Instead, she told me I wasn't normal. The memory returned of myself, five years old, knowing that I was *wrong*, that I'd deserved what happened to me, and that I deserved to die because of it.

The jumble of memories—my father, the Boston apartment, the copse of trees, so many things that I couldn't make sense of on top of them—teamed against me with the flames and stabs of agony through my brain and the ache in my bones from exhaustion and my mother rejecting me this way. I pulled the bottom of my pink t-shirt out to see that it had been almost incinerated, gaping holes ringed in black ash rending it apart. Red blisters popped up against my soft skin.

My mother did nothing, said nothing. She'd been the light of my life, the blanket from the dryer on a winter day. Now she was the fire that I couldn't run from.

"I love you, Rose," she said.

"I love you, too," I said. And I pounded toward them with all the strength I had.

Dr. Mortimer stopped me in the doorway, gently putting an arm across me. The simple touch sent shockwaves through me that erupted in what felt like a volcano in my stomach. I moaned at the pain, wanting to hide it inside me, but no.

There was no keeping the fire inside any longer. It had burned too hot for too long.

With a choked sob, a flicker of heat burst forth from my mouth, making Dr. Mortimer flinch away. But he still held me.

I was the one who had reason to wince and flinch.

I was the one who had suffered and not known it.

I was the one who wouldn't hurt anyone or anything and this *thing* inside me was forcing its way out to do exactly that. Another betrayal—this time from myself.

My stomach was a hole of fire, the pain blinding. But I saw through it.

From far away I heard Dr. Mortimer. For her own good as much as my own, he said to my mother, he was checking me into a wing of the giant hospital across the street from his office where they could help me "transition." I just fell into the x-ray vision, hiding behind it, the tiny threads in the arm of his sweater, the store where he'd bought it, the sales-woman who'd sold it to him, the shoes she wore, the scuff on the toe, the wooden floor under the semi-soft carpet, the grain of it, looking deeper and deeper…

But all this time, I'd been looking away.

My main office—Hell. Rotting meat and moaning. Viscera-soaked dirty hay and a red haze that mimicked a fog of blood. Time for a power lunch with the boss.

I burst through the vortex and landed on my feet, already in stride toward the Queen's nest. I passed the squawking wretches roosting in trees and huddled in thorn bushes. Except the trees were made of distorted human bodies eternally picked clean of flesh and the thorn bushes were host to lucid severed heads.

I couldn't help it. It made me hungry. I picked a finger like an apple off the nearest tree, an aggression so small it didn't even faze whoever it belonged to.

"Hissssssssssss!"

I knew that particularly desperate-sounding hiss.

"Jen," I said, stopping in my tracks, finger halfway to my mouth.

My rescue-soccer-mom friend had really hit the jackpot with me for a bestie. She'd since lost her stonewashed denim and her humanity. Never coming to the land of the living, feeding on the carcasses of those who suffered in the Wood eternally by taking their own lives. Not to mention playing bodyguard to the sex offender love of her life that we'd both managed to send there. Throw in a dash of quality time with the ancient myth bitches and her humanity never stood a chance. But she *had* chosen this over living a life without Evan Hale.

Mangled limbs, broken and rebroken to adhere to the shape of the dead tree, Evan Hale wasn't one of the many souls here who'd lost their will to scream. Evan cried out constantly, moaning, sobbing. Debilitating to listen to for a second, even for me. Especially for me. But Jen never left his side. And it had driven her insane.

"Why don't you ssssstay?" she hissed to me. Not *at* me. She didn't hate me like I hated me for getting her here.

"I can't, Jen. I wish you wouldn't either."

"You cannnnn!" she crowed, crouched and slithering around me, more snaky than birdy. "The Queen wantssss you by her sssside! Sssssstay with me. My friend."

Those last words sounded almost human. Tears clouded the crimson sky.

Forcing myself to face her, I grabbed her shoulders, pulled her upright to stand in front of me like a person, her wings folded messily behind her. She was ragged, a sewer Harpy. "Jen, I'm begging you. Take your life back. Have a real life, a human life. This isn't you, it's destroyed you!"

"*Life* destroyed me!" she howled like a heartbroken human. Evan's pitiful screeching echoed her voice from the tree behind her. Rotten meat and scraps of flesh lay in heaps around the base, the leftovers fallen from the other Harpies who'd kick them her way—because she wouldn't dare leave Evan, knowing they'd descend on him like the vultures they were.

"I have to go," I said, voice thick.

You can't help everybody. This isn't your fault. You can't help everybody. This isn't your fault. You can't help everybody. This isn't your...

More Harpies called out to me as I passed. I kept my head straight, didn't make eye contact. I'd defeated their Queen. Once. In survival of the fittest in Hell, that made me the Savior—a title I no longer wanted.

All I wanted was a reason to live.

The Queen was always waiting for me when I got there. That inflated sense of importance she gave me was her weapon like any other, meant to give me false confidence.

"Jesus Christ, do they never stop screaming?" I bitched as I sat beside the Queen in her nasty nest. It was really nice, actually. "What's this, velvet?" The lining was softer than last time.

"What do you want, Hazel?" she asked me, no pretense.

"None of the usual fawning today, huh? You super tired from eating people or have you given up on me?"

"You bore me."

As funny as I found this little triumph, it annoyed me that she was casting me aside. Not that I cared—but I'd been the big prize not that long ago. Now...

Well, now there was a new prize. Rose.

"You're following me, right? I saw the feathers when I went back in time to the kid's house, sans DeLorean. I don't care what you do. But you are Hell's leading authority on Harpydom, so tell me: How far can I go? Can I get trapped there?" and reaching to take her chin in my hand without so much as a tremble, I turned the Queen's face toward me. I had defeated her, after all; she answered to me. "Can I change the past?" *Careful. Don't let her know you've got plans, dipshit.*

Her dark eyes sparkled like black stars, and a sadness overwhelmed me. The intelligence there, the pain she must have known, the heart I knew still beat in her chest… We didn't have to be enemies, but we'd never be friends. I wished it was different.

"Oh, Hazel," she said without a hint of sarcasm. "You think anything will fix what you are? In a thousand lifetimes, you can't change a damn thing."

"Just answer me without all your goth staring-out-over-the-misty-moors words. Can I get stuck back there? Can I change the future by doing some Ghost of Christmas Past shit?" It dawned on me and I had to laugh. "Wait! You don't know! You can't do it and you don't know, you can't do it and you don't know…" I sang, dancing around.

"Of course I can do it," she scoffed, and I wilted. "You're barely real. You can't affect anything truly, deeply, where it matters. Nothing really changes, darling. Definitely not you. This is all you'll ever be."

"Wrong," I said, chin held high, getting to my feet. "I'm already more than this." I gestured to myself. "I can upend this entire place, I can time travel, and I bet I'll figure out a lot more I can do. More than you. If you're not scared, you should be."

The Queen leaned forward, eyes rolled upward, showing the whites underneath to meet my own stare. "Try. Me," she said. And leaned back in her nest like the queen she was, delicately plucking a juicy blue eyeball from the nest like a grape and biting into it.

"That right there," I said, "is all you'll ever be, too."

I leaped from the nest, sprouting wings in midair to the howls of the monsters and tortured dead surrounding me. I overpowered them all with a screech so mighty, Godzilla would have been impressed. I found the closest vortex and had never been so happy to high-tail it out of Hell.

I might go down in flames and take the whole fucking

world with me, but I was thrilled to try. I was goddamn going to make some changes, destroy this shithole if it was the last thing I ever did.

ROSE

"There she is," a woman said softly, like the whisper of wind through the trees at home. "Don't move too much, it will hurt your skin."

Burns.

I opened my eyes to first see her, a nurse with hair so luxurious and perfectly dark, she could've stepped right out of a magazine.

And beyond her, the beeping of machines, the harsh lighting, the spotless blinds over the massive window, the not-quite-noise of people trying to be quiet in the hallway, the voices through the walls, the stark white of those walls…

Hard to breathe. Skin burning, white walls.

White walls, a room without character, without flaws. A place that defied childhood.

Out the window, far below, the copse of trees where I picnicked with my dolls.

The boys walking by it off the bus from school, hooting, laughing, down the paths between apartment buildings.

I'd wave to the bus before it pulled away, then rush back into the copse of trees. Sometimes I went back there later in the day after dinner with Mommy and...

Daddy.

"No! No! No!" I was screaming and couldn't stop and the magazine nurse was holding my arms down, making me scream more.

Then she screamed, too.

Slow motion took over. The beautiful nurse stumbled back from me, both hands on one cheek, mouth impossibly wide as she screamed. Doctors and nurses rushed in, speaking hurriedly, until she finally took her hands away. In stark contrast to her peachy complexion, her right cheek was Hell-red, spotted with hot white blisters. But it was her eyes that made me shrink in and wish I could scream myself to death.

Her right lid was a milky, blistering cocoon around a seemingly flaming eyeball, a thing unrecognizable as an eyeball. But the glisten of the other eye, the quivering of those lashes... It saw a horror movie monster. I felt like one. Sobbing my apologies, the x-ray vision showing me the layers of burns, stopping just before the jawbone, her teeth chattering beneath despite the heat, one merciful nurse took pity upon me and gave me a shot. The last thing I saw was that beautiful nurse, porcelain skin destroyed, wailing that I was inhuman.

This happened more times. I don't know how many times. Between the doctors and nurses who gave me shots like I was an animal about to attack, I learned to keep that heat down, down inside where it had been for my whole life. Sickened that I'd hurt people who were trying to help me, I was lost during my lucid times, forcing myself into diminishing my x-ray vision and controlling my emotions. Because I could not, could *not* hurt anyone else and live with myself.

But below that, violent fury simmered over my mother's

lies. I was too angry to be afraid of why she was hiding the truth from me.

Not yet.

~

My mother didn't come to the hospital.

Dr. Mortimer did. Once I was in control again, and when my own burns weren't as painful, he came and he talked to me about what I remembered.

We'd leave my room—Room 6—and go to a different room with another big window and blue chairs with wooden arms, just the two of us. On the way there we'd stop at the nurse's kitchen and sneak out individual packets of graham crackers or chocolate pudding with a Coke or two. The nurses always smiled and waved little waves or winked when we passed by. Mostly at him. I was still a thing of nightmares to them. I heard them talking at night in the hallway—about how I was a "supposed" genius, a prodigy, that Dr. Mortimer was certain he could help me, that I was just a little girl after all.

"We haven't talked about your father, Rose," Dr. Mortimer said one day, and bit a graham cracker.

"I don't want to," I said before I knew I'd said it.

"You've talked about so many things that were very, very difficult to put into words. Why not him?"

I was very intent when I said, "Because I don't want to talk about my father."

That was where we left it.

But we did talk about the events that happened when I lived in the city with my parents. I remembered. Wrapped in a cocoon of drugs and fear and numbness, I remembered every second of it all.

Three boys got off the bus every day. I'd wave to the bus

while they laughed together on the way to their own apartments. Two of the boys, the skinny one and the chubby one, usually waved when they saw me. They'd say, "Hi Rose," sometimes. They knew my name. They knew where I lived.

The other boy had blond hair and dark eyes and wore a jean jacket with a big patch on the back. He didn't say hi often, and when he did it wasn't with a smile. He just looked at me. Blank. Sometimes he'd ask me how my tea party was, but he wouldn't smile.

After dinner I'd go back outside if it was light enough or if it wasn't too cold. I always went to the same hiding spot in the trees. The branches hung over me like a hood, making the shadiest and quietest spot in the whole city, probably. During the day the sunlight was just stripes across the grass. At night the fireflies made appearances. I remembered my doll with soft rubber arms and legs in a pink dress that I carried with me there. She was gone afterwards.

I didn't want to play with toys afterwards anyway. I very much remembered that.

The boys often came out after dinner, too, but most of the time they didn't know I was there. I remember the sound of the basketball, *thud, thud, thud,* as they dribbled it on the way home.

But one boy didn't go home.

I was picking up the sweater I'd been sitting on, and the tea set I brought with me and my doll, when he came into my space in the trees. When he pulled back the branches like a curtain, the sounds of the street came with him, a tumult of noises invading my quiet place.

"You have a friend with you tonight," he said, and pointed at my doll. I smiled a little. I remember that I smiled. I didn't know. "Can I be your friend, too?" he asked. But he wasn't really asking. I nodded.

If I hadn't nodded, it wouldn't have happened.

If I hadn't smiled, it wouldn't have happened.

If I hadn't always gone out alone, it wouldn't have happened.

If my mother and father hadn't let me go out alone, it wouldn't have happened.

"If we hadn't let her go out there so late, Sarah—"

"But she was only right there..." my mother moaned, that same moan from when I collapsed beside the car when we came back to Boston to see Dr. Mortimer.

If we hadn't come back to Boston, I wouldn't have remembered.

Taking it all apart, one layer at a time, trying to fix the past I'd hidden from for five years, and now... Now I was coming apart, too.

~

Cody Reese. That was his name.

He held me down, the dark all-encompassing inside the trees. My doll lay in the grass where I'd dropped her when he grabbed me. Just out of reach, staring at me. I'd squeeze my eyes shut, but when I opened them her blue ones still stared. I stared back, the back of my head rubbing on the grass, *shush, shush, shush,* her head bobbing before my eyes. I concentrated: felt the ants under my fingers, the droplets of dew, the ant hill as the soldiers filed in, the soil beneath that, the moles deep down in the dirt, the worms tunneling through, the rocks scattered randomly, I *looked* anywhere but at Cody Reese, hovering over me like a black cloud, muttering things like, "all the way in," and "feels too good to stop."

He cried. I remembered the tears on his face. He sat on the grass, breathing hard. And he said, "We're together, right to the core." When he moved, I flinched, curled up tighter on the grass. And when the trees parted again, letting the noise in from the parking lot, the cars on the street, neighbors talking loudly, I squeezed my eyes shut again.

The trees parted a third time. I remembered shutting off. Shutting off the noises of the world, whimpering, growling to hear anything but those noises, listening to my fingers dig into the grass, the dirt…

"Rosie, time to—" my father began. "Rosie," he whispered, "are you asleep?" And he knelt beside me, finally cutting off my view of the staring doll eyes that I couldn't look away from.

When my father saw that my eyes were open he let out a muffled howl. He picked up his hand from the grass beside me and sobbed, bringing it closer to his face in the dark. I could see it. His hand was coated in blood.

"Okay, okay." He smoothed my hair back, really just pushing it down into the grass where I lay. He touched my side and I grunted like the pig at the farm we visited on weekends for corn on the cob. But I still couldn't move. "Can I touch you, baby?" His voice was high-pitched, threatening to crack. I couldn't answer him. He murmured, trying to reassure me, trying to just fill the silence so he wouldn't realize I couldn't speak.

He lifted me, leaving the doll and the tea set behind.

He moaned, "My baby," over and over again the whole way home.

$\sim$

I was five years old when Cody Reese raped me. Dr. Mortimer told me that I spent a week in this very hospital then. And when that was over, I went home.

My father parked the big white car on the other side of the apartment building so I wouldn't have to walk past those trees. The sounds of being outside made me quiver, my whole body wanting to crash to the ground. We played board games at night to keep me from going to the window. I put all of my stuffed animals and dolls in the closet so they wouldn't stare at me. I didn't eat much and so my father brought me McDonald's, pizza, candy, cake, just to get me to want *something*. They didn't tell me the reasons for these things, of course—I just knew.

Days went by but I couldn't talk. Police came to whisper things to my parents, glancing my way, but I couldn't tell them anything. It wasn't a secret then—not yet—but I had no words.

The first sound I made was a scream.

I screamed when I heard the *thud, thud, thud* of the basketball being dribbled on the pavement outside.

I ran to the window—so fast in fact, that I ran right into it —and I watched that ball bounce, bounce, bounce on the pavement.

I don't remember much after that except waking up late that night, Mommy in bed with me. Tears gleamed in the dark on her face. I asked for Daddy, but he wasn't home, she said. He'd be home soon. Her voice was heavy, dark. Like the branches of the trees.

The next morning, Daddy was there. Deep lines creased his face. I didn't think he'd have the strength to eat his bowl of Lucky Charms. Mommy kept running to the window, until he snapped at her to stop. It wasn't that day, but it wasn't long after that the police started to ask questions about another child.

And it wasn't long after that when we moved to our cottage at the beach. But my father didn't come with us.

That was where my memory was gone. And I didn't ever want it to come back.

~

One day my mother came to Room 6.

I don't know how long I'd been in the hospital. I'd seen Dr. Mortimer many, many times. The burns on my own body had healed well. The leaves were turning orange, yellow, brown, red, outside my big window. I had come to think of the window as "mine." What wasn't mine were the pajamas. I didn't have my own pajamas from home, or my own pillow. I wore almost the same thing the nurses wore, just like the other people staying in the hospital for a long time.

Dr. Mortimer told me that my mother wasn't permitted to visit. I was okay with that. In this clean place where I had nothing to do except talk about my "trauma," and heal, my mother didn't belong. I didn't miss her. I'd come to see her as part of the fire in my body—and when I didn't think of her, it didn't come out.

When my mother came it wasn't to bring my pajamas. She'd come to say that Annie was dying.

Those words dredged up the filth of the world in a tornado. The x-ray vision that I'd made disappear, removed when I was truly awake without the shots, returned. The room spun, the time that had passed while I was in the hospital hit me, and I was suddenly terrified of what I'd missed on the outside, as if I had some accountability to live the life my mother had forced on me out there.

My mother, new grays streaking her hair, dark circles under her eyes, all the light gone from them, legs thin as if she hadn't moved off the couch for months, and yellowish teeth that smelled of smoke—listened with clear strain as Dr. Mortimer talked about what I'd been revealing in our therapy sessions.

We talked about the rape and memories of my father, he

told her. My mother only pursed her lips tight and nodded. I didn't remember much from the move to Manomet, and not a thing about where my father went; she immediately started breathing harder, blinking a lot, ready to defend herself and her income and her choices again.

But not before she let out a breath so deep that her shoulders drooped with it, a blink so lazy it made her entire face relax, jaw loose, lips slightly parted.

She was *relieved.*

From the bottom of my belly, the urge to *look* inside her welled up, a tidal wave of scorching *want,* to find what else she was hiding. It had been a long time since I'd needed that, been compelled to look so hard that I ceased to be and only the *other* was real.

She knew the rest of my story.

Faintly, I heard her babbling that she had no idea where my father was, he left us because he couldn't handle what happened to me, that it haunted him.

Lies.

I didn't have time to indulge my curiosities; curiosity that my brain didn't want to explore, but my gut did.

"We need to see Annie. Now." Heat roiled in my stomach, but I shoved it down and wouldn't show that I was in pain. I couldn't have felt less fragile, less childlike, less ruined or less afraid. I was a sharp and fiery and powerful dragon of a girl, and nobody would stand in my way.

As if they'd forgotten I was there, both adults scanned me, skimming up and down my body, considering their options. But they didn't defy me.

They knew danger when they saw it.

I'd never thought of Annie as vulnerable. But that's what she was in that hospital bed, in a fitful sleep, hair whiter than the pillowcase it haloed across. I rushed to her side and she woke right away, eyes as clear as ever despite what her body was doing to her. She grinned, no less mischievously than before. "I knew you'd come," she said, pain evident in her voice. My jaw set, my back straightened. Anger overtook my sadness that this beacon of beauty would be taken from me by something so commonplace as death.

Well, I didn't plan on giving her away.

Spinning on my mother, I spat, "I want to be alone with her."

Instantly defeated, she said, "Of course," and with one desperate glance back at me, I was alone with the beeping and the whiteness and with Annie.

Her hand was frigid as it took mine. "Rose, go easy on her. She isn't as strong as you."

"No one is," I said without hesitation.

My confidence didn't impress her. "Remember that you're a child, Rose. Don't become more than that, not for now. You've been dealt a wicked hand, my girl; I couldn't be sorrier that you're coming to terms with it now."

I narrowed my eyes, wondering just how much she knew of my past. A past that should not have been so tumultuous for only ten years in the making. "You know what I've been doing all this time?" I asked her.

"Of course, Rose," she said, as if it were the silliest question in the world. "You've been working with Dr. Mortimer for three months now. I've had to help your mother battle off those old bitty neighbors of ours that want to know what happened to you. Show no interest until they think they've got some gossip to spread." The smile returned. "No child should ever know the things you've known, sweetheart. My heart aches to think of it. I can't."

"Don't cry," I said robotically.

"Crying is okay, Rose. Children do cry, you know," she teased. "You know why you're here, don't you?"

"You are not dying."

"Rose, I can't live forever. Wouldn't want to—though a while longer might be nice." Her laugh became a wheeze, became a cough.

That was when I did what I'd known I would do all along. I *looked*.

I'd had too much practice looking inside myself in the hospital. Too much time spent digging and searching and recoiling. There would be no recoiling this time. There was no time for me to *try*.

"What are you doing?" Annie asked me. I swallowed hard to pop my ears. "Rose? Rose, stop. It's time for me to move on."

I shook my head, never stopping. I drew up my x-ray vision willingly, scanned her like a living medical chart, zeroing in all over. My temperature was rising.

"I know it burns," I said softly, wiping sweat off my forehead, "but it won't last. You trust me."

Annie's heartbeat quickened as I prodded it gently. I searched for where the cough came from, past all the failing organs, all the dark and unhealthy parts, all the pieces of her that were just plain finished working. I would not fail again.

"Rose," she wheezed, her heart fluttering dangerously fast. "Ro—"

Groaning, I squinted, dug deeper. *I'm hurting her*, I thought in disgust. She would never, ever hurt me. *I can't give up just because it isn't easy.* Annie was tough; tougher than me. Life without Annie wouldn't be easy, and far less endurable.

Tears poured down her paper-thin cheeks, and I knew, I *knew* she couldn't take much more.

And I knew, like I knew my own name, that I couldn't stop.

"It feels too good to stop," Cody Reese had said.

I growled through clenched teeth, holding in a scream that would certainly turn into flames. My tears matched her own now. I'd never looked so hard into anyone before, scratched at every little nook and cranny, every soft, pink tissuey hiding spot, dug into every dark corner and secret crevice.

"Right to the core."

She struggled as if she were pinned down. And I probed where I didn't belong, but I could *help*, if we could just get through—

The beeping machine beeped faster and faster and she grew paler and then the nurse rushed in.

"Rose…" Annie moaned, eyes wide and pleading. Then she didn't try to stop me anymore. She stopped fighting me, fighting her body, fighting at all. She took my hand again but I couldn't stop, not now. And I was focusing, so hard, but it wasn't me that heated up that time.

Annie's face reddened. Her fingers fiddled, grasping.

Her eyes pulled me in as she said, "Don't get stuck in those memories."

I shook my head, a sob bursting free, a hiccup without heat, and I looked deep, one more time, poured all my heart and mind into her. I should have known that no heart or mind besides my own could handle what I was.

"Move back!" the nurse cried, and more hospital people rushed in, and my mother and I were in the hallway and I just watched. Like the doll had watched me, both of us helpless.

I was not a little girl. I was a monster. And I continue to be.

Room 6 welcomed me after Annie died. I was glad I didn't have to go home. To see Annie's windows with no lights on, to be alone with my mother and our secrets, to not have Dr. Mortimer anchoring me when the heat of my insides became too much to stomach. I would have died. I would have wanted to.

My mother did return to Room 6 with me, though. The police didn't come, but only because Dr. Mortimer explained my "troubled past" and "childhood trauma" and "fragile mentality" to them when I was crumpled on the floor outside Annie's hospital room, clutching my throat. The police wanted to know where my weapon was, how I'd gotten into the room with it, sweeping their arms under Annie's bed, with her body still in it, getting colder, for a lighter or something that could cause the burn holes in the sheets. Dr. Mortimer calmly convinced them that Ms. Preston had been smoking and must have become careless.

When he said "careless," he glanced at me.

Yes, my mother had indeed been careless when it came to me.

When the words "suicide risk" came up about me and the policemen had gone, I had nothing left but the need for answers. Feelings had become a thing of the past for me at that time. I wanted facts. Nothing more could shock me, not after what I'd done. So when Dr. Mortimer and my mother and I were alone, I choked out from my scorched throat, "Tell me it all."

Finally, my mother spoke to me as if I were a person and not her fairy-daughter.

Pffft, fairy-daughter, I thought. *A changeling, more like.* That sweet, carefree girl had been replaced with a different child now.

"You weren't the same after that boy—"

"Cody Reese," I interjected, and gasped. The words scraped coming out, my chest a volcano, my mouth full of ash. Sunburnt all over.

My mother smiled a little, as if impressed, ignoring how burnt I was. "Yes. Cody Reese. You weren't the same, Rosie. It was like…you weren't a child anymore."

I don't know what kind of reaction she wanted from me. All I wanted was to scream at her that of course I was different, of course I wasn't a child anymore. She acted like I had to apologize for it. I tightened my jaw so I wouldn't say it, or else she'd stop talking.

"Your dad and I, we loved you so much," her voice cracked and my heart cracked at the past tense of *love*, "and you were so distant and sad and we couldn't risk you being in that place anymore. It was all over the news, the police in the apartment complex, the rapi—the person who did it still out there. We didn't know what to do." Her shame showed when she said, "*I* didn't know what to do." She had the saddest smile and took my hand as I lay there in bed. I let her. Her tears flowed freely. "You didn't know what to do either, baby. And one day… One day, Jesus, you were still only five years old, you tried to jump off the ledge outside your window. You were just a baby." She collapsed, her head falling onto my hand in the bed, her tears soaking it.

Like the blood had soaked my legs when my father carried me home.

"That's enough," Dr. Mortimer said quietly.

I wanted to be ignorant as I'd been just months ago. I should have let her hide it from me forever; she knew what was best. Now I'd destroyed all of my mother's efforts at giving me a normal life. The tears soothed my burning cheeks. I didn't deserve it.

"What about Annie?"

Dr. Mortimer spoke while my mother squeezed my hand. I couldn't squeeze back, I couldn't move at all. "It wasn't the fire that hurt Annie, we know that much. We weren't in the room, but when we arrived your lips were burned like they are now."

I licked them, felt the blisters.

"And there were holes in the blanket on Annie's bed." He glanced at my mother, but she was back to her head-hanging. "Annie is gone, Rose," he said with as much sympathy as I'd ever heard in Annie's voice, and the tears kept coming. So did his words. "You're no fool, Rose, and I won't keep you in the dark. Whatever happened in Annie's room, the authorities feel that you—took part in her death."

I swallowed painfully. "Do you think that?"

He contemplated lying to me. I could see that layer of him. "Yes. I don't think you meant to, but yes. Don't repeat it," he blurted.

My mother had picked her head up from my hand, blinking exhaustion from her eyes. "How is that possible?" she asked, voice scratchy. It didn't matter how, only that it was true.

Dr. Mortimer leaned in even closer to us in our huddle. "There are rare cases of what's called Acquired Savant Syndrome." Mom shook her head at his words. "I believe Rose's genius mind evolved with the trauma she's survived. Her understanding of mechanics, engineering, biology without ever having been taught, were acquired from her initial…ordeal. And the more Rose endures, the more powerful her savant skills emerge."

My mother's narrowed eyes were a window into her closed mind, her defensiveness, and it angered me to boiling.

My skin *sizzled,* and with a gasp she pushed her chair away from me. Refusing to see what was right in front of her, she jumped to her feet. "Rose is not an idiot savant," she started, but Dr. Mortimer interrupted her, snapping that 'idiot savant' was an archaic and cruel term. She heard nothing. "If you mean to tell me that Rose killed an old woman with her mind because she was raped as a child…well, I don't know if we've chosen the right person to help us."

"I can see anything," I said, my heart pounding, my breath too hot, "and you refuse to see what's plain as day because you're scared of the consequences."

"Rose, I see that this man has cornered us into trusting him—"

"I know the feeling well," I snapped, training my eyes on her. My mother deflated from her anger, raced from the room. Running. Always running and hiding.

We were alone, my trusted doctor and I. "I know something else, too, Rose," he said, and I was grateful that he'd written off my mother's outburst as inconsequential.

"Tell me," I whispered.

"Cody went missing days after he hurt you. His mother worked nights, his father was a terribly abusive alcoholic. Cody was known to get into trouble with drugs and the law even at his young age—fifteen. It wasn't unusual for his presence to be overlooked. The police investigations turned up nothing, and finally the case was closed, assuming he'd run away again. But your reaction to hearing the basketball being bounced outside that afternoon triggered your parents' suspicions. I don't think your mom wanted me to know that —but *your* mind put it all together." He smiled, and the burning protectiveness around my mind simmered lower. "I think in the days following your assault, your triggered psyche *took apart,* as you say, everything to the point where you—*you*—figured out Cody's name."

Surprising, a little. But I couldn't see where he was going with this.

"Now, I don't know if I'm right, Rose, this is all off the record. This isn't my professional opinion and it sure as hell isn't smart. Your reaction to the sound of the basketball, seeing Cody outside…it broke your parents. Rose, I think your father killed Cody Reese."

My head swam, pounded, burned.

"Your father is remotely paying for you and your mother to live in Manomet, I'm certain of it. There were too many memories in Boston for you to be able to heal. And your father had to disappear before the pieces were put together." Dr. Mortimer dropped his head into his hand, wiped his face with his palm as if trying to clear away what he'd said.

"You asked me to tell you," he said between his fingers, two pinched together to hold his glasses, elbows on his knees as if he couldn't hold his head up for another minute. How exhausting I must have been as a patient. He raised his head slowly. "It would destroy my career, I'd never work again for telling you, but I'll be damned if I'll lie to you."

I let myself touch his hand with my blistered one.

～

*A*nnie's funeral was no place for a child. That's what my mother told me, but I insisted on going. The real issue was that I was considered a danger to myself and others and not stable enough to be released from Room 6. In a heated argument in the hallway, Dr. Mortimer confronted a handful of people in suits and a couple of police officers through a haze of cigarette smoke. He told them that I was merely a traumatized child and had no chance of improving if I was treated like a criminal.

I was allowed to go to the funeral if Dr. Mortimer accompanied both my mother and me.

It had been a long time since I'd looked in a mirror, and longer since I'd seen myself in anything but hospital clothes. The sight of my hair, stringy and dull despite a gallon of hairspray, legs glowing pale, too skinny for any of my old dresses, was jarring. The black made my shadowy eyes and sallow cheeks ghoulish. The summer girl, tan and freckled, hair sun-striped and cheeks rosy, had been erased, replaced with an autumn golem.

"Very pretty, Rosie," my mother said as I walked by her into our kitchen.

"Liar," I muttered at her in passing.

We were driven in a black car with Dr. Mortimer to the cemetery. There weren't many people there. The driver opened our doors, murmuring condolences on behalf of Bartlett Funeral Home. He smelled like the peppermints Annie kept in a bowl.

The whole collection of mourners turned to watch us cross the dismal scene of black mourning clothes and gray headstones freckled with dead leaves. My mother kept her head down but I met every set of eyes, anger flaring in theirs. I wanted to yell at them, "You all care now, but *I* was the one with her when she died!" I kept quiet and squeezed Dr. Mortimer's hand. Whispers followed me as we passed, but I would not put my chin down.

They didn't have to know I was ashamed.

The priest talked for a long time about the things Annie had done in her life. She'd been a nurse, driven for Meals on Wheels, had three children (only two of whom I saw). He even mentioned how she'd helped me recover from a rare tumor. That was when the two women who I knew must be her daughters began to cry louder. I sneered.

Where have you been all this time? What right do you have?

The wind picked up, leaving all of us shivering, bundling into our sweaters and coats as the priest said final prayers. Annie's daughters stepped forward to place white roses on her casket, followed by the rest of the people dressed in black. When I let go of Dr. Mortimer's hand and went to the casket with my white rose, one of the daughters spoke through her sobs.

"What is she doing here? My mother is dead because of her!"

I spun around, still clutching the rose, the thorns biting into my palm, and heat bubbled in my chest. *No, not here.*

She stopped and stared at me. They all did, as I stood there, blood dripping down my arm as I squeezed the rose, angry and afraid.

I can admit now that I was afraid. To be faced with a dozen mourning strangers that equate you with the death of their loved one is daunting. All I could say was, "She was old," in the tiniest voice imaginable. A sound that barely existed in a sea of people that couldn't do the things I could do.

As if that's all there is to you, I thought. Sudden weariness enveloped me, made my knees shake. Exhaustion of…everything. Images assaulted me, trapping me in place there on the mushy grass of the cemetery in front of all those people, my best friend's casket at my back.

Sean Singh ripping my skirt down.

The doll staring at me, my head rubbing the grass up and down up and down.

The seagull wrapped in a t-shirt in the cellar.

Amelia's face brightening as I took apart her cold.

My piteous teachers.

Cody Reese.

Cody Reese under the trees.

Cody Reese dribbling the basketball.

The thud, thud, thud *of the ball moving in time with my head rubbing the grass, the doll staring at me, staring at me.*

My father handing me Zebra Stripe gum.

The white walls of Room 6.

My mother smiling at me through the kitchen window.

Annie pouring tea.

Annie's radio, working again.

Blood on my hands.

The mole in my fist.

A cacophony of faces and voices telling my mother what a princess I was, what a fairy I was, what an angel I was, how perfect I was.

The two words, Cody Reese, *like black magic marker bubble letters in my mind, handed to me when I heard that basketball* thud, thud, thud.

His name had been a gift. From the voice in my head.

I swayed. But I didn't fall down.

Didn't find myself with my cheek on the grass, pulling apart the topsoil with my mind down to the pebbles at the Earth's core. I stayed right there in that moment.

Then the voice in my head chimed in: *"Be stronger than your coping mechanism."*

That's when I saw the woman. One who hadn't been there before, in black like the rest of us, but glistening like oil-slick stars, tall and proud, angelic and demonic, monster and savior. She smiled at me, showing all her teeth.

I closed my eyes, regained my balance. I straightened up, letting myself feel how strong I was, could be. I took a deep breath, my throat still raw from the fire inside me.

In a slow, measured voice, meeting the eyes of everyone in the crowd, I said, "I. Am the only one. Who tried to help her."

"I want her out of here," Annie's daughter, the mouthy one, said.

I *looked* past her anger, past the blame, past her sadness and I found her guilt where she'd hidden it from the mourners comforting her. She hadn't visited her mother in years.

I *saw* the color of that guilt in her heart—a pink-gray lump. And with one fraction of a thought, I set it alight.

She stumbled back from her sister's embrace, where she'd been slumped in tears, and clutched her stomach, gasping for breath. Her sister grasped her shoulder, eyebrows knitted, mouth open, while other strangers put their hands on her arms, one around her waist. "It burns!" she cried out, and then again, "It burns!" and terror swept over the mourners, subtle, black and gray, quiet terror. All the attention she'd been aching for.

I finally let her guilt go from my fiery hold. Simply stopped looking. The color of her guilt faded away. I felt my eyes narrow, the smirk on my lips at the newfound power I'd created.

Dr. Mortimer had gone ghostly pale. I closed my eyes so I didn't have to see.

The woman in black was gone when I opened them again, but I felt her as I walked back to my mother's side. Invisible to me, but she was there, watching, as I took Dr. Mortimer's hand again. He stiffened.

And when I heard more than the rustle of the autumn breeze shake the tree leaves, and a black feather the length of my arm fell at my feet, I smiled.

~

*I*t was nearly dark when my mother and I got back home. A light was on in Annie's window, probably left on from the daughters staying there before the funeral. So careless. Thoughtless.

I slumped on the couch, vaguely uncomfortable in my own home after having been at the hospital for so long. Home had become a place where I had choices, like the end of a race when I was supposed to rest but was really gearing up for the next thing to do. Aside from Annie not making tea in the house next door, nothing could have made me sadder.

I cried. My mother sat beside me, and every ounce of fury at her melted. I clung to her more tightly than I ever had.

"It's okay, baby," she crooned, running her hand down the length of my hair, nestling my head in the crook of her arm like a puzzle piece. After all my resentment, shutting her out and blaming her, she didn't hesitate to hold me and tell me everything would be all right. Like no time had passed since we played Atari together and ate Bugles on that same couch. We laughed and threw Bugles at the TV every time we lost.

I cried harder. I didn't want to know as much about the world, as much about myself as I did. I wanted the hardest loss to cope with in my life to be at video games. My childhood corroded as my abilities fortified.

"Where's Dr. Mortimer?"

"Staying close by. We'll be okay," she whispered as I dozed off.

I knew better.

⌇

"**. . .** *C*an't stay here and she can't go back to the hospital. If Rose doesn't go to this facility where she can get the right medical attention, keep a close eye on her brain, receive greatly advanced psychological help to help her understand and control her abilities—"

"You mean to help *you* understand and control her abilities."

He sighed. "I have little choice, Ms. Preston."

I'd woken up in the middle of that night, having slept more peacefully than I had in years. In complete darkness but for the slightest sliver of moonlight through the window. Patchwork quilt pulled up to my neck, still scented of dryer sheets, mattress pulling me in. Mommy must have put me to bed.

"I just got her home, Dr. Mortimer. Don't take her away again," my mother pleaded in the living room. The best part about our cottage was that you could hear almost anything in it no matter where you were. For the first time, I took no pleasure in hearing my mother in the next room while I tried to sleep.

"Sarah. We have to be honest with each other, with ourselves. I care for the girl too, more than I should as a professional. She needs more help, more *protection* than I can provide for her."

"Protection? From who? Goddammit, I knew they'd come for her, that sonofabitch Cleary—"

"Word travels fast through government agencies, Sarah. The FBI, and someone—someone not from the FBI—showed up after Annie's funeral at my hotel. Between the malignant tumor that Rose made go away, the nurse she burned, the burn holes around Annie's body, Annie's death… They knew I've had the most contact with her."

"How convenient."

"If you think I want my name associated with the discovery of her abilities at the expense of her sanity, then you've put your trust in me without much basis, haven't you?" The heat in his words made my heart swell. He truly cared. I wondered who did anymore besides my mother.

"She is all I have left in this world," my mother said as if she heard my thoughts. "I need her to be safe."

And yet she'd left me in that hospital for months without insisting upon seeing me, speaking to me.

"Sarah, how can I say this? If Rose doesn't go to this government facility, she'll be slaughtered in the public eye. She won't be able to live a functional life—"

"She doesn't live a functional life now!" my mother shouted. She had to know I wouldn't sleep through that, but I was frozen.

So quietly I could scarcely hear him, Dr. Mortimer said, "Then wouldn't you take any risk at all to try to make her life better? Livable?"

My mother said nothing.

"There's no choice to be made, Sarah," Dr. Mortimer said, his words razor-sharp.

And in one sentence, I'd been surgically removed from my home forever.

"What are you doing skulking around here, Queenie?"

"Look at her, Hazel. Where else would I be?"

Rose, the girl of the hour, was indeed a nightmare to behold. Her hair alone.

"Hey, this is the eighties, right? Can I drink in here?"

The Harpy Queen glared at me intensely, but not as intensely as I wanted a beer. I knew for a fact that people smoked in hospitals in the eighties—doctors were flicking ashes on the fucking floor in front of me, as I live and breathe, second-hand smoke! Whenever I betrayed Robbie, myself, basically all of humanity, and became the Harpy, I always got the dirty guilties after. I wanted to dig that hole deeper, darker, see how low I could go, and absolutely shroud myself in bad habits. Second-hand smoke was a retro twist, but booze was my favorite killer.

Where exactly did they keep the beer in this hospital?

"She's spectacular," the Queen cooed, tracing her finger on the splintered glass of the itty bitty window on Rose's room door.

"What's her deal exactly? Not that I'm surprised she landed in here, not after the last time I saw her playing in the dirt."

The Queen's eyes glazed over with love. Like a real creep, she never took her eyes off the girl. "Raped at the age of five. Child genius, past hidden from her, father disappeared, coddled and manipulated, her mind became a trap full of holes that gifted her with exquisite abilities."

"Let me guess, you've got designs on these 'exquisite abilities,'" I said, making the snottiest imitation of her words with accompanying asshole air quotes.

"Perhaps," she said, smirking, and tapped one black fingernail on the glass, spiderwebbing it. No one noticed— no one could see us. And thank Christ for that, because if Dr. Smokesalot caught a glimpse of Queenie in her black spikey sparkle crown and her pretentious-as-shit black ballgown, well, he wouldn't even glance at me. Not to mention the black wings that took up half the hallway. Her thing for bad-guy-black was so stereotypical.

I didn't love playing wingman to her.

"Rooooosssse," she hissed through the hole in the tiny window.

The girl grunted as she lifted her head off the bed. All she could do, really, strapped down as she was. That had to be killing her, to be strapped down when she'd been raped as a kindergartener. Like having a mountain on top of you.

I shuddered, shook off memories. *If all goes well, I could rip that mountain to shreds before he ever knew what hit him.*

The Queen hissed for her again, and Rose thrashed and muttered, "Mommy?"

"She's obviously drugged, Morticia," I said. "What the hell do you think she's gonna do for you strapped into a bed anyway?"

"Watch." She had this way of infusing you with a feeling

of power like you've never dreamed of, but you knew she controlled you with it, too. Just another form of being beaten down, but with the promise of so much more. "Rooooooosssse."

Rose stopped resisting and just lay there. It hurt to watch.

The Queen pressed on. "You can hear me, can't you?"

The child stuttered but said she could. "You're the one. From Annie's funeral," she said with alarming surety. She sounded far less out of it than I'd pegged her for.

"Yes, child," the Queen said, lips curling. Through Rose's spiderwebbed window, she whispered in an ungodly voice that carried in a way it shouldn't, a list of instructions just for Rose. Bitch made everything sound simple, way simpler than life really was. Anything to gather her minions.

Finished with her trance of false promises, the Queen turned on me, eyes hazy as storm clouds and sharp as lightning. "You'll help her."

I put my foot on the wall I leaned upon, examined one talon. "Oh yeah? Says who?"

"This girl is more important than you—" she began, stepping closer to me.

"Yeah, yeah, the new chosen one, huh? You can only use that line once before it's not chosen *one* anymore." Sneering, claws digging into my palms, I growled at her, "I won't do a goddamn thing I don't want to. Said it once, saying it again for those of you—only you—who's not listening. I want nothing to do with your Skipper to my Barbie and you have no hold on me. I'm stronger than you. I beat you once, and I'll do it in every time warp we rendezvous in. You won't use me anymore."

She reached out, ran her fingers along my collarbone, ready to kiss me or throttle me. "Sweetheart. You were born to be used."

With a final glance at the moaning child tied to a hospital

bed, the Queen disappeared into the cosmic tornado that would return her to the Wood of Suicides. She was gone for now, but she'd always be back. Another revelation—Hell doesn't play in the bounds of time, so that fucker could always show up.

I went to Rose's broken window, could hear her whimpering, frozen in that bed. Finally, with the Queen gone, I could follow the Predator-type heat signature of the bastards who deserved to be ripped to shreds and stored in my freezer. But like the night in her yard, the heat signature here came from a defenseless child.

"What are they doing to you in here? You know this is a weird long-distance job for me, yeah?" I whispered. Whatever these doctors were up to, the Queen's plan would be worse. To Rose, it would feel better, but it would hurt her more than being tied to a bed. "The Queen didn't put me in your yard that night, didn't bring me here—it's *you*. So whaddya need?" Nothing. Just the sad noises from the other side of the door. "I eat people, you know. So tell me, who do you need me to turn into a distant memory?"

At the word *memory*, she stopped moaning, lifted her head up painfully, the heaviness of the medication weighing it down. I saw her eyes for the first time. Wide. Alert. Not so hazy after all, despite all the tubes hooked up to her. The child looked me right in the eyes. *You can see me?* I thought, glancing at the passing nurses who couldn't.

"Yes," she said out loud.

I backed right into a cafeteria tray cart, knocking a bunch of them to the ground, eggs and toast and all kinds of crappy food splattering the wall and floor. The pair of women pushing it screamed and ran. They couldn't see me—I was as good as a ghost when I wanted to be.

Plenty of ghosts haunting this place, I bet.

But what the hell is she?

"Psssst. Hey, kid." Nothing. She heard me, her body stopped its restless wriggling. "Seriously? You'll talk to frigging Maleficent but not me," I muttered. "Hey! Red. I know you hear me."

A series of clicks, scraping of metal, a couple of soft *clunks*.

Rose Preston sat bolt upright. The restraints hung at the sides of her bed.

"Whoa, what the *fuck*?"

"Why did you call me Red?" she said.

"What? Oh, like the tea. Red Rose. What in the ass did you just *do* though?"

Her face crumpled for a millisecond. "Annie drank Red Rose," she said.

The kid was so little. Too little for this, but not defenseless. I'd been wrong.

But what struck me more than her presence alone were her eyes. The way she looked at me, *into* me through that tiny, shattered window in the door. They never wavered, she didn't even blink, as if she'd been waiting for someone to invite her to look and couldn't get enough of the feeling. Her stare was a needling pair of tweezers pulling a layer of my brain off, reading, searching for memories, for something I couldn't give. Pain shot through my eyeballs, searing my skull. *She's tearing my brain apart...*

My vision blurred but I could see beyond that stare; her shredding me like a butcher knife gave her the same high I got from eviscerating a rapist.

"Don't look at me like that!" I yelped, claws burrowing into my hair. *How is she doing this to me?*

But I knew the answer before I'd ever walked in there. She was a weapon, itching to be used.

"Sorry," she said quietly. The brain invasion...stopped.

"Cool trick," I breathed, holding myself up on one side of

the door, sweat pouring down my forehead while she propped herself up, comfy in bed on the other.

Her eyes darted around the corners of her room like a pointing finger, telling me something while my head still swam and pounded. Of course—she was surrounded by cameras.

I wished I didn't know that feeling she was experiencing.

The feeling that even the slightest change, a tiny movement would upset the silence, bring attention to me, *remind him that I was close, a green light to come in and do what he wanted to me...*

"They'll come when they see me talking," she said, snapping me out of it. The claws on my feet clicked restlessly on the tile floor, echoing in the empty hallway.

"I know." I did. Girls like us didn't get left alone for long.

Her head cocked sideways and like flipping pages she went from little frightened girl to a quiet predator. *How smart is this kid?* It sent a chill down my spine. This is what the Queen saw in her, right here. And just like everyone else had, the Queen would use her.

"Tell me what you're doing here," Rose said, tiny interrogator.

"I...I uh, you probably need some help, right?" She didn't waver her gaze or move, the little weirdo. "Well, do you or what?"

Glance to the cameras, but that wasn't what she was talking about when she said, "You can't help me. Not here." She put a thought into my head, making me about choke on my own tongue at the speed and force, the intentional hurt. *"You could have gone anywhere, anytime to help me, and you waited until now."*

She'd been hurt long before I knew her.

"I...I didn't know."

I didn't know a world of protecting people long-term, of

wanting to fix past wrongs, of wanting to change someone's future, despite all the blood-red-collar work I did. A sudden shift of power occurred when I spoke to Rose. Mythical beast or not, that little girl had the power now.

Because I understood on the deepest level of my soul, that I would do anything to fix her life.

"Miss Preston?" a woman's voice said over a loudspeaker, vibrating the walls and the door I leaned on. *"Is there something you need?"*

"Ask for water," I said.

"I'd like some fresh water, please." There was the sweet girl; dirty sandy hair falling around her shoulders, freckles, bright eyes. She switched effortlessly—and I don't think she knew it. This place had split her apart.

"Of course, Rose," the woman's voice said, warmer this time. That little girl had a face that nobody could say no to.

"Just…just let them open the door and I'll do the rest," I said.

Rose tightened her lips. "I don't want your help. I'm fine here. It's getting better. There's nowhere else for me to go."

"That's not true," I said, shaking my head, frizz and feathers brushing my cheeks, making me spit them out of my mouth. "You don't want to be here. Who the fuck *would* want to be here? You've got someone on the outside."

"Move," Rose said.

I got out of the way and a nurse brushed by me, making more hair get in my face. She saw not a thing. She used a keycard and the door buzzed open. Pretty high-tech shit for the eighties.

The nurse carried a pitcher of water that made me wet my lips. I was so dry, hadn't realized it, as absorbed in this kid as I was. And I was fucking starving. I wanted meat.

Then what are you doing here? *Go eat a rapist's intestines. You're doing exactly what the Queen wants you to do.*

I watched the nurse pour the kid water, hand it to her with a genuinely kind smile, and gasp when she realized Rose's hands were free. With a side-eye at the camera, the nurse muttered, "Child shouldn't be restrained anyway." She patted Rose on the head.

I thought of Robbie. How gentle and kind he was with me. And how despite that, he was still ashamed of me.

The kid knew that feeling, too.

She wouldn't be ashamed of me.

Rose sipped the water, watching the nurse with the eighties-brown hair. You know the color, campsite brown. She was telling Rose something silly to make her smile. I remembered Robbie telling me silly things when I was near to turning into the Harpy, and I'd so wanted to, just for a little while, be free of my own monster.

Nobody can save us. This kind of gentleness doesn't save the weak.

Harpies save the weak.

The nurse came toward me, leaving the room with a little smile on her lips and a self-satisfied swagger. She did her good deed for the night. Yippee. Still hung around when the little girl was tied to a bed, didn't she? But when she passed through, opening the door from inside with the black keycard, I stuck a feather in the doorjamb in a moment of fucking genius. She never saw a thing and was probably already lighting a cigarette.

I nudged the door open, edging inside but not getting closer.

Why am I so scared? I hissed at myself. *Probably because they've got this kid in max security and I just wandered in like the cheerleader in a slasher flick,* I answered.

Rose sipped her water, eyes on me, cameras on her, with the open door. Perfectly relaxed.

Who exactly was I trying to save?

This kid is different. She needs more than I can give her. The only thing I had was the ability to help. Just *help.* If she didn't really need it, what good was I?

You're not capable of real good, dipshit. You can do what feels good. That's about it.

Adding someone else to the short list of people I cared about, then eventually destroyed or was destroyed by, was not an option.

Robbie. Jen. Evan. Painter's daughter, Maggie, the worst of all.

This kid is no Maggie Painter.

I had nothing to offer. Nothing but risk.

Rose watched me as she sipped, the bottom half of her face distorted through the water. Zero surprise registered in her eyes that I was letting the door close between us.

"Told you so," she said.

"I'm sorry," I choked out. And I ran from the Facility on clawed feet, my wings unable to lift the heaviness of my heart.

CHARITY

I sure as fuck needed to be drunk on something stronger than beer, and the *craving* for meat—real, fresh meat—hit me like a freight train when I rushed out of the Facility.

Leaving Red in there, where the lights were always on and pretty nurses brought her fresh water was a far better scenario than anything she'd get with me. I'd end her life faster than death by "helping" her. God, she'd said she didn't want my help.

You could have gone anywhere, anytime to help me, and you waited until now.

I kicked the Facility wall as hard as I could, and in beast mode, that was pretty fucking hard. A chunk of gray brick crumbled out, and I kicked it again and again, wanted to knock the whole building down. Fucking place, made to look abandoned and left to rot when inside it had some futuristic-for-the-eighties sinister shit going on. Hiding in there.

I hadn't left Rose in the Facility because I knew I'd ruin her more. I'd left her there because I didn't want to face that

I'd failed her already. She'd needed me and where the fuck had I been? Probably spending too long ripping the heart out of a molester somewhere while she suffered. Kid was right: *Now* I show up? The damage already done, and now I show up?

Screeching, I took to the sky, knowing I wouldn't have to go far for a motherfucker to eat in this part of town. Nothing good happened around here.

Then why are you leaving the kid?

Tears streamed down my face, from the wind, I told myself, until the old familiar glow showed up moments later. Crappy train station. Typical.

I dove hard, faster than ever, down the tunnel of a stairway to the underground station, the cement walls whipping past me, scraping my sides. I needed some pain, to be scared, some other feeling besides this regret.

The station hadn't been used in forever.

Used. The word made me scream louder than any train that might have torn into this old station.

I landed with a *whump,* as heavily as I could on the subway tiles below ground, rupturing them into a fountain of ceramic debris around me. A good entrance. I stood up straight from my shock-absorbing superhero crouch, imagining how terrifying I must have been with the tornado of dirt around me, spreading my dirty wings wide.

This lady was homeless for sure. A real shitstorm of rags, smudgy dirt, backpacks and bags. I cocked my head at the guy, trying to figure him out.

"You homeless?" I asked him. He still had his back to me, even after all the noise I'd made. Drunk, then. When he faced me I saw that his clothes kinda matched, still had most of their normalcy. "Not homeless, just a dickhead. My mistake. You lost, dummy, or are you specifically down here to ruin this lady's life? Well, worse than now."

A face full of Harpy and he sobered right up. "What the—" the motherfucker blubbered out. "Who *are* you?"

"I'm Christian Bale."

"Leave me alone!" he yelped.

"Do you not get it? 'I'm Batman?' Wait, you're not even at Keaton yet in '87… Anyway, you're not a movie-watcher, you're too busy attacking—" But the girl was gone. "Well, how do you like that? She's gonna miss the show."

I twisted like Ali throwing an uppercut and sent him airborne with one slap of my wing. *Slam!* Right into the crumbling wall. Crumbling like the wall in the Facility I'd kicked in. Before he slid down I plowed into him, bringing the wall down in pieces, with him among them.

"Jeez, that didn't hurt a bit," I said, rubbing my shoulder, smiling. The comedian rolled around moaning, covered in a sheet of white wall-dust. And I descended upon him like seagulls at Burger King, ripping chunks of his skin out through the new holes in his shirt with my claws as he screamed.

I bet Rose screamed, I thought.

The more violent I became, the more I thought of what Rose might have endured when I should have been there, saving her.

Standing on his stomach as his broken limbs flailed, I dug my claws in until I felt the gush of intestines. Blood pooled around my scaly ankles, stained the downy feathers further up. Robbie would be so disappointed in me. The Queen would have loved it. I found myself sobbing and laughing at once and knew this was what it felt like to lose your fucking mind.

Hunched over, sucking the marrow out of his broken arm, eyes raised enough to watch his head loll back and forth, in and out of consciousness.

Had Rose gone unconscious when she was raped?

I'd gone unconscious when Painter whacked me in the back of the head, and when I woke up, there was Maggie, waiting, terrified.

I burrowed my human teeth into the dickhead's throat, squirts of bright blood on either side of my face.

Again, I left her. I failed her without having met her, and I failed her when I did.

Without her, I was just a murderer.

"Hey, asshole," I said, sitting up, cowgirl-style, my voice thick with blood. "Ever feel like you *could* have been better, but you just plain weren't? Like," I slapped my clawed hand into the pool of blood that had been his stomach. I twirled the stringy organs around my talon. "Like you had the opportunity to be free, but you just shut the cage door, you know? That's how I feel." He moaned, definitely dying slowly. My stomach turned at his suffering, because I didn't want it to be over. He deserved it. Rose hadn't deserved to suffer. This guy did. "Wake up." I slapped him across the face, but too hard. His neck snapped, leaving his eyes wide and staring.

"Fine." For a while, I considered the mincemeat his body had become. I wondered where the homeless lady had gone, if this guy had an apartment somewhere around here that she could have now. I pried the blood-soaked pants pocket apart and found his wallet. A few twenties fell out.

I sighed. That would have been plenty of beer and meat money for the week. But I pictured Robbie's face when I pulled the cash out of my own pocket and knew that somehow that would be worse than what I'd just done in his eyes.

I grabbed the sonofabitch by the hair and threw him like one of those Olympic disc things onto the old train tracks. Out of sight, out of mind. Out of my mind.

Slumping against an old broken bench, I cried. For what felt like hours, I cried, until I could finally say, "I wanna go home." As if I had one.

"I've never been much of a planner," I said through the door, "but this seems like a good time to get you out of here."

Shaking, a sheen of sweat coating her hot pink cheeks, Rose gingerly lowered herself into the puffy white chair in the corner of the room—a thing put there to make her feel at home, like she was wanted, a person and not a thing. But she was still a prisoner behind a locked door, the shackles still lying limp on the bed, people in uniforms deciding her moment-to-moment existence when they got to go home at the end of the day to a life they chose.

Rose swiveled the chair my way. It had been two days. Two days since I'd been home to Robbie. Two days since I'd left the kid. Two days where I sat in that train station, immobile, too sick of myself to be afraid or care what happened to me next.

But freedom called to me in the form of a little girl, the heat of her anger a beacon that I could see through time and space. I had to come back. If I wanted to *live* at all, I had to help her, to help myself.

"I'm not trapped here," Rose said.

"Right, you must love being isolated and what? Running laps in your eighties gym shorts outside? Why are you so sweaty?"

"Eighties gym…" She smiled. I was amusing to her. "I um, just show them how I do things."

"What, Jane Fonda aerobics? What things?"

She just swiveled back around in her chair. "You're a mess," she said when I couldn't see her face.

Definitely. Two days in an abandoned train station rolling in viscera will do that to a girl. "That's neither here nor there. I always wanted to say that. Anyway, whatever you're in here for, whatever they make you do, I can help you escape."

"There's no escaping what I am."

There's no escaping what I am. There's no escaping what I am.

I ran my fingers through my hair like Robbie always did, a habit I guess I'd picked up. My fingers got caught in there, though. Never an easy way out for me.

"You know, kid, I'm a complete fucking stranger to you, offering you a way out, a fresh start or a chance to go home, whatever you want, and you don't give me an inch, do you?"

When do I get to go home? I thought, then shook my head to get rid of it. *When are my tests over, when do I get to stop sweating for everyone else, when do I get a fresh start that's real? Any good I do is sucked up in the bad that I am. There's no escaping what I am, Harpy or not.*

No escape.

The thought brought into perspective what the Queen told me—time doesn't exist for a Harpy. I slid down the door, felt the cold floor under me, solid. I'd never be different than this right now, never change.

Never heal. I wanted to try, for this kid. So she didn't end up anything like me, and so that I could end up like someone else, too.

Impossible, probably.

Leaning over, I threw up on the tile floor. Chicken bones and spaghetti and bile swimming in blood and half-digested flesh.

I heard a clicking noise over my head, the distinct sound of a lock being picked, and got to my feet fast no matter how shaky. You could never know what was coming through a locked door.

I fell back against the wall behind me, far from the door, a vision of Carl Painter on the other side. *It's not his time now but time isn't real and I was never safe.* I came back to the now with every click of the lock. *He is* not *real, not now, Charity,* I told myself. Time might mean nothing, but reality was always there, promising some new surprise. And there was my surprise, clicking away.

The door lock popped open. The wide bolt, the size of a credit card, slipped to the left. *Kid can pick locks.*

Then her eyes at the window, the only part that could reach if she stood on tiptoe.

And she opened the door.

Rose Preston glanced at the puddle of puke on the floor, and back at me. She pulled on a green tracksuit jacket. "You'll be okay," she said with a little smile. "I feel sick sometimes, too."

~

White coats came from everywhere when the door opened, and we ran. Sure would have been easy to open a portal to the Wood and get outta town altogether, but Red needed to be kept as far from Hell as possible… She could *never* know about such a place. The Queen would never get her hands on Rose.

But *shit,* trying to make a quiet getaway as a human, *with* a human was hard.

Too many locked doors, passing people in suits and lab coats and other suit-like lab coats. We slipped into a broom closet—classic hiding spot—to catch our breaths. "They'll find us here," she said, hint of a smile on her face. I shoved a broom under the doorknob.

"Maybe just the janitor. Maybe he'll bring a sandwich."

Rose stared at me in the dark, eyes shining, but not with that weird looking-through-me thing like before. Just like a kid excited for adventure. "Shouldn't look at people like that, Red. Makes it too easy to be seen yourself."

I hated hiding in small, dark places. I hated hiding at all, actually. I'd tried to hide from Painter once. He found me because who the hell doesn't hide in the closet as a kid? It was a safer place within the once-safe place of my bedroom. Hiding did nothing for me. A lock hadn't even done anything for me.

"They won't be long," she said, but she wasn't scared. *I'm not trapped,* she'd said.

I screamed when the doorknob beside my head jiggled fiercely. Great.

"Told you," Rose whispered, little peach-fuzzy knees against mine.

"Open up, Rose," a woman's voice said. "Nothing to worry about."

"I know," Rose answered.

My mouth hung open at the kid. "You're really not afraid, are you?" Rose shook her head. Then the woman on the other side was talking to someone else, and a third person, and then banging that made me stifle a scream again. My face grew hot with embarrassment.

"Rose, let's open this door before you're in trouble," a man said. I sneered, growled, willed myself not to attack them. *Stay a people person, Charity.*

The kid noticed my discomfort. Turning her head toward the doorknob, a wave of heat came from her, making me fall back in surprise, clattering against a mop bucket and dust-pans. Shimmers, reddish, barely visible flickers crossed the space, and the next time one of the Facility people tried the doorknob...

"Aaaaaghh!" A garbled scream and rushed voices.

"How the hell did you do that?" I gasped.

She shrugged but smiled that shy smile again. "They call it acquired savant syndrome. I can do things."

"Like open the lock on your door?" Rose nodded. Nice. Hidden powers, an ace in the hole, never a bad thing. *But her power isn't all that hidden—she's in here because of it.* What were they planning to do with it? With her?

I swallowed hard. "I'm getting us out of here, kid." She sorta shrugged, unhurried.

I opened the vortex fast. Really small one, like *really* small because we were in a frigging broom closet. A black, swirling hole in the air, hiding a bunch of janitor stuff behind it. Flashes of purple, blue, pink inside it, so beautiful it could make me forget where I was going.

"Like the Milky Way, right?" She nodded, oddly unim-pressed. Whatever. Kids these days. Those days. "Okay Red, jump in."

She did it without hesitation, and was in another world, with me right behind. A worse world, but a clearer one.

CHARITY

THE WOOD, NO YEAR

"**D**on't open your eyes, not for a second, understand?" I held Rose's face between my hands, trying to cover her ears but she'd already heard the screams, the groaning, the souls pleading with the Harpies picking them limb from battered limb. There was no drowning it out.

Her eyes were closed but it didn't matter. "I've been here before. Charity," she said, pulling my hands away, letting her eyes flutter open. "I know this place."

No. "What? How?" But I already knew. "The Queen brought you here."

"She told me…that I'd seen worse than this…in my own backyard," she said, nodding her head, trying to remember the bitch's exact words.

"Oh my God," I mumbled. "Was she right?"

The kid's face went blank for a minute. "Sometimes I think so."

"Well, we aren't staying."

"There's nowhere to go but the Facility."

"We'll go to my apartment." *Shit, Robbie.* "And you can stay there for a while until I know what to do next."

Fucking hell, I hadn't thought this through at *all*. Can't bring a stray kid home to Robbie. Not to mention, people would figure out real quick how weird it was that the town trash suddenly had not only a kid, but one with a track suit from the 1980 Olympics. And for what? I didn't know anything about her, not even what I was hiding her from. For fuck's sake, the worst thing I could hide her from—the Queen—was right where I'd brought her.

"Grooming her," I whispered. The Queen grooming her, the Facility grooming her. I knew that feeling. I knew it, I knew it, I knew it…

Drawn to the thing that hurt me, in true Harpy style.

"You keep saying *grooming.*"

"What? No, nothing, kid, nothing."

She pushed past me, walked into the bloodbath that was the Wood with the questioning eyes of a kid dissecting a frog. Like, I could tell she noticed the odor—unforgettable odor—but it didn't move her. The Harpies stared, silent now that she'd made a move, unsure if they were predator or prey.

"Human," one said in its gargly voice, full of fresh blood. It threw a clump of innards to the ground with a *thud.*

"Shut up," I said reflexively. But I was too intrigued to call the kid back to my side. She sure didn't seem like she needed my help now. She didn't go to a flesh tree the way I had my first moments in Hell; she walked straight into the center of a cluster of Harpies. In what I recognized as a singularly Rose way of looking at stuff, the kid gazed around the circle. Inquisitive, not intimidated. If anything, she commanded attention.

Kid knew she could incinerate those bitches.

A child who could destroy Harpies. What was the Queen's endgame in bringing her here?

Culling.

The Queen was preparing to clean house.

No. She's preparing to eliminate the bitches who cross her. Or, bitch, singular who crosses her.

She planned on using Rose to get rid of *me*, and as an extra bonus, get me to help the kid do it. Queenie-pie loved irony, and she was too good at subtle planning not to get away with it. After all, here I was, with the kid I said I wouldn't help, bringing her right to the firepit itself.

I watched Rose, short enough for me to rest my beer on, the green shorts with the rainbow rings around the legs, bright green track jacket, two thick braids, with a group of more than a dozen Harpies glued to her every move.

And make a move she did.

Smiling so as not to scare them off (scared the shit out of me), the child dug her heels into the bloody ground, ducked her head down for a second—her shoulders relaxed as she breathed out meditatively—and when raised her head and opened her mouth? A fucking ball of fire was inside. Like where a tongue should be? Ball of fire.

The Harpies, all crouched down like vultures, inched forward for a better view. They made the most human sounds I'd ever heard them make, *ooh*ing and*aahhh*ing at the human Roman candle on July Fourth. She laughed, cute chuckle that should not at all be heard in the Wood of Suicides. The Harpies laughed...I guess...along with her. Change in this timeless, ancient place, was happening before my eyes. The Queen couldn't possibly like this. That made me like it a helluva lot more.

The Harpies were riveted, even the really gross ones—the ones that never leave, just eat the rotting flesh that falls from the trees like crabapples, can't speak, the least human of all of us. The fools shifted from foot to foot, bobbing their heads and chattering in some weird dead language between them, watching Rose. So Rose amped up the show.

"You want to see more," she told them. I wondered if she could read their minds or if she was telling them what they wanted. The monsters all hopped up and down, jabbering away. "Here goes!" I held my breath like everyone else.

The souls in the ashen, twisted trunk of the tree in Rose's sightline howled louder, longer. The branches, with human arms impossibly elongated and contorted around them, shivered, raining severed fingers and blood clots to the ground.

"What the shit is happening?" I said to myself.

The crowd grew. A Harpy with dreadlocks that hung to the ground asked Rose, "What is this you do, child?"

"Watch," she said, never taking her eyes from the tree. And watch we did.

The entire tree shifted, a living dead thing getting comfortable. The moaning and screaming changed—different from the usual agony. I spotted a space by a knot in the trunk that hadn't been there before. Again, the tree shifted and the space grew. An arm popped out of where it was buried in the dead bark, and hung lifelessly, flapping as the tree wiggled more and more. Branches swayed, heads smacked into limbs, human and tree alike, as the entire thing unraveled like a knot of wires. Until a half dozen human bodies tumbled to the ground in a squishy splash of torsos, legs, ragged amputations, let loose from the tree like vomit. They writhed and rolled on the ground, worms in the sun, hideously out of place, but free.

Free.

Rose straightened up, put her shoulders back, held her head high, and popped a piece of gum in her mouth from her jacket pocket. I rushed over to her, reluctant and eager at once to be closer to the disassembled nightmare tree. Because…what was it now? What did we do with these half-alive stumps of souls?

"Dude," I breathed, putting my hand on her shoulder, as if she were about to bolt outta there. "What did you do just now?"

Her eyes met mine, just a kid, not the weird kid who did whatever *that* was, and she simply shrugged and said, "I took it apart." And she held out a piece of gum for me. Which I took. Because I wasn't about to say no to the fire-breathing dragon girl.

"Wha—how? You did that with your fucking—oh, sorry, your *mind?* Did it hurt?"

She laughed, sweetly. She was just the prettiest little thing. "No! It feels *good!*"

"You've done this before?" *Duh, obviously, Charity. Can't you tell by how fucking perfectly and easily she did it?*

Her face fell. I don't know what I'd said, but my heart constricted to see her get sad. "Yes. I've done it before."

We both quieted and watched the Harpies inspect the tree, restored to just being a big dead plant, bodies littered on the ground like a bomb hit them. A Harpy put red-taloned toes onto an amputated leg and ripped loose veins from it with her teeth, wings tucked back to keep them clean.

Rose shuddered beside me. "So, what do you want to do now?" she said.

~

The Queen would know. She'd know what the kid did, and in that *Cops* moment, I said, "We gotta get out of here." I took the kid through the closest vortex and right home.

Well, not her home—Robbie's and my apartment.

We fell into a heap of AstroTurf-green polyester/terrycloth and naked bird bitch in the middle of the living room, me cracking my head on the coffee table, screeching, "Fuck!" while the kid rolled pretty much under the couch.

"What the fuck?!" Robbie yelled, jumping onto the couch like he saw a mouse. "Charity! Holy crap, are you okay?" He jumped back down and put a hand to my head, coming away bloody.

"Yeah, yeah, watch your mouth around the kid."

"What! You watch *your* mouth around the—" My vision focused enough to see Robbie gaping at Rose as she brushed under-the-couch dust off her jacket and fixed her braids. "Who…"

"Hi," the kid squeaked.

"Hey," Robbie answered.

"Robbie, Rose. Rose, Robbie. She's from the eighties, this isn't the eighties, I'm naked and in trouble probably." I left the room to get some clothes, Robbie right on my tail.

"Char, what, who—"

I pulled on a black tanktop I'd left on the bed, glanced in the mirror. "Ugh," I shuddered. "Her name's Rose. Remember I started telling you about a new girl, but then we started talking about your new kid? Well this is my new kid. I mean, not *my* new kid, but she needs me. I think."

It was always worrisome when Robbie just stood there. Like, not running his fingers through his hair or smiling, but just stood there. "Charity, you've been gone for days, and *she* cannot be here. She's…from the *eighties?* We can't have a kid, we're struggling just to keep you…you know. And not to mention, a *kid.*"

Letting out a huge breath that emptied my entire body, I squeezed the nearest unicorn pillow—purple fabric, space unicorn—and formulated an actual plan. Or tried to.

"She was in this Facility, kinda place that doesn't do anything good. Hiding in plain sight, the second-hand smoke alone… I don't know where she goes if she isn't there." The bed creaked as Robbie sat beside me. Breathing a sigh of relief, I rolled over, put my head in his lap, trained on his face, got grounded in this world, even though I made far worse decisions here than in the Wood. "Don't get mad—but the Queen has a hand in this. She's grooming Rose, wants her in the Wood…and I saw what Rose can do there." *You're blinking too fast, he'll know you're afraid of what he'll say, calm down.*

"You've been there all this time? You left me with no clue. Charity. Jesus Christ."

"I had no choice, it was bring her to the Wood or let her be locked up again, and they've made her think she's got no other options. I don't know what they're trying to do to her there, but if it's anything like an eighties movie, they want to make a weapon out of her, experiment on her or something."

Robbie's eyes narrowed. "What do you mean? What can she do? Who is she?"

The sound of cabinets being opened. I smiled a little that Red was getting hungry. She was settling in.

"She has this thing with fire. And she—now, don't get mad—but she got up real close and personal with the suicides in the Wood and she freed them from a tree. Like, took the tree apart and freed them with her mind. As free as they can be, anyway." I tossed the pillow aside, sat up, brain as on fire as Rose's mouth. Robbie made a little grunt, his horror slipping out. "She can set the suicides free of the torture there, Rob. I don't know what the Queen wants with her—kid could take the whole place apart—but she's being groomed, by the Queen, by the Facility. So I got Rose out of there fast and brought her here."

Robbie put his hand on my cheek and my body became a puddle of relaxation. *He's still here.*

"I thought of something else, Rob."

He laughed, lit up my soul. That was the thing about Rob—he never held a grudge. "You've got room to think of something else in there?" he joked, tapping my temple.

"Yeah. Yeah, I guess." I glanced toward the door, knowing the life-changing power beyond it, and focused on my shelf of unicorn statues, hating them for a second. "I can go back in time. I don't think too hard on that one, because what am I, Isaac Asimov? But if *she* can take the suicide trees apart, and *I* can go back in time—"

Robbie's eyes widened bigger than I'd ever seen them. He played it so cool most of the time, I didn't think I could scare him anymore, past exploding in the kitchen or coming home wearing intestines like a feather boa. He whispered, "You think you can bring them back to before they killed themselves."

I cracked my knuckles. "Yup. Uh-huh. Because who the hell else is good for a job like that? Is that even a fucking job? Robbie, I can't cook, I've never paid a bill on time, I don't remember drinking anything but alcohol and coffee before last week." Fucking hell, tears welled in my eyes. Stupid fucking unicorns everywhere. What childhood did I think I was holding onto? What fairy tale ended with returning mangled dead people to their former lives? "Robbie," I sobbed, losing my grip, "I don't know what to do, but I know what I *can* do, or at least try to do, and I know that kid has more power than me. I can't bring her back to a place where they'll use her. Bad things have happened to her, and instead of eating the guy who did it, I think I can do something for her now. I should have been there, Rob, and I wasn't. But I can help her *now.*"

There'd been times when I'd been soaked in blood and the

metallic taste of it overwhelmed my senses and I'd felt whole. Simple again.

The way Robbie wrapped me in his arms then was the same acceptance of the most basic part of me. My soul let out a sigh.

"Um, hi." A soft knock on the door, then it pushed open. "What's wrong with your Oreos?" Rose asked.

"*Wrong?* If Golden Oreos are wrong, then I don't wanna be right. That, my small friend, is the best goddamn—"

"Char…"

"—the best junk food since cookie dough ice cream."

"She doesn't know cookie dough ice cream."

"Yeah, well…she would *like it*, and that's what I'm getting at, Rob. If she likes regular Oreos, Golden Oreos are like Nilla Wafers had sex with—"

"Char…"

"Yeah, I know," I said, putting on my best dufus face to mock him. "I'll clean it up some."

"Wouldn't be hard," he muttered.

Rose laughed, out loud, and I was a kid right along with her. But the way she studied the Golden Oreo snapped me right out of my little kid moment. "Red," I said. She looked up. "Whatcha doin'?"

"I took it apart in my head," she said simply, like it was totally obvious. "Same stuff that's in a regular Oreo, mostly." She popped the whole cookie in her mouth and chewed for a second. Then her face lit up like a Christmas tree. "Whoa!"

Robbie laughed first, all heart and zero bite. The kid would totally have a crush on him. "Come on," he said. "Let me show you the wonders of the Uncrustable."

I mouthed, "So. Bad," to her as he crossed the room, and without even a glance at me, Robbie added, "No they are not."

~

The in-my-head movie, *Night With Red*, was pretty awesome.

Because Robbie enjoyed it right along with me, I didn't feel like quite as much of a weirdo in this half-assed kidnapping/sleepover with a little girl. But the sadness of how happy it made me was just pathetic. And Rose definitely needed the quality time as much as I did.

"I haven't…talked…to anyone…well, I don't really talk to anyone," Rose said as we laughed over the differences between my wardrobe and hers, which consisted of the single outfit she had on. Nothing I owned was appropriate for—well, anyone, but definitely not a child. I gave her an Avengers t-shirt of Robbie's that stumped her pretty good. I don't think she had a whole lot of exposure to superheroes, despite being one.

"Nobody ever gave you a comic book in the Facility? Or your…parents?"

She hid in the closet as she changed, calling out to me that she had a mom but hadn't seen her in a very long time. That she had been in the Facility too long to remember much outside of it, which struck me like a proudly waving red flag of WTF.

"How old are you?"

No answer from the closet. I took that as an *I don't know* and skipped to much harder questions that were sure to cross some boundaries.

"What do they make you do in the Facility, kid?"

"I'm not talking about that."

Expected. "I just kidnapped you from the past and brought you to Hell—and say nothing about Hell really being where my macaroni and cheese comes from because you said it was good when I made it. Point is, I'm going on little more than a feeling that I'm better for you than the Facility or the Queen of the Wood. I just…" Big sigh, lots of silence. Kid had to be changed by now and was literally hiding in the closet from my questions. "I want to be there for you."

"Everybody. Says. That," came her muffled voice, and the closet doorknob glowed bright red with heat.

"Okay, okay, chill out, literally. No setting my apartment on fire, it's hardly even mine."

The knob went back to tarnished brass, and the door opened.

"You're the cutest thing ever, huh?" So damn adorable in the giant t-shirt with her braids that I couldn't handle it. She didn't smile. And in a beat of my frigid heart, I remembered Painter's daughter in an oversized, holey shirt, her feet so pink it didn't look like she'd ever walked barefoot. The purest part of her. All that was left.

"Sorry," I said. "I won't hurt you. I know…someone has, and probably has said a lot of the same stuff I'm saying now, but not everybody's out to hurt you. I'll protect you." *What am I saying, what am I saying, holy crap.* My face burned with embarrassment. Whole time, she just stared at me like she didn't know if she should run or attack. "You know, I don't really talk to anyone either."

She sat on the bed with me, knee brushing mine. I tried not to flinch or to think of Painter's daughter—Maggie. *Her name was Maggie.* I forced myself to think of it. I'd ruined her life. We'd ruined each other's and yet it was neither of our faults. I wouldn't ruin Rose's, too. *Rose isn't Maggie, isn't you, isn't Jen. You can't help her, you can't fix the past.*

"Everybody says they can help me," Rose said, getting up to look at one of my unicorn shelves. "But I never needed help. I had a tumor, you know. They couldn't help me—so I helped myself. I took it apart."

"You what? What, like, self-lobotomy?"

She laughed. I loved hearing her laugh. "Everything is made of other things. I see it and take them apart. That's what I did with the tumor, but I couldn't…stop. Sometimes—most of the time—I helped by taking things apart. But not always." Her voice lowered, she dropped her head. "Do you have any gum?" she asked out of nowhere.

"Nah. I like bad habits, not just habits."

Another smile from her. *Win.* "I'm sorry I snapped at you," she said. "It's just that when people try to help me, they really only want to help themselves. My mother left me at the Facility because she was sick of being afraid. She never wanted me out of her sight because of the bad thing that happened when I was five, and then even more because the doctors and scientists wanted me. So she gave me away when she couldn't take it anymore."

My chest hurt. "She gave you to the Facility because she couldn't keep you safe," I said.

Rose kept going. I'd sparked something more than fire in her—the kid wanted to keep talking. Psychiatrist might have called it a breakthrough. "I miss home," she said. "My mother lied to me about a lot of things, but home was *real.* Not the apartment in the city; that doesn't feel real. Home, by the beach, with my mommy." I cringed when she said *mommy.* "I got hurt there, too. Nobody liked me, and there was Sean Singh… But I had Annie, and she made me feel more real than anything in the world."

I stood up, put my hand on her back tentatively, and was flooded with relief when she didn't pull away. She suddenly smiled brightly, even if it was sad. She *was* brightness.

Picking up a dusty unicorn in a waterfall, she said, "These remind me of the tiny animals that come in the Red Rose tea boxes." Bigger smile now, all teeth. "Annie always said, 'Our zoo is growing,' when she opened a new box, and she put them on her windowsill, even if she had two or three of the same one."

"Why didn't you bring the doubles home, make your own zoo?"

Her face hardened, and she put the unicorn down. "Because with Annie, they mattered."

I pictured the windowsill zoo of fake animals, real to Rose. No cages.

"You matter here, Rose," I said softly, throat constricting. Without warning, she kissed me lightning fast on my cheek. In a weird metal unicorn I caught my reflection; no lipstick mark, but a flaming lip print, glowing like a brand and sizzling on my skin. Good pain. *Kickass tattoo.*

"I mattered at the Facility. Mr. Cleary knows I'm important, he doesn't want me to hide. He doesn't underestimate me. He *sees* me. With him, I was real again." Her eyes searched mine, not the scary way, but just needing to know I got it.

"Listen." I picked up her braid, waved it around. "I don't feel real a lot either. Most of the time nothing feels more real than that voice in my head that tells me I deserved it. All of it, not just the touching and all that, but everything nasty that came after, this whole *life*. I had it coming because it was just prep-work for this monster I'd become one day. I never stood a chance. This life? People working stupid jobs and having babies, frigging college, and stupid shit like getting oil changes and being annoyed about bad customer service, people living lives like that couldn't be real when *my* life had been about being knocked out and raped until I couldn't stand. *My* real was a drugged-out mother and knowing I had nothing good coming, not ever. And now I *am* nothing good. That voice, that real voice, it knows me. But I know you, Rose Preston. You make me feel real. And you, and how much I care about you, that is *real.*" *Humiliating.*

"I love you," she blurted out, grinning.

"What?" I gasped, squeezed my eyes shut against…what? That the kid still could love someone so easily, that it hadn't been burned out of her despite what she'd been through? That she, anyone, could love *me*? What did it matter that we'd just barely met? More time didn't necessarily make love grow—it just provided more opportunity to be lost.

The word *sister* popped into my head, that this was the closest I'd ever felt to one, even though Maggie should have been, in a perfect world, in one where people cared. One with boy talk, sharing clothes, arguing, beating each other to the single bathroom, getting in silly trouble together. What we'd had instead—sleeping with one eye open or not at all. No time together to trust each other. Nothing simple, nothing easy. "I love you too, Red," I said solemnly. "I'll protect you."

Suddenly all the love was gone. "I don't need protecting *now*," she said, voice cracking, showing me not a scared kid, but a despairing miracle made of steel. Her entire being seemed to harden, the child being torn away to reveal decomposition beneath. Her chest glowed stronger and stronger orange through Robbie's t-shirt. I found myself breathing hard, breath exploding out in cold bursts, no match for the boiling of my insides. My face and arms feeling like I'd been in the sun too long. Then my blood ran hot, my hands felt like they'd caught fire first, then the rest of me.

"No!" I yelled at her. "Why are you doing this?" *Don't scream, the cops will come.*

"I would never have been so different if you'd *seen* me and saved me before that boy—"

God, she's right, too little too late.

"Where were you, Charity? I was only five years old!"

"Hazel, stand up for yourself or die right here and now." The

Queen's voice squeezed into my mind between the burning and guilt.

"I'm sorry, Rose!" I screamed through sobs.

She shuddered, drooped so that the heat and hardness left her, releasing me from the flames. "Sorry means nothing."

"Stand up for yourself, Hazel."

Goddamn Queen always knew what I needed. "Rose. I'm sorry I couldn't save you."

"You could have."

"No! I couldn't have! Women, kids, victims, you're not fucking Pokémon. I'm not gonna catch 'em all! I have limits. I'll never be everything to everyone."

And then "everyone," Robbie, cracked open the door on cue. The blast of truth came through the doorway with his open, trusting face. He could never be everything to me because I'd always believe he had one foot out the door. He was better than me. Part of his love for me was the need to fix me.

I wanted something unconditional, even though I didn't deserve it.

One relationship crisis at a time, Charity. I waved him out. There'd be plenty of time for movies and pizza and laughing. Sometimes not laughing was way more important.

"You're right," Rose said, pushing sweaty strands of hair from her forehead. Blinking her tears back, she asked me, "What's scary about you?"

I belly laughed so hard I thought I'd black out. "Oh shit, kid, you have no idea. I mean, this fucking unicorn collection, for one."

Her laugh was quiet, hidden. "You don't have to stop swearing in front of me," she said with a conspiratorial smile. "I like the way you talk to me."

I pulled her against my side. "I like the way you talk to me, too."

~

*R*obbie ordered six pizzas.

"Dude, the pizza kid only gives *me* a discount and that's only if I'm wearing fishnets. You should have waited for me."

Grinning, he handed me a plate of anchovy, which I ate only to annoy other people who might see me eating it. Being off-putting semi-professionally. "Well, well, well, suddenly so money-conscious," he said.

"Just saving a buck in case I have to hire a guy to clean up bodies for me."

I sprawled on the floor, leaning against Robbie's legs, Rose's cheeks pink and puffed up with a face full of food. She smiled as wide as she could without opening her mouth. She'd even tried a piece of anchovy but spit that shit out fast.

"I like your bird," she said, wiping her mouth.

"You don't need to compliment my bird because you don't like anchovies."

"I really do! I never saw one like that."

"Yeah, me either," I said, smiling at Keegan. Ah, Christ, might as well let my soft side shine through. "You know, I got him because I wanted something to take care of. Something I could be good for." When the kid's eyes looked into mine a little too deeply, I turned away. Didn't need her digging around in there to "take me apart" when I was exposing myself enough as it was.

"Sorry," she said.

I rolled my eyes at her. "No, I'm sorry for being an asshole and not trusting you to poke around in my head. But my brain is mine kid. I got that brain, that bird, and that boyfriend, so I get a little claws-out about them. Pun totally intended." I snatched a pizza crust off Robbie's plate, shrugging at his disbelief. "You weren't gonna eat it."

"You're a Harpy," Rose said without context.

"Wow. Yeah. You win a trip through time to a bird bitch's apartment to watch her eat anchovies."

"I can see it inside you."

If possible, Robbie's body went more still.

"You ever wonder why the Queen comes to you?" Changing the subject was easy when the kid was so ill-versed in conversation.

She peeled a piece of pepperoni off her slice, studying it quizzically. I wondered what she saw in there. "I don't ask questions," she said, distracted. "I give answers."

"Wow. That's creepy as fuck, kiddo."

"Charity…" Robbie warned.

"She likes it. Besides, she's seen some shit; a well-placed f-bomb won't scare her."

"Right," she said, grinning. She picked a meat circle off her slice, shoved it in her mouth, wiped her hand on Robbie's big t-shirt.

"What happened when the Queen brought you to the Wood of Suicides?" Robbie asked robotically.

"I met bird bitches." She grinned at me, I clapped for her. "She talked to me about being raped." Jesus, just like that, zero emotion. "And about the boy at my school who's terrible to me."

Robbie flushed, hung his head. "It's okay," Rose said. I was proud, she was starting to see feelings more than just brains. "You want to know if I like the Wood of Suicides; I don't."

"Thank Christ." I relaxed—for a second.

"It's horrible there. I love *life*. She doesn't underestimate me though, different than Mr. Cleary…"

Panic. Panic. "She uses people, Rose, she has nothing to offer you—"

"Everyone has something to offer," she replied.

"She isn't everyone. There's no one like her. You don't

know her. She double-deals worse than the devil, she'll chew you up and spit you out. Please, *please* don't go back."

She'd watched me calmly through my outburst, then pointing a pizza crust at me, said, "*You* don't know her either, and you're scared I'll replace you." Caught a side glance at Robbie spinning his head toward me. "And no. She won't. I can take care of myself," she finished coldly.

She stared at the pizza box. I wished I could dig deeper into her thoughts then. There was a memory there, I could feel it. Something that started good but went bad.

"We were eating pizza when I first realized my mother was becoming afraid of me," Rose said, certainly having read my mind. Then back to me, "I don't deserve to be feared."

"Fucking hell, you're just a kid, like what, twelve? I agree. You don't deserve it, and that even sounds too old for you to say."

"The Queen says fear is good in the right hands."

"You can't listen to her, kid."

"She's really smart, Charity," Rose pushed. "She said that medicine and psychology have come a long way since the 1980s, and that they can tell me much more about why I'm like this."

"And why do you think she's telling you that?" I said snidely, unable to hide how fucking stupid she was being, little kid or not. "She's not just being nice, she wants something."

"Everyone wants something!" Rose shouted. "The doctors, the Queen, my mother, Cody Reese, Sean Singh, you. Me. We all want something, don't we? What good is this life if we don't?"

"Charity…" Robbie's voice warned yet again. Except now he was scared.

The fire in her chest had burned a hole clean through Robbie's shirt. Yes, less laundry.

"Cut it out, Rose. I just don't want you to replace one mother with another who sucks. You don't need anything from her, from either of them. You want a mom, I get it, you're just a kid. But you…you're more than a little girl. You've gotta control that chest furnace of yours or you might as well spend the rest of your life in the Facility."

The kid collapsed onto her side then, staring straight ahead, whimpering, "more than a little girl."

Flashbacks. I knew them well.

We watched helplessly as she quivered on the floor, burning holes in the shitty carpet. I couldn't bear to think what had been done to her, the names on her list of people who want stuff from her written in Sharpie on my brain.

"Still don't see why I want to be a Harpy?" I spat at Robbie.

He had nothing to say.

Except, "Did she say 'Cody Reese'?"

~

*R*obbie carried an exhausted Rose to our bed to rest while I gnashed my teeth, itching to Harpify, enraged over the kid's damage, despising the memories her episode conjured up in my own head. I groaned, my toes turning into claws, digging into the carpet beside Rose's burn marks.

But I had to stay for her. And I wanted to hear this fucking bombshell I was pretty sure Robbie had for me.

He clicked the bedroom door shut quietly behind him, finger to his lips as if I might wake the baby.

"What do you know about Cody Reese?" I said, putting down a bottle of water, reaching for the cabinet with the whiskey, but going for a Bud Light. God, I hated Bud Light.

Robbie ran his fingers through his hair, eyes narrowed like he was in pain. "His kid is at the boarding house."

I coughed on my beer. "I'm sorry, *what*? How is that possible?"

He shook his head, popped the beer I handed him. "I'm so confused, Char. Rose time-traveled with you, right?"

"I can't believe I'm a fucking science fiction story now, but yeah. Time-traveling Harpy with a telepathic orphan or some shit, that's me."

"This kid, Turner, he came to the boarding house after his dad killed himself. That's his father, Cody Reese, he was forty-nine. It's got to be the same guy."

I sat on the kitchen floor—or more like my legs folded underneath me, claws clicking on the tile, when I heard the words *killed himself.* Robbie sat beside me, and I threw my legs over him. I needed contact, him, to keep me from turning into a Harpy. I watched my claws turn back into ragged toenails, then back again. I wanted to be there when the kid woke up.

What will I tell her?

"It's no coincidence, I'm meant to help her, I knew it. The son of the guy who raped her just turns up at *your* boarding house?"

"No, definitely not a coincidence," Robbie said. "It's a trap. The Queen knows she's losing her grip on you. She did this to reel you in. Cody Reese killed himself, Charity. He's got to be in the—"

"Wood of Suicides," I said coldly, pissed off that Robbie was making sense. *God, I'm such a wishful thinking bimbo.* "Rose can't know."

"Why not? She might be able to get some closure—"

"Don't be an idiot, Rob."

"Hey."

"Sorry, don't be a *fool*. The Queen knows Rose is powerful, special. She orchestrated it so the kid would be in that Facility, made it so I was drawn to her, that I'd seen an opportunity to, I dunno, help her where I couldn't help Maggie. Help myself when I was her age. Fuck, I sound like Psychiatrist. She *made* Cody Reese kill himself—you know how the Queen is—and she knew, she fucking *knew* I'd bring Rose here, where the dick's kid is. She's trying to drive me crazy and she's trying to make herself a new Harpy that can upset everything. She loves chaos, the bitch."

"It's all a ploy to get you back at her side," Robbie said stiffly.

I shrugged. "If it doesn't work, she'll have a new and improved Harpy to take my place, won't she?"

"You won't let that happen," Robbie said, resignedly. "God, you'll never be free of that place, will you?" His head fell back against the battered cabinet.

"Probably not. But this…feels like change. I *want* change. I can't ever get better, be different if I don't do something solidly good; this is the way to do it." My mind raced. I chugged my beer, turning to him, lighting up with revelations. "The Queen thinks I'll try to fix my own past, Maggie, Painter, Jen… But she's not counting on… You should see what Rose can do, Rob. She could take the entire Wood apart, and if we play our cards right, I can bring those suckers back to the time before they killed themselves! I can *reverse time* with her help."

"Holy shit, Charity, that's impossible. You need to let it go."

Itching legs, prickly arms, feathers stabbing through my skin slowly. "Fucking *excuse* me? I tell you I have a plan to get rid of the Wood of Suicides and you say no?"

"Charity, I know you mean well, but the list of reasons

you can't do that… Rose doesn't belong down there! You know that. Don't do to her what you've done to yourself."

I could've caught flies in my mouth. "What did you say?"

He wiped his hand over his face. "You know what I—"

"You're…blaming…*me* for becoming…" My bones went limp.

He squeezed my hand and I wanted to punch him. "I don't blame you. It wasn't your choice. But it is now. Yeah, that's right," he said louder when I was ready to attack. "You're choosing it now. And you think you can undo everyone else's choices? You have no right."

"I have a right to do whatever the fuck I want with what I have, and you're an asshole to tell me not to try. You don't want me to hunt down criminals, you say I'm better than that. Well, this is a better plan. This is real change I can make happen, not this one-kind-act-at-a-time shit that you love so much."

"I'm sorry that's what you think of me." So cold. So unlike him.

Holes were being torn in my heart. "I remember when you loved *me*, no matter what I was."

"I still do! Stop doing that shit to me, Charity! I stick beside you all the time, I love you despite all of it—"

"Oh, how nice of you. What a martyr."

"You know, you might stop calling me names, let me finish a sentence. I'm not against you. I want—"

"Me to be normal? Not likely. You want normal, go check out the other coffee shop flunkies. You took home the wrong one."

I got up fast, slammed out the door on my way out, well aware I was leaving Rose behind and knowing she was used to it. But I couldn't wait another second to do what I did best.

Standing on the hill outside the apartment building, I

threw my arms back, hugging the sky, and let the feathers pop out of my arms one at a time, feeling every single quill tear through the skin. My legs scaled over, the talons grew out of my hands and feet. Feathers emerged from my torso, ripping my clothes as I pulled off my pants. And I was the monster again, ready to do monstrous things.

CHARITY

inutes later, in a hot, dry place that made me want a margarita for the first time in my life, I found him.

He was nobody. Not the quarterback, not the rich kid, not the disturbed kid. Just a kid, maybe seventeen? He had her in his car, they'd obviously been messing around in this park that sucked because there were like, zero trees. *Phoenix? Vegas?* Didn't matter. Dickheads were the same worldwide.

Roosting on a telephone pole I watched my target. There was giggling, murmuring, steamy windows, the whole deal, but then it got louder. Not the good kind of loud.

"Ahhh, there's the jerk."

I swooped in, landed with a *thud* on the top of his car just as the "get off me" call for help sounded. Of course, then it turned into a scream because something—me—landed on the roof like a ton of bitch bricks. I stretched out across the roof, smashed the driver's side window with my claw and hung my head upside down to see in.

"Hey, asshole," I said with a big smile. "Let's get off the lady, shall we?"

She kept screaming, and he started to do the same. "What *are* you?" the boy cried and I told him—Harpy, here to avenge the girl he was about to rape, yada yada. Like Wonder Woman's usual speech but less inspiring.

He was terrified, which was never easy when dealing with a kid this age. You know, at one time it wouldn't have mattered to me how young he was—he was about to rape this girl. So, goodbye intestines for you, dink. But now…I thought of the maybes. Maybe he hadn't been taught that no means no. Maybe he deserved a second chance. Maybe he wouldn't make the same choice, maybe he'd never been listened to either, maybe he was just a stupid kid and didn't deserve to die. Maybe that girl wouldn't have agreed with me.

Maybe Robbie's boarding house shit was rubbing off on me.

Until he said the magic words: "She knew what we were gonna do!" And I ran a single claw down his neck.

I let the claw run deeper.

Red gushed out, the usual gurgling noises abounded, the girl got out and ran.

I licked the blood off my talon, remembering when it was simple and the taste of human blood had soothed me. Back when I was uglier, not so long ago. But this…didn't feel good. It didn't taste good. It felt backwards. If I hadn't been a Harpy and just been Charity Blake, would I want him dead? If I'd been Hazel Harrington, would I want him dead? If I was the girl in that car, what would I have wanted?

"Fuck." I ripped the door off the car and dragged the kid out, trying not to make him bleed more. His eyes were getting faraway already; not much time.

I ripped through the sky to the nearest hospital, not bothering to conceal myself, and landed on the roof of a parked ambulance, making every paramedic and wandering person screech like tires.

"He needs help," I said calmly.

One of the paramedics stopped his bumbling and pulled a gurney out of the back of the ambulance, tripped on it and fell down, got up like the Scarecrow in *The Wizard of Oz*. Two more ran over to help lower him down. I jumped to the ground to hand him off, not meeting anyone's eyes. And before they said a word to me, I took off, the wind drying my tears.

"*H*errrrrrrr," the feral Harpies hissed as I strolled through the Wood of Suicides, blood squishing underfoot.

I made monster fingers at them. "Yesssss, meeeeeeee."

That isn't who I am, I thought for the first time in a long time. But then again, I wasn't like them and that's why they hissed at me when I went by. I was the second coming of the Queen. I wished I wasn't proud of it.

I had two stops to make. First, Big Bird herself, as always. Nothing happened in the Wood that she didn't know about. Turned out, I didn't have to go far.

"Hazel, what a surprise."

I spread my wings wide in response, impressively wide, white and dirty. "Is it a surprise, though?" I said, screwing my face up. "You know, I beat you once, and I can do it again. Probably a bunch of times, actually."

The Harpies looked on, screeching my name for various reasons. "Is that why you've come today, Hazel? To show your dominance?"

"No. I came to tell you that I've taken Rose Preston and

she's mine now. Just like you took me, I took her. Don't interfere with her again—the kid's had enough abuse." Deep breath. "The Wood is mine, I let you stay here. Don't test me."

The Queen's chin tipped up as she took me in. She was tall, stately, put-together macabre sophistication. I was wiry, scrappy, meant business and had played in the dirt and blood to prove it.

"This is my place since always and will be forever. Get out, Hazel. You are no longer welcome here."

"Pfft, I'm not *welcome* anywhere—doesn't mean I stop hanging out. You should hear what they say about me at that one 7-Eleven." I stepped closer, and the other Harpies inched in, wanting to miss nothing. "I have an agenda. And that's all it takes to run a place like this. You don't scare me," I hissed as menacingly as I could. "You mean nothing to me, and you'll never beat me." I spit at her feet, to the delight of the crowding wretches, and turned my back on her.

Mission one: accomplished.

I didn't relish my second.

The tree that imprisoned Evan Hale was a small one. He didn't require a lot to hold him there—that was Jen's job. But maybe not for long.

I let my wings drag on the ground behind me, at ease, hoping to come across as serene. Like I had something to offer this girl who had been my friend. I couldn't put into words what we were now.

"Jen," I said when I came face to face with her. She squawked at me. Once, I'd seen Jen as a plain "nice" girl, but she'd become a symbol of simple beauty to me quickly. With her own scraggly feathers, the wildness about her as she protected Evan's tree like a clutch of eggs, it hurt to see that simple beauty still peeking through. "You were never really simple, I know that."

"What do you want?" she crowed, bobbing up and down, pacing back and forth, ready to pounce.

"Jen, this place makes you a violent motherfucker, but listen to me—"

"Youuuuu want me to leeeeeave!" she shrieked, backing against Evan's tree, making him scream in pain or fear, who knows. The Evan Formerly Known as GQ Model was no more than conscious sinew and rotting flesh now, hideously distorted into the tree limbs. His eyes were pleading, but couldn't focus. My stomach wrenched as much as my heart.

"I think I can get you *both* out of here."

She stopped pacing and scrambling against the tree. "Impossssible." And for a second I saw that woman I'd known: the way her lips went sideways when she spoke, the naiveté that showed how much she wanted to believe everything would be okay. I longed to see the infuriatingly inappropriate smile she'd always worn when we met. I'd taken that away, like I took everything away, always.

"Probably. Let's try, though."

More of Jen, less of feral Harpy, the more we talked. "You're talking about resurrection," she said, shaking her head, her voice the same I once knew.

"Yeah, I guess. Time travel, too. Fuck it, we've done weirder."

Blood dripped from Evan's eyes. He squeezed them shut.

"What do we do?" Jen said.

"You gotta leave him now if you want to give this a chance." The pain in her eyes brought back memories of that denim-clad, eternally scared woman from Psychiatrist's office. I hadn't wanted to know anyone for so long before her, not again until Rose.

"We have to go," I begged, pulling her arm, feeling scabs on the skin between her ratty feathers. "I need to get back."

To Rose. Wouldn't be that easy. Not that it had been easy at all. "Oh, fucking hell."

Just as the vortex opened for me, a giant black hole in the red sky, guess who fucking shows up? Goddamn Insecty, who'd brought me here to begin with way back when. "I know what you are," I said through a smile. "Queen Bee's alter-ego or some shit, her true monster face. Whatever, get out of my way, I don't care."

"A conduit," Insecty said. "A vessel for the strongest." God, that voice would make anyone believe Satan existed. The sound of knives slowly slicing skin. Chainsaws grinding bone.

"Oh, like a real live Room of Requirement! Where's your idiot buddy?" I asked, pushing Jen behind me. Insecty came with a half-witted backwoods Harpy on the reg, but not this time.

Those giant fly eyes of hers never blinked, and her skin was still almost clear, showing off all her beating, quivering organs inside. Nasty. "Not important. You...you are important."

"Yeah, I know. Move it or lose it."

"The Queen—"

"Can kiss my ass, currently. Unless you're coming along." *Say no, say no.* "Never mind, you're not. I have things to do."

Insecty opened her transparent buggy wings, hovered just over me, daring me. Daring *me.*

I'll say this for the Wood of Suicides: it brings out wild power in me to fill all my voids. I didn't give a shit about who Insecty really was, what she wanted, what she meant by *important.* I didn't care that she'd been ruined like the rest of us, that she'd been a person like me, that she'd been taken advantage of and stolen from a shitty life to become this monster. She'd had her share of choices and chances, and this was the thing I faced now. No guilt, no holds barred.

My tongue hung from my mouth, I let out a throaty noise that grossed out even me. *Hungry. She'll have to do.* My wings roared up and around me, blotting out the crimson sky, sending bloody hay flying. I screamed—God, that fucking scream seared my throat, sex couldn't feel better—and my jaw shifted, moved, making room for the most inhuman thing I could conjure.

A massive, clacking beak, sharp as hell. Total commitment to the fuckery I'd unleash on this bitch.

Insecty's mouth opened, the sound of a thousand cicadas emanating from whatever hell was in her belly.

"God, you're gross," I said, and I fucking pounced. Felt like I'd been waiting all my life for this fight, it had been so long—too long—since I'd been *this*. All that anger, all my trying to be *good*, all the wrongs I deserved to have righted, fuck them all, just *violent*. I landed on her, knocking her to the ground, blood puddles squelching underneath, and I tore into her flimsy chest where her black heart was pounding, sucking. Fuck me, she was terrified. *Delicious.*

A swarm of buzzing bugs flew out of the chest cavity, surrounding my face. I dove right through them, stung on all sides, right into her chest and ripped the beating life out of her, consuming it with my head thrown back in one swallow, black cloud of insects whipping around me in a tornado.

Sitting back on her legs, I ran my claws through the blood spattered on my chest, the heat of it sending shivers through my body. I blinked more and more slowly, staring at the gaping hole in her chest, ragged at the edges. My breathing slowed, satisfaction buzzing through me like the flies, gone now, on to the remains of their host. "Uuuungh," I moaned.

"Charity," Jen's voice came from behind me, penetrating my haze.

I shivered all over, snapped out of the afterglow as best I could.

Hundreds of Harpies circled us, licking their lips, dancing back and forth, clacking their claws, waiting their turn with the fresh corpse. "Let's go," I gasped, still quivering, "before the hunger gets me again."

The vortex welcomed me like an old friend.

The wind burst out of me when I hit the black water. Tepid, overpowering smell of moss with a hint of decay.

Jenny Pond. Across the street from our apartment building.

Finding the mucky bottom amidst the green swirling pond nastiness, I pushed off and broke the surface fast, soaring into the dark air with dripping wings.

"Jen!" I called into the pitch dark. Night—the only pedestrians would be downtown, not here at the duck pond unless they were making out. "Jen!"

I hovered over the trees, water pouring off me. No Jen.

Diving down, I pushed through the dirty duck shit water, couldn't see a damn thing, panic rising. *Where is she?*

Then I got spun around in a whirl of bubbles, fast despite my wings slowing me down. There she was!

She was pissed.

Jen, her Harpy wings and claws disappearing slowly, blonde hair swirling around her like a mermaid-monster, face twisted with rage, bubbles flowing out, fist coming at my face.

Too slow. I grabbed her with my superior demon bird strength and dragged her with me to the surface again, throwing her in one move onto the shore.

"What the actual fuck, Jen?!" I yelled, stalking after her onto the grass on my sodden scales-and-feathers legs.

She tried to push her naked body up, soaked and covered in scabs and scars. Made me stop for just a second. Wiping wet waves of hair out of her face, she screamed at me, "You *killed* her!"

"Who?" Total confusion. "Who, Insecty? Yeah, I guess. So?"

Her face crumpled in desperate sadness, body slouched on the ground in the dark. So vulnerable. "She was one of us, Charity! One of *us!*"

"What, you made friends down there? You and Insecty have blood tea together?"

"Get off your fucking high horse for one minute, Charity!" She *swore*. She meant business. "It doesn't matter if she was my friend or not! She was in pain every minute of her existence, don't you get that? Do you see anything past your own goddamn face?"

"It was me or her, Jen."

"No. It didn't have to be. You didn't even try."

I swallowed hard, pond water making me gag. Hating myself for it, I still fucking defended it, refused to say I might have been wrong. Horrible things, hard to think about things, were my specialty, and if I started second guessing suddenly? No. Gotta stand by my actions, or I'd lose what was left of my mind.

"We're demons, Jen! One less heinous animal won't tip the scales of good and evil! Those bitches would have picked my carcass apart just like they did to hers. We aren't alike. Stop thinking that way."

She shook her head, disappointment all over her face. "You're right. We aren't alike."

She got to her feet and elbowed past me, turning around as an afterthought and taking my arm. She pushed my head to the surface of the murky water, showing me my own foul face, marred with floating splotches of bright green moss. "That's *your* reflection, Charity. Don't blame it on the wings."

My stomach pinched as I pictured Keegan in his nest with the other birds at the pet store. How he'd stayed away from them, but was still a part of them. No harm, no foul. Oh, what he would have thought of me.

Having Jen close like that, both of us at our most naked and base, I contended with knowing she'd seen the worst of me and still got this close.

I'd never felt more broken.

~

We rolled into my apartment like two homeless girls on a bender.

"Holy shit, Charity. *Jen?*" Robbie's head swiveled, obviously afraid Rose would see us like this.

The two of us fell naked onto the couch. Any other time Robbie would have been perfectly happy to see it, but in our current watered-down-blood-and-pond-muck condition, probably not.

"You know Char, this is getting old," he grumbled as he went off toward our room to get clothes for the hundredth time.

"Here's a story for the grandkids, right?" I said, elbowing Jen, throwing a blanket on her. She didn't laugh. Might have been asleep. Keegan chirped though, so I knew it was funny.

Robbie liked me best in sweatpants and a tanktop, so I had about seven hundred pairs of sweats. They were a get-out-of-clothes free card. He tossed me a pair of blue ones, Jen got gray, and a couple tanktops, which we changed into while Rob put on tea. I wanted whiskey and a steak and cheese sub, but tea was better for negotiating with Robbie.

Jen's breath was shallow, hard, shoulders curled over as if she could hide under her wings in human form. Her fingers twitched, and I knew she was subconsciously flexing her claws. "Why did you make me leave?" she asked. "I left him. Evan is alone, he's alone, why did you do this?"

"Work to do."

We stared straight ahead, bodies one with the couch, smelling it up worse than it already was. Robbie brought us tea, and we talked through her shell-shock. Or, more like, I explained myself as she breathed a little more steadily.

"Jen, I can't let you rot away down there. You never belonged there. I think I know how to make things go back to the way they were. Better than the way you were."

"I belong with Evan."

"Yeah, well, I don't 100 percent support that either. But I need you to meet Rose."

Robbie stared daggers at me from the armchair across the room. "You didn't tell me you planned on bringing Jen back."

"You know me. The planner."

Jen turned on me. Again. "You didn't have a *plan* after tearing me away from him? Let me tell you, this girl had better be ready to go right now, because I won't leave him for another minute otherwise. And don't you dare come find me again, Charity Blake. This is it. This is your one chance. After this, I never want to see you again."

That hurt. Because man, did she mean it. I was the trigger for all of her bad choices in one punk rock trash mess.

"I don't want to wake her, and Jen, you could use some rest." Me, the voice of reason. "It can wait a few hours."

Robbie came to my rescue. "Charity's right. Get some sleep, I don't think you can stay awake if you try. Want me to get you a straw for your tea?" He grinned, and Jen, as pure of heart at one time as Robbie was, gave him a crooked smile back. There was no triumph in me when she began poking around the apartment, feeling the softness of the dirty old couch with her fingertips, her shoulders relaxing.

"Okay. Okay, just a few hours. Maybe a shower." Her eyes welled fast with tears; she knew she couldn't hide them. With an explosive laugh, she said, "Who knew the thought of a hot shower would be the thing to crack me?"

"Oh, don't get excited. I'm gonna get up like, fifteen minutes before you and use all the hot water. You know, to ease you into life slowly."

She smiled at me, eyes apologetic. Poor Jen, always apologizing for nothing. I resisted the urge to hug her because one smile didn't change anything.

I had one chance to fix her life and Evan's or I'd lose her, Rose, probably Robbie, and definitely my life to the Queen in one fell swoop.

~

We lay staring at the ceiling in the dark.

"Where's my night light?" I said quietly.

"Rose took it."

"Thief."

Robbie chuckled, which is a stupid sound unless Robbie does it. Then again, a green light-up Pegasus sounds stupid unless it's mine. "She took it to the living room."

"Well, she's not gonna land herself in jail that way, she's gotta work harder."

A bigger laugh. But that didn't mean I was out of the woods, no pun intended.

"Charity, you can't do this."

Saw that coming. "Sure I can. With a little coaching I can land the kid in jail quick."

"I'm not kidding."

I really had to have a good answer. Because the "this" that Robbie was saying I couldn't do, was a lot of things. "I know you're not kidding. But I gotta follow this through."

"Why? Char, whatever your original plan was, whatever good you think will come of this—"

"I could reverse a lot of suicides. Maybe give those poor bastards being tortured in the Wood a chance to right their wrongs without having to eat them eternally."

"Or they could make the same choices all over again!" He lowered his voice quick, because of course, there was a sleeping child in the apartment. "And that's if this half-cooked plan even works. Charity, I thought you wanted to take care of Rose, to help her out of that Facility, get her away from the Queen, give her the chances you didn't take."

"Take? You must mean the chances I never *had.* I do nothing *except* take chances."

"That child is not a chance to right your wrongs, Charity! You can't undo the damage you've done. Don't take *her* chances away by putting her in the exact spot that made Jen what *she* is. That made you what you are."

"And what exactly is that spot, lover?" I spat, pushing up on my elbows, ready to run out of there if that's what it took. Playing house with Robbie was fun, but this bullshit was too much for me. "You tell me all the time how good I really am. Bullshit."

"You know, Charity, you're right." My heart stopped. "I do tell you that all the time, and you never, *never* believe it. I'm

always here for you—and you'd give up on me in a heartbeat
if the roles were reversed. I'm on eggshells all the goddamn
time, waiting for your next freak-out, waiting for you to
show up covered in blood and guts, waiting for the cops—"
He threw the covers off, sat up, a shadow in the darkness. My
heart sank, but I wouldn't cry.

*What the fuck, he was walking out on me and I wouldn't let
him see me* cry over it?

"Robbie, I promise—"

"No." He'd never said it to me like that before. "Don't
make promises. I promised I'd never leave you; breaking that
promise is the best thing I can do now."

"No, no, give me a chance to—"

He took two long strides toward the door, zero hesitation. "You've had plenty of chances. I won't watch you take
Rose's, too."

~

$\mathcal{I}$f Psychiatrist had taught me anything, it was that
victims got blamed first and often last, and it was
usually by themselves.

As usual, I hadn't done *that* good of a job. Robbie had
taken Rose away. Jen had disappeared at the first sign of a
clean day, deciding my shitty plans weren't good enough. I
had no company except woulda, coulda, shoulda thoughts;
one of which bristled me like a goddamn toilet brush.

*If I'd killed Evan as soon as he'd told me he craved sexual
violence, both that woman I'd "rescued," and Jen would be saved.*

*If I'd been a little nastier, if I'd thought about my friend before I
thought about her boyfriend, I could have prevented so much. Too
much.*

Growling, I jumped off the couch, threw the throw pillow

harder than I meant to and stormed off to the kitchen for something to do. Ripping the fridge door open, I went for the bottle of water, knowing it would make me feel best—but I stopped short and went for the shelf of beer cans instead. They'd make me feel pretty goddamn good, too, despite Robbie telling me otherwise. Saint fucking Robbie.

"Gah, fuck," I yelled, throwing the beer can into the sink —not at the destroyed cabinets. Even in this moment of anger, I was trying to minimize damage because of how I'd disappoint Robbie, when we both knew I was pretty much born to disappoint. *Excellent bumper sticker idea.*

Pacing the little kitchen, I went over it and over it. "If I'd killed Evan before he'd done anything wrong, would that make *me* wrong, or just proactive? Jen wouldn't be playing fucking human tetherball with the Harpies in the Wood at least, would she? Moron." God, I was such a fucking moron. The answer was that I could do nothing right. I wasn't built for *right*—I was built for survival. Not love, not goodness, not healthiness, not happiness. I was built to just make it out alive.

"Fuck it," I said, and barely reined in the wings poking through my skin, leaving dime-size drops of blood on the backs of my arms in a neat couple of rows. No, the bird bitch wasn't called for this time. This was a job for Stupid Charity.

~

Time travel isn't just for space geeks. Here I was, unemployed and unenthused and time travel was like, as easy as eating innards for me.

I'd toyed with the biggest what-if ever: If I could go back and murder Painter before he got to me, would I? Would I trade in an eternity of power for *possibly* a less torturous childhood and conscience?

Nope. End of the day, the power was too much. Too much good I could do, too much of what I deserved, too much freedom. Becoming the Harpy was worth the suffering.

I wanted to think Rose would disagree when the Queen gave her the choice—if she did—to become a Harpy or not. But no kid, genius or not, should get that thrown at them at Rose's age. A twelve-year-old, scared, weak, hollowed-out Hazel Harrington wouldn't have survived one minute of the shit I saw on my murder missions. I'd been filled with as much horror as I could take back then. The notion of anything scarier than Carl Painter at Rose's age would have killed me. Made me kill myself.

I huffed at the realization: as a tiny girl, one choice could have banished me to the Wood of Suicides for eternity, too.

Oh, irony.

I walked up to the boarding house door, rang the bell. Waited on the rickety wooden steps, listening to them creak under my feet.

"Hi. Can I help you?" Tall dude, black rings below his eyes like Lurch, haircut like Fester's, telltale pinprick scars all over his arm showing as he leaned against the door. A volunteer from the big boy boarding house across the street, then.

"Yeah, hey, um, is Robbie here?" They all knew who he was. He was like Cher, Prince, Mother Teresa.

"Sure," he said. "Do you have any—"

"No drugs on me, no blades, no guns, no chewing gum or money. *You* got any money?" I rattled off, pushing him aside and walking right on in.

"Uh…"

"Charity?"

"Every time, yes."

Robbie's voice spun me around. Despite coming here in part to see him, *actually* seeing him stopped me short. The way he was so in his element here, flanked by adoring, cast-off kids who listened when he told them how good they were, so casually at ease with them right down to the relaxation of his shoulders. He wasn't that relaxed with me anymore. He had been once—before we moved in together. Before I tried to *not* be the Harpy and ended up with a series of bad trip seizure transformations and lied to him and closed myself off. Before he'd lost faith in me. Before Jen and Evan had damned themselves to the Wood. Before Rose.

One little girl would seal the fate of my relationship with Robbie. But this was the right thing to do—if you were me. If "right" meant something far different than what the world would call it.

"Hey, Rob," I said in the same tone I used with Keegan. The bird wouldn't leave me, but Robbie sure would. "Can we talk without the juvie entourage?"

He huffed, pursed his lips, but mumbled to them and they left the room. Huffy Robbie is a person I awoke, not his natural state. "Sit down," he said, pulling out a thrift store wooden chair at a mismatched café table. It made me think of my apartment before Robbie's, how nothing belonged to me first. For me, those lackluster things felt used and discarded. But for the kids here, it felt like home. Once-loved things brought back to life.

"I'm sorry."

"I know."

Awkward silence. "You knew I was trouble, but you couldn't have seen all this coming. It's not fair to you, and I apologize that I've put you through it."

He leaned back, eyes narrowed. "You know, Char, when you say stuff like that it makes me think you're going somewhere."

I put both elbows on the table, put my hand over my

mouth as I thought, wishing I could keep the words that needed to come out in, my eyes blurry as Rob waited for me to respond. Pulling my hand away, I blurted, "I am. I have to."

He snickered—another snarky habit he'd picked up from me. It only solidified that he was one million percent better off without me. "I should have known you'd bolt the second I had expectations of you."

"*Expectations*? This isn't my yearly performance review, this is my life, our life. When you asked me to move in with you there wasn't a contract with *expectations*. There was a lot of bullshit about how you loved me for me."

"Yes, I had expectations!" Shouting—another thing he picked up from me, probably. "You should have them, too! Of yourself, and of me! What the hell good is being together if we don't want more for each other? Goddammit, do you really want me to be okay with you destroying yourself?" Hands through the hair. My heart melted. "I love you, and that means I will never stop wanting more for you, I will never stop wanting you to be *really* happy, and I'll never stop pushing you to be better because you deserve me in your corner, Charity. You deserve me telling you the shit you don't want to hear."

Exasperated, out of breath, finger probably sore from jabbing it onto the tabletop to emphasize all the points that made me cringe, he fell back in his chair again. He ran his hands through his hair one more time, left them there like it would help hold his brain together.

Fuck, he always said the right things, though. And it was for that reason I had to do what I had to do.

I got up, went around the table and wrapped my arms around him, kissing the top of his head between his hands, letting my lips stay there, breathing in the green apple shampoo. He never got the same shampoo twice; I'd always thought that was funny. I knelt at his side, as close as I dared to get, wanting to be closer.

"Robbie, I...I couldn't love anyone in the world more than I love you." I fucking despised how hard it was to say those words, even though I meant them from the best hollows of my soul. "No one is worth more to me than you."

"That's what I'm afraid of," he said, voice cracking. He took my hand, pleaded with his eyes. "I'm afraid you'll never love yourself." Then, in a whisper, "I'm afraid that you'll always be the Harpy, no matter how much we repair your damage. And if you can't love anyone as much as you love me...that isn't the kind of person who should have the power of life and death at their fingertips, Charity. Not the kind of person who should make the judgment calls you do."

"What's that supposed to mean?" I growled.

"God. Don't make me say it."

"No, please do. Say exactly what you think."

"Fine. A person filled with as much hate as you carry shouldn't have the right to decide anyone's future, no matter who they are." He gnashed his teeth, shook his head. He'd lost hope. "You don't gut rapists out of some sense of justice, to be a *hero*," he said, incredulous that he had to explain it. "Don't you think you're the Harpy just to satisfy your hatred?"

It was too easy to drop his hands. To stand up over him, tip my chin up, crack my neck, put my hands on my hips. To feel like that fishnets-and-corset-wearing overgrown delinquent I'd been before I loved him. "Thank you," I said, voice flat, cold, "for thinking I'm not doing enough by loving you. I have to love the whole fucking world before I start eviscerating predators, I guess. I'm not the poster girl for self-love but I think enough of myself to go with my gut, to know when I can do more. *Now* is the time I can do more." Deep breath. "Where's Rose?"

Tears clung to his eyelashes, but he didn't let them fall. "I'm not going to let you near her," he said, a sad resolve making his voice hard.

"You can't stop me," I said, swallowing back my self-loathing, the thought that I'd built this ultimate wall between us in one sentence. No back-pedaling now. "You want what's good; I want what's right. They aren't the same."

Rose appeared, ghostlike, in the doorway, the way I used to when I was her age and my mother would be fighting with some rando druggie dude. The blank fear coupled with an expected disgust left Rose's face pale.

"Hi," she said to me, voice as small as she was.

"Hey," I said gently. "How are ya, kid?"

Her dark intelligence returned once the fright spell was broken. "I'm confused, and I don't like being confused," she said.

I turned on Robbie. "Is that a kid who knows what she wants, or what?" Rhetorical and he knew it.

"Charity, leave," Robbie said. That voice sealed the tomb of our relationship for sure. And now I had nothing to lose except the remnants of my own conscience.

"You're not the boss of me," I said. "Rose, there's something you should know about—"

"Charity, no!" Robbie yelped.

"Shut up!" I yelled back, and pushed him out of my way, knocking him back into the chair he should never have gotten out of. Rose glanced at him with concern. "He's fine," I said.

"Tell me," she said hurriedly.

"There's a boy here—"

"Char—"

I delivered a backward kick to Robbie's chair, knocking it off balance, taking Robbie and the table down with it. He slammed against the wall, and a shelf of glasses crashed to the floor, smashing everywhere. Robbie yelled at the kids pounding down the stairs in the next room and across the floor that everything was fine, to go back to what they were doing. While he tried to gather himself, I told Rose what I knew. What she had the right to know.

"There's a boy here named Turner. He's Cody Reese's son."

"What?" she said, inching forward.

"You call the shots with this information. You've probably heard 'the apple doesn't fall far from the tree.' I'm giving you a choice—a *chance*." I glared at Robbie on that word, throwing it back in his face. He'd frozen on the floor, staring at me like I was the thing under the bed. The more I spoke to Rose, the easier it was to distance myself from him. Broken glass crunching under my sneakers—a fashion statement I planned on trading in quickly—I went right to the kid and took her by the shoulders, intent on her totally understanding how serious I was, how real this could be. "I can finish him before he does the same thing his father did, if he hasn't already. We can stop this from happening before it starts. It's your call. What do you want?"

Her mouth worked up and down, eyes wide, her body trembling violently. I gripped her harder to help her stop, to show her the world was solid and she was safe—more than safe. She was *protected.*

"Wh—how does he have a… Cody was fifteen when my father killed him."

Oh, right. I smoothed her braided hair. "I'm sorry you've been lied to so much, kid. Cody's dead now. But not before he lived a life." Words like poison.

Rose stopped breathing, blinking. In the long silent exchange between us, we were sisters in every way that counted. We both thought the same things:

Cody Reese hadn't deserved a life.

If only he were here to see his own son die.

The kid shocked the hell out of me when she spoke, though. "I'll take care of him myself," she said.

"No, no, don't go down that path, Red," I blurted. "That's not why I told you. I'm a monster already, doing this for you even if he's *innocent,* it won't...I'll be fine. But you...you'll destroy yourself."

Amid a sea of broken glass and upended furniture, Robbie came to my side—classic de-escalating—and put his hand on my shoulder. I wasn't having it. Robbie's eyes darted to the other room where kids were trying poorly not to get caught spying. It dawned on me that he was looking for Turner. To get him out of harm's way.

"He hasn't done anything, Charity."

"Yet. But you were willing to let her unwittingly share a crappy common room with him for what? To see if he would? Give him a *chance?* Oh, you love talking about chances. How about choice? You lied to her. That's not a chance, not for her. It's a chance for *him* to fill Daddy's shoes."

"You knew," Rose said, her stare as hard as bullets at Robbie.

Heavy sigh. That heavy sigh that just...was so befitting of a good martyr. I rolled my eyes.

God, who was I now? That I could turn on him like this?

"I couldn't think of any reason to tell you, Rose. It would only dredge up memories and feelings you aren't ready to deal with."

Tears welled, her fists clenched. "I wasn't *ready* when I was five."

"That wasn't him, Rose," Robbie said quietly, ever the negotiator.

"It could be him. The next kid walking by. There's an elementary school a two minute walk away!" Her chest heaved with exertion as realizations, possibilities, flooded her head. "What does he see when he looks at me? Now I see…why my stomach flutters when our eyes meet, and why his voice gives me goosebumps. His hair…"

My stomach lurched at her misguided understanding. Fuck, if she'd been developing a crush on this kid and had found out after kissing him or something? Yuck. What a first kiss memory that would be. Even now, she didn't know the difference between her brain *feeling* his frigging gene pool and getting tingly over a cute boy. Already the kid couldn't distinguish between butterflies and brain tumors.

"A part of me recognizes a part of him. My *brain* knows his," she said to Robbie, tapping her temple hard. "You put me in the same room as him when you didn't have to." Her face tightened, pinched, froze over anything childlike about her. "You made an *experiment* of me."

Well, shit. He'd managed to equate himself with bad memories of the Facility. Fear clutched my stomach, anticipating the next moments.

Don't hurt him, Rose.

Who would I protect? Who could I save?

Robbie wilted. He glanced at me; he knew what he'd lost. Or more accurately, what I'd lost. Tension and hopelessness sifted through the air like dust from the crappy old furniture.

There was a millisecond of relief when Rose spun and took off through the house, me and Robbie close behind, yelling her name over the pounding footsteps—because whatever she was planning to do, she hadn't planned enough.

We followed her, racing up the stairs, a few of the more curious kids tagging along on our heels. We had no time to shoo them away as Rose burst through a closed door and slammed it shut behind her.

"What is this room?" I called to Robbie over my shoulder as we made it to the top of the stairs.

"Turner's."

I grabbed the doorknob and ripped my hand back—it was boiling hot. White blisters popped up all over my hand, my flesh sizzled, the shock forcing my claws through my fingertips, in and out again, searing pain making my stomach turn.

I kicked the door in, toes tingling with the aggression of it, the Harpy wriggling in me, my only friend, *aching* for what could come next.

Turner writhed on the floor, and I watched, actually *saw* his fingers getting longer as she dislocated the joints by just looking at them. "Rose," I said softly. "Think about this before you do something you'll regret."

She stopped and whipped her head around at me. Turner went limp, clutching his hand with the other. *Pimples. Skinny legs, sandy hair a little like Rose's, big brown puppy-dog eyes. Just a little boy, really.* Rose said, "You offered this to me, Charity."

"I offered to do it *for* you. You don't want this on your hands, kid. Leave the killing to me." But the thought of killing this *child* made my head swim. He wasn't his father— but he could be. Right or wrong, the claws stayed out anyway; my toes had become talons, bursting through the tops of my sneakers, ripping them to shreds.

Hungry.

The lust for fresh meat had me licking my lips, mentally gnashing my teeth and vibrating out of control with want. That part of me could rationalize just about anything if I didn't convince it otherwise. Charity Blake, voice of reason.

Turner, whimpering, got to his feet. Rose took in his height, his face, pausing when he frowned, studying how it reached his eyebrows and the space between. The way she blinked, how her breathing stilled… That face, that body, the similarities only she could see with his father, they cried out just the way she must have under the trees. Rose trembled harder, harder, harder still.

Part of me regretted telling her about Turner at all, knew Robbie was right.

But that part got buried quickly as he stepped toward her, snarling, hair falling in his face. I didn't know what he was gonna do, but I refused to find out. I felt no pulsating heat that gave me the big KILL IT vibes, but it was enough that Rose backed up, her trembling anger replaced with a trembling lip.

Who would hurt who more—Rose or Turner?

Faster than I knew my brain could move, I worked through it: how much I wanted Rose to take her power back from the Reese men, how apocalyptic it would be for her to hurt him, that she'd never come back from it.

But the thought of her as a little girl…

The horrid image replaced by Maggie Painter.

What I'd done to her. Who I was.

Who I couldn't let Rose become. I had no control then, but I had control *now*.

He reached for her, a glint of malice as he backed Red into the corner, her stomach still burning through her shirt in a vengeful blaze that she was too paralyzed to use. But shit, I wanted her to, and that told me enough.

If she did, she'd be seconds from going Harpy, right where the Queen wants her.

The need to *save her* from Turner was as strong as the need to save her from herself and from a fate like my own. Not when I had the opportunity to end her pain because my life was already ruined. Red was the only part left to save.

A volcano blast of feathers sprayed everywhere as wings exploded from my arms, propelling me across the room. I grabbed Turner as he yelled obscenities. Pulling his back tight against my chest, much stronger than I would ever be without my wings, I said, "Sorry kid, but you never stood a chance."

With one ragged claw, I dug into his throat, a spray of blood dousing the floor in front of him.

Before I could drag my hook across, it suddenly blazed red like a branding iron as a scorching heat ate at my hand, sped across my wrist until the nerves were useless, twitching as my claw jerked helplessly in his flesh.

Rose ran forward and grabbed my arm.

My body quaked with the heat as if my skin could wriggle away from it.

Tears lit up her baby blue eyes. "If someone could have stopped Cody before he went bad, wouldn't you want them to?" she said. My mouth bobbed open and shut, unable to form a yes or a no.

And with all her might, from her hips and her back, she yanked my arm hard, slicing Turner's throat open.

~

Screeches, unintelligible whimpers all around, white-noise terror. I was faintly aware of the wetness of my lips, blood or snot or tears, a split-second fantasy of it dousing the flames racing through my arm, torching it from the inside out. Paralyzed, I still clutched the boy, vacantly noted the blood sizzling against my boiling arm.

Everything stopped.

As fast as I could move but still in slow motion, I pressed my hellfire-glowing talon to the chasm left in his throat. He tried to scream, I think. I don't think he could really have tried to do anything, eyes rolled back in his head, limp but for the occasional spasm. His skin around the wound bubbled, popped sickly.

But the wound was closing.

I moved on to the next part of the gash. *Come on, come on, kid.*

Rose, dreamlike, lightly touched one of my wingtips, oblivious to the mayhem she'd caused, that she stood in the middle of Turner's blood pool. And she looked into my head.

My brain screamed, shook, burned like my hand did, world blackened, brain blackened. She dug around like a mole in there. I clutched my head with bloody claws, praying for it to stop, heard my own voice as a child, *Please God, keep Carl out of my room.*

I fell to the floor, one leg splayed across Turner's, hitting my head on a nightstand. Pictures of my "childhood" zipping through my mind so fast I had no time to linger on their horrors, only *feel* them, rapid-fire.

She's reading me like a book.

Then suddenly, she wasn't.

Paramedics busted in, Robbie running over to them with explanations as they unfolded the gurney with lightning speed. Boarding house kids screamed, crying. Rose watched, detached and expressionless. I knew how she felt: wondering what will become of you next. I bet this felt a lot like that first time the door locked at the Facility.

The sirens—the police ones—came next.

"Gotta get out of here," I said, sounding drugged even to my own ears. I tried to roll over; my foot slipped out from under me, knocking me back to the ground. The room spun, paramedics pushing each other to reach for me like on a dare, as they reached for Turner, touching me and pulling away, yelling *what the hell* is *she*. Then Turner was gone and I had to *go go go* before more came to get me. To get Rose.

No, she's fine, it was my claw, my bad record. Anyone would think she was trying to help him by grabbing my arm.

No focus was needed to see the void as it stirred in the

air, sucking up the screams of the approaching children in its vacuum. Black on black on black layers that went as deep as Hell itself, swirling with the cosmos in one hole in the atmosphere. I ambled toward it, half on my knees in this messed-up crouch, and threw myself into it, hearing nothing but Robbie calling for me through its thick silence.

CHARITY

THE WOOD, NO YEAR

I'd become way too accustomed to tumbling in a dirty heap into a mess of blood-coated hay and red dirt. Harpies screeched all around me, taking to the air in a horrifying flock, circling. I remembered in my daze a meme that said *a large group of people is called a Fuck No.*

Stumbling, I got to my feet and wiped my face with a bloody hand. I started walking the best I could, tripping every other step, aware of my own groaning.

"Wait for me."

"What the actual fuck?" I turned—too fast, falling on one knee—to see goddamn Rose. I should have known.

She trotted to catch up with me. "I couldn't stay there," she said. "They saw me hurting him before… I'd be sent back to the Facility."

"But they'd forget that part! You grabbed my arm, it looked like you were trying to help him! Shit, Rose!"

"I won't lie and say I didn't help you."

My heart collapsed. I'd just about killed a kid to help her and she was so fucking determined to doom herself that it didn't matter. "You know, I thought you had a better sense of self-preservation than that."

She stuck her chin up. "The apple doesn't fall far from the tree."

The Harpies circled her closely, the freshest meat they'd seen in a while. Obviously they'd missed her magic tricks in the last visit or they would've steered clear.

"Queen. Now. She knows everything that goes on down here and a lot that goes on up there. The rest of this place… has no direction. It's like wandering a nightmare."

Jesus Christ, the kid was twelve or some shit, and I absolutely loved talking to her. To be able to talk about this place, this terrible home of mine, was a luxury I wasn't afforded, and was absolutely judged for. She saw what I just did, what I could become, and still, she was with me.

Yeah asshole. In it *with you now.*

Detestably, I thought how Robbie would have stopped me. He was too good for me, and in the end, he knew it.

"You're the only one who always tells me the truth," Rose said.

"I never tell the whole truth," I said, unexpected tightness in my throat.

"You don't treat me like I'm about to break. I've said it before, but it bears repeating."

My throat constricted. "You sound so much older than me."

She took my hand and the tightness went away. "Time doesn't matter when you're like us."

It took everything in my memory and body and bones and heart to not burst into tears like I never had before. Finally, *finally,* someone got it, and she was someone who'd been so much better than me—but I'd ruined her. In trying to help her, I ruined her.

"You're okay," she said, leaning forward as we walked to look into my face.

"Probably," I said, laughing. "Christ, I shouldn't laugh in the Wood..." *of Suicides. Shit. The Wood of Suicides.*

Cody Reese is here.

"I know why you like this place," Rose said.

"I like it for lots of reasons," I choked out, panic setting in as the rush of *she can look into my head, she'll know, I have to get her out of this place right the fuck now.*

"I could learn to like it."

I stopped in my tracks, alarming her a bit. "Don't you dare like the Wood of Suicides, kid. Don't even fucking try it."

"You wanted me to work with you here. I saw it in your head. You told Robbie."

Get a hold of yourself, jackass. "I'd been thinking of these people," I said, waving my arm around, "and how you could free them from the trees and I could bring them back to their lives to make different choices. Maybe put this place out of business altogether, right? But if anyone's gonna get a second chance down here—shouldn't it be the Harpies?" *Why did I say that out loud?*

Her sweet face was more delicate, younger down here with the red haze behind her, a mist of blood raining on this fresh, pink flower.

Every one of these Harpies had been that innocent. Once.

The man who undid her is here somewhere.

The nest glittered and shined as always, brilliant, gleaming black against the crimson sky, with those bright blue eyes winking at visitors.

"Let me go first," I said.

I climbed the nest rather than flew to the top. There was something altogether human about having to pull oneself up the rungs of a ladder, knowing nothing good lay at the top of it.

"Hello, Hazel."

"Hey, Queen Bee, what's happenin'?" I plunked down beside her. "Never mind, I'll tell you. I've got the girl with me. You know it, of course. She's not yours. That's all there is to it."

The Queen's lovely red lips parted in a satisfying moment of surprise. "Really? You'd choose to disrupt time, take on a child, rather than return her to her home and live your own life however you choose?"

"We both know I don't have much of a life and less of a choice. And the kid hasn't got a real home. Her mother just left her at that Facility. She abandoned her. I won't do that."

The surprise dissipated then, and the red lips curved into a smile that made me want to punch her pretty face. "Yes, of course," she said. "Why don't you bring Rose into the nest with us to discuss this?"

Bitch, you think I'm going back down there, then all the way back up again? But I didn't want Rose alone on the ground any longer than she had to be, whether she could incinerate the place or not. So I stood up tall, flung my arms out with a grace befitting a pole dancer, let out a predatory cry, and spread my wings triumphantly. Go big or go home. With a hawkish scream, I swooped down to gather up Rose in a single move, and just as quickly brought her to the Queen. The eye of the storm.

"Hello," Rose said reverently.

"Hello, sweet girl," the Queen said. "I'm both sorry and thrilled to see you here." The Queen stood in a grand gesture and opened her arms wide as I had done, just to show me up. Rose went straight to her to be wrapped in a dark embrace. I only shook my head when the Queen met my eyes. *Well played.* Truth be told, I was actually pretty jealous that Rose liked her at all. "Our friend here," she said, batting her eyelashes, "thinks we should no longer speak to each other. What do you think?"

"That's not fair!" I shouted, too quickly. Like I was admitting guilt. "Of course she wants to be friends with you, you're a goddamn magic queen!"

"Why don't you tell her the real truth, *Charity?*" the Queen spat. Jesus, I lived a lie.

"The truth is I would take this place down in a heartbeat if I thought it were possible. I sure as hell don't want Red here, now, anytime, ever. This place…it's a sickness. A disease. An addiction." I swallowed hard. "I *hate* you," I said with as much venom as I could muster.

The Queen threw her head back and laughed more heartily than I'd known she could. "Of course you do, darling!" she said when she recovered herself. "Do you think anyone can *love* me?" Her condescending tone slipped away for a split second when she said deeply, darkly, "Do you think anyone ever has?" Right back to the Queen of Mean, though. "Love doesn't translate here. The Wood is unlike anywhere in Heaven, Earth, unlike any other Circle of Hell. And yet, here. You. Are. Time and again."

I suddenly wanted to go back in time for every one of the Harpies before they ever met the Queen, before they'd been violated. But I shoved the errant thoughts down to focus on the one job that needed to be done like, yesterday: get Rose out before she learned too much.

"Come on, Rose," I said, turning my back on the Queen. "This was a pitstop, quickest and, uh…safest…and I didn't expect you to come along. We aren't staying for dinner."

But the scary side of Rose was edging out. "Tell me what she means by 'the real truth,' Charity. Or Hazel."

"I was born Hazel Harrington. The fewer who know that, the better. I don't want to be found ever again."

She nodded, but she wouldn't take her eyes off me.

The Queen laughed. "The two of you have created such *truths*, do either of you know any reality anymore?"

"Well, we won't figure it out here, freak. So, bye." I took Rose's hand, pulling her toward the edge of the nest, but she remained firmly planted.

Oh no.

"What are you talking about?" Rose asked the Queen.

"Red, no," I pleaded.

"Don't call me that."

"She loves to remind us of the past. It makes savages of us," I said, nodding in the Queen's direction. "The kid is no monster and you will not make one of her."

"Are you absolutely certain of that? Do you know what she's done?"

I gulped. "I don't need to. I know Rose."

"He deserved to die," Rose said, and I whimpered. How could I ever have thought she should have a choice in the matter? "I haven't done anything wrong."

"Haven't you? If you don't remember, Rose, do what you do best—take your mind apart and find it. I'm not talking about what you did to Turner Reese."

"Rose, don't listen to her."

"Right! Listen to *Charity Blake*, who you believe has told you the whole truth! Why don't you both lay out your lies on three? One...two..."

Rose's head swiveled back and forth between the Queen and me, her chest heaving in her anxiety.

"Rose, let's go back home—"

"Home?!" Rose cried. "What home? The Facility? Your place, where we're murderers?"

"Turner won't die, he just won't forget..."

The Queen delighted in this little exchange. "Oh, do tell me more about Turner, would you?" She stood gracefully and glided to the child like a dripping tar fairy godmother. "I can tell you things that would change your entire vision of the future."

"Leave her alone!" I shouted, but the Queen had her hold on the kid and I'd be curious too, if I were her.

Rose's arms wound around the Queen's in an elegant embrace, stray strands of hair blowing in the hot breeze. "It's okay, Charity," she said, muffled, but like a scream to me. My stomach plummeted. "No more secrets."

Before I could say another word, the Queen gently turned Rose's chin up to face her, and told her the one thing I'd have done anything to keep from her. "The man who raped you has killed himself in an overdose, my dear," she crooned. "Which means he's out there." She swept a long, lean arm out, indicating the hellscape below. "You're aware of what we do here, yes?"

"Ro…" I tried to say, but my throat was dry with the Hell-hot air and my peaking fear, and I knew I'd lost the only playing card I had.

"Say it," Rose said, entranced.

And the Queen leaned in close, that intimacy every one of us craved and couldn't get quite like the Queen gave it. My eyes lost focus as I imagined all the horrible, wonderful things Rose was hearing from this beautiful beast.

Stay in the Wood and you'll never be imprisoned again.

No hiding, lying, and calling it protection.

I will protect you by standing beside you. I will help you bloom rather than cut you off at the root.

I'll let you be a child. I'll take care of you, heart and mind.

And I will never make you lesser.

The things that make you strange in the world above will make you exceptional in this one.

You'll become a Harpy unlike any other. I'll see to it.

You'll have nothing but truth.

And you'll make Cody Reese pay for eternity for how he hurt you.

I couldn't breathe as I waited for the Queen's speech to be over.

When Rose's body relaxed, she was ready to tell me that she wanted to be a Harpy. She was tired of being simultaneously caged and abandoned, powerful and imprisoned.

But that wasn't what she said.

"You knew my rapist killed himself."

Dammit.

"Yes."

"I won't ask why you didn't tell me. I'm familiar. You were *protecting* me."

"And everyone else!" What the hell, the bitch was out of the bag now. "You're dangerous, and you know it. There's an amazing kid in there, and you've been treated like…like…"

"Like nothing. Like what I am is too much."

My throat closed up to see a deadness emerge from a place deep behind her eyes for the first time. I wanted to throw my arms around her, squeeze her and tell her she wasn't *too* anything, that she was just right, just perfect, but I couldn't breathe through the despair.

Two sentences. She felt it her whole life and it was so untrue.

"I don't see you that way," I finally choked out. "I know what *she* tells you," I said, jabbing a finger in the Queen's direction, "and what's worse is, I know she can make it happen. That heat thing, the taking stuff apart thing, she'll make you feel like you're perfect the way you are. But she'll give you what you *want*, too, and it will be… It won't be the same, kid. Not the same as what you really want. It won't change things with your mom, it won't fix what the Facility did, it won't change what happened to you. It will *feel* good, it will feel *right*, like everything you ever wanted, but it's just another lie, and more hiding. You don't want to end up like one of those poor women down there, evil, feeding on scraps, wronged again."

"I could feed on Cody Reese."

"Yup, and how long will that hold you over? You want to do that and nothing but that until the end of time? You'll never grow up, super fucked-up Peter Pan deal?"

"I've only ever been a *little girl*," she snapped, and her skin reddened—her arms, her bare legs, her neck. Heating up like a tea kettle.

"Not yet you haven't, kid. You haven't had *fun*. Just been ridiculous, not reading too much into everything. You've never lived with just feeling, not thinking. I know, because I never did either. Eternity is a long-ass time. Leave this behind. Come with me. I'll be your family, I *want* that with you. I'll take care of you. We'll both move on and get *over* it, just change. We can change."

"Easy for you to say," the Queen stepped in. "You've had time to avenge yourself. This child hasn't had the chances you have. She's been pinned down, unable to evolve, and you speak of her moving forward? She hasn't lived yet." Her eyes glittered as she said, "You've got a vivid imagination, Hazel, I've seen it in your kills. This little one would be a goddess with her gifts enhanced and expanded. One I would be proud to serve one day."

"Bullshit. You'll give up on her just like you did me. Nothing changes here. Gets worse, but doesn't really change."

"You," the Queen spat. "You can offer her change? You can't even go home." Her sly smile told me exactly how much she knew about my personal life these days. "Are you certain your life is going so well that you'd like to bring a child into it?"

What could I say to that? I was a terrible influence. I'd be using Rose to try to turn my own life around. I already had been.

"You'd leave me because you don't know what else to do with me," Rose said, her voice cracking.

"Rose, no, I *want* you to come with me—"

"But. You want me to go with you, *but.*" The poor kid's face turned a sunburn-fuchsia in her anger, then the rest of her body followed; the skin actually bubbled on her thighs from the bottoms of her track shorts, then raced down her legs in miniscule blisters. Her hands shook as they burst out in the little bastard blisters, too. *Poor baby,* was all I could think, watching her fight with her deep sadness and fury, the battle coming out of her very pores. And yet, I was rooted in place with terror.

Her power was bigger than she was.

The hot pink showing through her shirt grew brighter and brighter, until the fabric began to smoke. A hole blossomed, peeling back the fabric like the tip of a cigarette. Her belly underneath glowed so brightly with heat that it illuminated her insides. The palpitating outline of every organ shined through, moving faster and faster as she panicked, became more and more angry, more and more sad. She looked down at her belly, tears streaming, and shouted, "My own mother hated who I was!" And on that word, that one all-powerful word, "mother," a ray of heat emanated from her stomach, straight through her tender skin. It set the closest black branches to smoking, the blue eyeballs tearing up like I didn't know they could do anymore until they exploded into ash. The curls of hair that had popped out of her braid had become licks of flame framing her sweet face, falling over her big blue eyes. Her lashes set alight.

Holy shit, she's burning to cinders!

"Rose! *Red!* You have to calm down! You'll kill yourself!"

Then she'd be here forever, both suicide tree and Harpy. A true freak.

The highest tree branches shook and bowed as Harpies flew up to roost and watch, drawn to all things violent and unhealthy. Their squawking and hissing, calling out my name, had Rose quivering, the heat waving around her in the bloody sky. Fist-sized bursts of fire popped in the air like popcorn all around her, igniting out of nothing.

"Charity?" she whimpered in fear and despair.

Resisting the instinct to run like hell from the flames, I stayed, screamed inside but put my hands on her glowing shoulders, my fingers smoking, my stomach burning so close to her, and I demanded her attention with my voice. "You. Must. Breathe. Breathe, kiddo. And trust me. Please trust me."

The war in her mind came across in a succession of blinks and tears that evaporated as soon as they touched her cheeks. Until she stared deeply back, concentrating, breathing out long, longer, longer through the little O of her lips, turning from soft pink to a blistering crimson. I nodded, murmuring to her how proud I was that she was doing it, taking control of something so powerful. I shuddered, sweat pouring into my eyes, unable to stop my face from screwing up in pain though I didn't want to scare her. I fell back to the nest floor, blowing ridiculously on my hands, talons aflame like candles, slapping them against the ground, my body, anything to put the fires out.

"Charity!" Rose fell at my side, pulling off the remains of her tattered shirt to wrap around my hands, sitting there in just the ugly little Facility-issued sports bra.

But the babyish skin of her belly where that inferno had come from was unmarred, no different than before. Rose was a child, but she wasn't as soft as I thought.

"I'm okay, Red," I muttered. So not true. "Are you okay?"

Her face crumpled. Her eyelashes were normal, the flaming tendrils of hair restored to blonde, her skin normal but for faint white spots here and there where blisters faded as quickly as they'd come. She slumped against me, sobbing, mumbling apologies while I rocked her back and forth, shushing her softly. The kid was healing before my eyes.

The Queen was enraptured, a smile on her face for the whole show.

"You whore," I mouthed to her. She waggled her slashes of eyebrows at me.

"How exhausting this must be for you, dear girl," the Queen said to Rose as she sniffled against me.

Fucking hell, this day would never end.

Rose sighed, lifted her face from my shoulder. I wished she didn't have to face reality, this insane reality, again after what she'd just been through. The bird bitch supreme was right—exhaustion seeped out of her like tears.

"I don't know what to do now," Rose let out in a breath, defeated.

"Let us decide for you," the Queen said in a surprisingly human way, like someone with actual concern. That was her trick—she really did care in her warped way. "Let us handle this, the way your mother should have done."

The kid curled up against me, nearly asleep, while I had the most civilized conversation possible with this bitch I'd murdered once and would kill again.

"You care about her," the Queen said.

I patted Red's hair as her body rose and fell with snores. "Yeah."

"Of course you do. She's your chance to live again. Charity, I don't want to fight with you."

She used my actual name. "Goddamn right you don't."

"We both want her for our own reasons."

"No. No we don't. I want the best for her. You want her for an ulterior motive that ain't even all that ulterior."

"I run a *world* here, Charity! I have more in mind than just one child's well-being, but I certainly do have her well-being in mind. We just have very different ideas of what will nurture her best."

"I won't let her life be destroyed anymore. You want to take it from her completely."

"And you want to steal her from her own time, let those wounds and mysteries lie open! Do you believe she won't become beastly that way as well? She'll never stop remembering new, worse things about her childhood. Now throw in a lack of continuity? Her brain will work so hard, she'll burn herself to death if more tumors don't take her down first."

My mouth fell open, the taste of the stale death air filling it. "Did you give her the tumor?" I gasped.

"What? No. No, that was all in her own mind. I'm not actually responsible for everything horrible, contrary to your beliefs."

Jesus, was that guilt I felt? "I know you aren't. I didn't always hate you."

Self-deprecating laugh. "I did tell her Cody Reese's name, though. That was me."

She did a thing I'd never seen her do before—tucked her cheek against her shoulder, eyes closed, both like a content mother bird and a genuinely humble royal. I *believed* it. I believed in her for that blink of a moment, and I grabbed onto it, let myself trust her. For Rose's sake.

"Charity," she said, and I softened even more, "the girl has power that would serve a Harpy immeasurably. *Unprecedented* is the word she hears a lot." The mix of regret and strength and loss showing on her face cut me. "But she's a child."

"A child," I repeated.

She nodded rhythmically, our hearts matching through that soft quiet in a Hell world.

We'd all been children. Once.

She broke the trance between us to gaze out over the Harpies. Some beautiful, like Loretta, the ruined flapper. Others that could never be mistaken for human again. Embodiments of a guilt they didn't deserve, given to them by fiends who dismembered their souls as humans. As people. As women. As girls.

As children.

"They would despise me, Charity," the Queen said, dreamlike, lost in her own guilt. "I can't take the child's life, whatever that life will become, good or bad, and use it. I would bring her to a point of no return, and while her singular, stunning ability would make her a wonder to behold…" She trailed off, and a tear splashed into the closest blue eyeball embedded in the nest. Her tears were falling freely, leaving a sheen on her face that seemed to peel away layers of emotion she'd forgotten. "As a mother, I cannot take her life away from her. She has to live it. The tiny beauties…"

And she gave me a gift then, as she'd once made Carl Painter appear in a tawdry film in the thick red air, a real-time vision she could conjure and project. She gave me a larger-than-life image of something so simple and pure I thought my heart would explode.

A buttercup.

I'd loved them as a child. Finding the stray ones here and there in the sidewalk cracks in Boston, stumbling upon a surprise patch of them under a shady tree that had outgrown even the city. I'd entirely buried the memories of that feeling.

"The tiny beauties," I repeated, my own tears salty on my lips.

A series of other images. "The enormous ones." The

ocean, Rose running into it in a buttercup-yellow sundress, laughing as strongly as the sun shone.

"The sorrows." An old woman in a hospital bed, Rose at her side, tears pouring.

"The victories." Rose smiling up at the same old woman as she handed her a radio.

"The agonies." Rose on the floor, skirt around her thighs, a sharp-eyed boy reaching for her.

"The falling apart." Rose huddled under the bed covers, sobbing.

"And the taking apart." A bird on concrete, neck twisting unnaturally, with Rose sitting too close to not be instrumental in it.

I had to look away. Lesson learned. "Her life is hard but it's hers."

"Her triumphs will be as spectacular as her downfalls. And her choices will be monumental no matter where she is."

Guarding the little girl as she slept, head resting on my knee, our wings a dome around her, the hush in that whirlwind of horror, was as close to Heaven as the two of us death angels would ever come.

The Queen was an unthinkable devil, but apparently, love brings even the most vile beings together.

Fuck, I hated that. The sheer Disney movie-ness of it, and yet I didn't get to kill the mother. Instead I got *feelings.* Caring about someone other than myself was tiring as fuck, never got easier, and always ended up with me alone.

This time would be no different.

"Charity?" Rose croaked. Christ, she even sounded like I'd put her through hell.

"Hey, Red."

She pushed herself up in the hospital bed with a grunt, and the reality of where she was blinked into existence through a cold tile floor, one-way mirror, some sad attempts at personalizing the room she'd spent so much time in.

"What did you do?" she said breathlessly.

For once, I'd found myself speechless. For all the words I'd prepared, all my reasons, I was mute in the face of her accusing glare. I let out the breath I'd stifled when she shifted those too-deep eyes to the cameras in the corners, no doubt wondering what the Facility was cooking up now that she was *home.*

"Kid, bringing you back to my life with Robbie—I don't even have a life with him anymore—it was impulsive, irresponsible, childish." All the stuff I liked best.

"Don't make me your penance, Charity."

"Yeah well, you're not my shiny new chance either."

Silence where I waited for her to dig into my brain to find anything I wasn't revealing. Better to just come clean. I'd sworn I wouldn't lie to her anymore.

"Here it is, Rose. The Queen knows things. Your buried memories, the ones your mom buried *for* you, caused the tumor. And there's only going to be more, worse ones, ahead."

"She doesn't know that," Rose said dismissively.

"She does, and I'll tell you why. Queen Bird Bitch is really fucking good at planting seeds to turn the world her way. She regrets reeling you in now, but it's too late to un-plant them. Now you're stuck with this side effect of patent-pending Queen-Induced Memory Retrieval. And we both know, kid, you won't stop digging and disassembling, especially now that life isn't a tidy little seaside cottage with an adoring mommy and you remember *why.* Babe, you're too sharp to ignore what's been hidden from you."

"So, what? I keep remembering my past, keep making tumors grow, kill myself with them and that's what my life consists of? I could be like you, with you."

"That won't be me anymore." *It's gonna get ugly now.* "No more Harpy."

Rose gave this snotty laugh. *She didn't get that from you, she's getting older, teenagers are jerks.* "And everyone you'd save as a Harpy, they don't get a way out anymore."

"I...I can't move on if I keep doing this—"

"You think you're moving on, but all you're actually

doing is giving up again. Abandoning me, then abandoning the Wood and all the Harpies in it. You're so preoccupied with changing yourself that you're leaving them to suffer the way they always have. You were supposed to bring *them* change."

"I'm no hero, Red. I'm one person and not a particularly good one at that. The best I can do is lead by example. Show the Harpies there's a way out."

"And you found a way out of me, too. You won't be able to come back here then."

I shook my head, biting my lip, trying to harden from the inside out. "For once, you can have a clean break, Rose. From me, the Queen—"

"She can come here whenever she pleases."

"But she won't," I said firmly, to convince us both. "We promised each other. This place might not have the best intentions…but maybe it *does*. Me, the Queen, we *never* do. Nothing turns out good for us, we can't let that become you, we can't drag you down that road. This is *your* future."

She huffed. "You could never see the future for what it is, Charity. It's not a path to be forged; it's building blocks for someone to pile up without any reason other than to see them fall. But me? *I* can see where the next block will go. You don't have the foresight to see that everything you do is a *reaction*. Avenging, saving these victims—destroy the victimizer first. Take down the next building block before it's placed."

I could tell she was getting more and more excited by the glint in her eyes but she was so incredibly careful to speak evenly, matter-of-factly so I would believe her.

So I would follow her.

She went on with her measured appeal to me.

"With your power and my ability to see into the heart and the brain when I try, we could stop these events before they happen. Take out the monstrous risk factors that walk among us."

I'd done this, by giving her the choice with Turner. Telling her where he came from so she could decide what he was. Before even he could decide who he was on his own.

It was as heartbreaking as it was chilling to watch her mood go from calculating to completely innocent in a second. Tears gleamed in her eyes, so she looked away. She'd seen that I wouldn't do this thing she asked—even if it had been partially my doing, her wanting to make this nightmare team with me. "Why not bring me back before we knew each other?" she mumbled. Fuck, the hurt just emanated from her, in the slouch of her shoulders, the way she'd closed up, rubbing her arms.

"I wanted to, but the Queen… It wouldn't work. I can't bring you to a place we haven't been together in time, it's so confusing. But what's not confusing is that if I could go that far, why wouldn't I bring you back further? Before anyone hurt you? When would I stop?" I hiccup-sobbed at the thought of how much pain the child had seen in such a short life. "Besides, no more stealing memories from you. I won't do that."

Warring fury and anguish twisted her features. Her voice cracked when she said, "But I'll miss you too much."

My head tilted of its own accord like a sad puppy's. My throat closed, my heart thudded in my ears. "You won't. Not too much," I choked out. "And Mr. Cleary, he's good for you, even though he's messing with your head." I charged on. "He'll make sure you get through these memories of yours, that the tumors get the medical attention they need. He's smart, the best person to help you grow up and be healthy, every way there is to be healthy. He *loves* you, Red. He won't let you take more than you can, and he won't treat you like a flower."

Tears poured freely. "If you love me how can you never see me again?"

"Because I love you more than me." My own splashed on my hands. "This is *your* time." I found myself leaning forward, licking my lips, heated with my passion for this girl to take the world by storm in her own way. "With everything you know now about your brain, your past, you can determine your own future. Use all your gifts, take control of your life. You're more powerful in every way than anyone I've ever met, and kid, these Facility folks will be at your beck and call. They'll do anything for you, and if you have to? You can make them. You sure as shit don't need a mess like me pulling you through my train wreck of a life. Get all your questions answered, open and close all the doors, Red, before they leave a hole in you. You're destined to be someone the world could never imagine. I'm so fucking proud of you for everything I know you'll do."

I'd been clutching both her hands, tears pouring down my cheeks, and it felt *good* to believe in her so much. But the tears began to sizzle, and I yanked my hands away in shock. Rose's sadness had given way to anger. Being sad pissed Rose off.

I did *not* want to piss Rose off.

Her voice was falling volcanic ash, dark and dry. "You think you're doing me a favor dropping me back into this place, to rip my way through life alone? You'd leave me with questions about a dimension and a time I should never have seen? You're proud of me?" she snickered. "Just wait."

"Rose, please—"

"Get out, Charity. Get out before I give you something to plead for."

CHARITY

*S*itting at Dunkin's against my better judgment, knowing the type of riff-raff I picked up there, I shook my head. My regular Charity Blake platinum hair replaced the enormous halo of zig-zags and tight curls and kink that it morphed into when the Harpy showed up. Then had come the kick-ass mohawk. I'd miss that hair. It went well with red and black raccoon-eye makeup and a corset, not to mention giant nasty wings and claws, and the occasional beak. And disembowelment of villainy. No, I'd traded it in for brown roots and a near-mullet at this point in my lack of self-care, and a black tube top that required constant yanking up. Black track pants maybe gave the impression I worked out—certainly not in that tube top—and slip-on Chuck Taylors. Zero makeup.

Just how Robbie liked me.

I didn't like myself as much. The average-girl-in-summer tube top showed off all my scars; not something I cared about, but when I was wearing a corset and fishnets and a leather skirt and a shit-ton of makeup, the spectacle *dared* everyone to gawk, begged them to see it all. This…this felt like I should have to explain, and I most certainly would not. I was rail-thin as usual. Probably looked like a junkie, but I'd never cheat on my alcohol problem.

I was bare like this. Normal. Held to the same standards as the rest of the world. A world that had beaten the hell out of me almost as much as I'd beaten myself.

Returning Rose to her time was easy in the end. How could I let her run from her past and to a future alongside *me*? What kind of a sociopathic hypocrite was I to get all high and mighty about living a life, good or bad, when I scuttled away like a mole from anything resembling a real life? No, I preferred to be an *honest* sociopath.

So I went to the pink and orange counter for another cup of coffee. The coffee girl was always new these days, and I'd been there since the change of shifts. She didn't know me from a hole in the wall. It was kind of okay, actually.

"What can I get you?" she asked with not that big of a smile. I understood, having toured the behind-the-counter scenes of local coffee shops as much as Guy Fieri did diners, drive-ins and dives. She liked her job, but had been working since dawn and wasn't tired—she had better things to do. Girls like her didn't get tired, not really. They wanted to go to the beach, and meet their friends at Pinz for drunk-bowling and axe-throwing, and take long car rides out of town just for fun. I'd never been one of those girls, but I'd known them for as long as I stayed at any given coffee shop job.

"Hey, can I get a medium, black, no sugar?"

"Sure."

While she rang me up she didn't linger too long at the cigarette burn scars on my belly and arms, or the less identifiable ones. And when she took my money, she still smiled at me, met my eyes—even when I paused, having seen the vertical white lines from her wrist to her inner elbow.

"Thanks," I said after she handed me my coffee made by the other girl, and I smiled at her. A real-life smile, not even my intentionally scary one.

When I turned around to go back to my table and wait for probably nothing, Probably Nothing was there.

My feet were numb, but I plodded to the table, knowing I couldn't avoid it, not wanting to, but also wishing I could just go back to the Wood where I didn't have to do this. The Wood was just my hiding place. Nothing more. For all my talk, I was a coward.

I stomped forward now, setting my coffee down, not shyly, on the table and sitting with a *thump.* Not ashamed. Not afraid to apologize. Not owing anybody. And not ready to fight.

Robbie put his phone down with a sigh. He'd been at the boarding house for over a week, since I returned from the Wood and the Facility. It was yesterday that I started waiting here until I was too tired and just went back to the apartment and Keegan. We did love sharing a cage.

"Turner's okay," Robbie said, without a smile for me. Anger simmered in his eyes. Wariness that I'd put there. He'd been the most trusting person in the universe before I'd gotten to him.

"Thank Christ," I breathed, my shoulders dropping—but only a little. "I haven't seen the cops..."

He glared away, out the window rather than at me. "That took some doing. You're lucky I know the police from the right side of the bars. They won't arrest you."

"What? How is that possible?"

"I was there when Turner woke up the next day in the hospital. He agreed not to press charges. And he agreed not to tell anyone about the Harpy. Matter of fact, they all did. Those kids are quick to give second chances and forget the past."

I understood just how big a mess I'd left him, and I'd never felt better about evicting myself from Rose's life than I did then.

Rose. A child that never existed in our timeline anyway. Nothing to cover up there. Besides, I knew plenty about wiping away a kid's existence.

"How did you do that?" I asked softly, doing my best not to show how ashamed I was.

"They all wanted to do me the favor."

"Of course they did," I said with a sheepish smile.

"Turner wants something from you."

"Anything."

"Never say again that he's Cody Reese's son. He's not that person."

"Okay." I'd never been good at admitting when I was wrong, but there was no way out of it this time. The kid had saved my ass. I didn't want to owe him, and I still thought he was capable of more bad than he knew, but it hadn't happened yet. And just like Rose, he had a life to build, no matter what and where he came from.

Life Lessons with Charity Blake.

Encouraged by my lack of argument, Robbie went on. "I'm helping him get his name changed."

"Cool. Something I should probably do legally. I am a sucker for doing stuff on the straight and narrow," I joked.

"It wasn't so long ago that you tried." The anger in his eyes flashed to hurt, and then back again.

My head bobbing up and down, up and down, like constant nodding would help me succeed, I said, "I'm giving it up. For good. I talked to the Queen, and a lot—a real lot has happened. Rose is home, or at least back to the Facility. She wasn't thrilled about it, but she's there. I was wrong to take her out. If you love something—"

"Set it free,' he finished, and cast his eyes down at the hot pink tabletop. My stomach plummeted, I felt disemboweled. But I'd known. I'd known.

"Robbie—"

"I'm sorry, Charity. But no. I'm not a punching bag. I'm not a doormat. I'm not your savior. I was wrong to enable you, be there for you no matter how much you hurt me, through the deception… I hate to see you struggling more than anything. Anything in the world." Tears welled in his eyes, and then in mine. "I do love you. I love myself, too."

There went my world. There went all the goodness I'd ever tried for. I couldn't even say it was mine one minute and gone the next. I'd proven myself unworthy of his love more times than I could count.

"Told you so," I said, voice cracking.

"I'm staying at the boarding house, there's plenty of room, it's comfortable. I'll come get my stuff later."

"No, I'll go. That's your apartment, I just live there."

The guy Robbie was, he'd been my safety net, putting me first and saying it was okay, that we'd work it out together. But not anymore. He'd taken the net with him, fell into it himself for once. "It's okay, Char, I'll find a new place fast. Just stay there, stick to it. Stick to *something*. Have a regular life, take care of your bird. Rent's paid for the next two months, that will give you plenty of time to get started."

Two months. Fuck. He was really leaving. This was it.

All that bullshit about trying to salvage this with dignity and not owing anyone and not being ashamed, that was dust in the wind.

"Please don't do this," I begged, tears flowing freely, hands shaking until I steadied them on the table. "I love you, and I've hurt you, and every time I said you should've known, every time I fought when you insisted I could be better, and, and… I've abused you. Really, really badly." Shaking my head, wiping snot from my upper lip. "The Harpy is gone. I promise. I've hit bottom, Robbie, you don't need to dig a basement. Please stay with me, and I swear to you, I will not be back in that place again for as long as I live. I promise you." Gulp. "I promise *me.*"

He took my hand across the table, squeezed it. I saw spots behind my eyelids at the relief that flooded me. "I don't believe you," he said.

And then he left.

ROSE

*E*ndings come more quickly than beginnings.

Breaking free of my stagnant life at the Facility, with no visitors, no change in scenery, nothing to do unless they gave me something to do, and even the "challenging" experiments and tests growing mundane, had been a mountain climb. Once at the summit, the drop-off was immediate, and while expected, still a shock.

Charity Blake was a traitor.

The scientists, with their faraway, dreamer expressions, would say that I was a "superior human being." That my mother abandoned me in recognition of her inability to nurture me the way that I deserved. Charity Blake, on the other hand, was herself a superior human being, and she'd abandoned me even more quickly.

Apparently, a superior being doesn't require nurturing, or "coddling," as I'd heard one of the nurses say when the depression set in upon my return to the Facility. I hadn't known that depth of darkness since I was a little girl under the covers trying to block out the sound of hope that the ocean waves brought.

To have been given a taste of my true capability, to catch a glimpse of my potential and have the possibilities stolen from me, in addition to the loss of the companionship that she and the Queen provided, was a double hit that I couldn't see to the other side of. The Queen, who wanted to raise me right, and Charity, who threw the word *sister* at me like she was feeding the birds. I'd say I didn't know which was worse to feel betrayed by—but I do know.

My hands clenched until my palms ached. The nurses learned to keep my nails very, very short, because I kept making my hands bleed this way, the frustration tearing me open.

I certainly wasn't the little fairy princess the world thought I was not so long ago.

No, not the world—*my* world. My mother.

Home.

Yet again, I thought of home at the beach: our cottage, Annie, the yard and the garden, the basement with its cold cement floor. My mother.

She'd always said that I never asked questions, I only answered or raised them. But that was Rose then. The Rose I was now had been assaulted with memories that had literally tried to kill my brain, and I was left with newer holes, new gaps. I wanted to ask questions—where my mother was and why she hadn't visited, being the big one—but I stuck firmly to *Rose doesn't ask questions.*

The only thing worse than hidden truth is finding it. Taking apart that fabric so carefully woven.

I wasn't home, but I was *back.* Back in the Facility that I knew. Where I was never underestimated, where I'd be encouraged to set my gifts free. Mr. Cleary said my abilities were "strengths, not secrets."

The Facility didn't want to make me better—they wanted to make me better *for them.* Not ideal, but it was a means to an end. I wanted simplicity—they would give it to me. If they kept me happy, I would perform, give them what they wanted. And in turn, they wouldn't underestimate me, and they wouldn't coddle me.

And if they knew what was good for them, they wouldn't stop me.

~

The Scientist—Mr. Cleary—came to visit as soon as I returned to the Facility.

I didn't want to like Mr. Cleary. I didn't like that he pretended to be a *mister* when he wasn't a neighbor, or a teacher, or a hardware store owner. He was Scientist, and he could disguise himself all he wanted—but I could take him apart, down to what he really wanted.

He was a simple man: single-minded, with a goal that ruled his life, which made him easy for me to understand. More than everyone else, he wanted a knowledge that no one could take away from him, and he wanted to share it with people who could use it and make him important. This knowledge eliminated any pretense.

"You came back," he said, sitting down in the comfy chair from before.

I had a new chair now. A new bed, actually, too. This one was a real bed, not a hospital bed. I had wallpaper—pink, with red roses. *The evolution of sweetness,* I'd thought. And I had a window now because I made them give me one. Not a new room with a window, but *my* room with a new window made just for me.

I wasn't about to give up what was mine.

The Facility would give me just about anything I wanted now. Just about.

My request for tools and parts went unfilled because of

the *danger*. I was testing them before they ever tested me—how ridiculous, to think that I couldn't make tools and parts out of anything I dreamed up, that I couldn't take apart their will to *protect me* from myself. Now…now I saw new ways to rebuild. To rebuild my whole world. The Queen had shown me.

"I came back," I confirmed.

Mr. Cleary leaned forward, a hungry glint in his eyes, a sparkle in his teeth like the Big Bad Wolf. "Tell me what you learned," he said.

I grinned. "More than you could ever grasp."

"I think you'd be surprised," he said, leaning back and mentally preparing for a fight.

"I've been to another world."

He tried to figure out if I really was insane or not.

"Tell me about it," he said casually, while internally salivating. He was waiting to use his next tactic if I refused.

I pulled his intentions apart without him ever knowing it. "So you believe bribery is the best way to get to me. You think I'm an ordinary kid who'll be swayed to give up information with candy."

"I don't think anything of the sort. I have information that you don't. I know what really drives you, Rose Preston. I won't offer you anything that you don't have a use for."

"I traveled to a Circle of Hell."

He stopped, assessing me again. I let him. "I find that hard to believe."

"I don't care if you believe it."

"That's fair." He reached into his pocket and took out a pack of gum, offered me a piece. It wasn't the kind I liked and he knew it. "Will you tell me more about it?"

"Not yet. I want to know what you've got for me."

He laughed drily. "You run this place like a prison yard, don't you?" he said, and I noted a tone of affection. He *liked* me. I immediately began to notice things I liked about him and gritted my teeth to stop myself. "Well. Let me start by saying, I know something I don't think you're ready to hear. I also know that you don't like having information kept from you. It's truly an interesting yin and yang of a complex you have there. Perhaps you can tell me, to help me better determine what would best suit your needs, why it is that you returned to the Facility."

Emotional need was a rash that resurfaced again and again. Part of the whole machine that I was. Mr. Cleary, when he'd just been Scientist, once told me that my ability to bury childlike needs was the result of a combination of things: my extraordinary genius, my "acquired savant syndrome," my abandonment issues, and my childhood rape. In short, I was too smart to trust anyone and it made me better. Stronger. But still young.

"I want to be stronger. You'll help me."

"Stronger how?"

"I think you know."

"I would love to hear it from you, Rose."

I chose to trust him with my thoughts. "I want you to make my powers stronger."

Nodding, he smiled, wide, wider, wider. "Yes. Yes, let me help you with that, Rose. We must work together. A business relationship. I—not just the Facility, but *I*—want to know more about this place you've been, because Rose, you defy explanation. And therefore, I believe you when you tell me you've been somewhere *else*." He began tapping his knee with one hand in unbridled excitement. "When we found you, Rose, you showed us a raw talent to 'take things apart,' as you've said, yes?" I nodded. "And you grew it, *you* did that. We have so much to learn from you, my darling."

My darling.

And with those two words and the joy in his eyes…something sunny that I hadn't seen since…

"Tell me where my mother is," I said. But not as firmly as I would have liked.

The sunny brightness was gone, just like she was. "I'm going to ask you to trust me, Rose, in that I don't believe this is the time for that information. It is yours, but to have it now would quite possibly destroy the impact of our exercises to strengthen you. I would ask if you understand, but I know that you do."

Exercises were actually experiments, but I let him have his safe word. What mattered was that Mr. Cleary knew where my mother was, and why she'd left me so entirely. And he'd told me that he was keeping it from me, but not because I was a child—because I couldn't perform properly in the experiments if I knew. He didn't hide the information from me, though he didn't hand it over. For my own good, and for his.

I couldn't help it; love moved in, quickly and without hesitation. *Hide it,* an inner voice said.

"Understood," I said with a nod and a smile I couldn't hide. "Now. There's someone I need to see."

CHARITY

THE WOOD OF SUICIDES, NO YEAR

My last walk through the Wood of Suicides was nearly peaceful. The suicides were fairly quiet, as were the Harpies. I stopped to say goodbye to Loretta, my old-time-movie sorta friend. The first thing she said was, "It's about time you blew this joint, doll," and I blinked a bunch of times, ready to open them somewhere, anywhere else.

"Uh, yeah, thanks? Anyway, you were pretty nice to me here, and you helped…" I didn't want to say her name, to think about her at all, inevitable though it was. "You helped Jen. Please, keep helping her. I think I uh, lost that one. She's here for good, you know? But I can't be. I can't." And in an unprecedented idiot move, I threw my arms around her. She was stiff, cold, like a corpse, but smelled like champagne when I moved the right way. Champagne and dead bodies. Not likely to forget that particular aroma.

"Don't come back, Charity Blake," Loretta said, then smiled with her black, bee-stung lips; a dreary reminder of who she'd been. I squeezed my eyes shut, hating that she wasn't that person, despised that I knew anything about her, and vowed to avoid all the other Harpies on my way out of this hellhole. Couldn't afford to think of any single one of their lives, who they'd been. Couldn't think of them chewing gum like Rose did, or wearing bad jeans like Jen, or having a cat or eating Chinese food, or doing laundry or collecting coins. There was no way to help them now, not if I wanted to help myself.

I didn't go to Jen and Evan. Total pussy move, but then again her running out on me like a walk of shame on crack was no better. And the Harpy was like crack for her. She'd fallen hard for the power, the escapism, the badassery, even harder than she had for Evan. Nothing I could say would bring her back to her bad jeans-wearing, baking-for-fun, sad clown life, not even the long shot possibility that I could give him his life back.

I wasn't one to beat a dead horse. I was more one to leave a dying horse and wish him good luck.

The Queen was always expecting me. Sounds really cool, to have a queen always expecting me, but not this time. This time it wouldn't be some get-off-easy deal like a fight to the death or anything. No, this would be a heartfelt goodbye.

To someone I alternately despised and admired. To someone who gave life to my desperation and anger. To someone who manipulated me, lied to me, mistreated me for her own ends, just like Carl Painter had. To someone who played mother to me when I hadn't had one in so long, who was furious that I'd been so horribly wronged. To someone who gave me an actual mythical power and told me that whatever I did with it was okay. That I was okay. That I was enough. To someone who had *seen me.*

Saying goodbye to her meant saying goodbye to a recovered part of me, a rebellious, vicious side that needed to be heard.

But I'd given it a voice until that's all I was.

I wasn't willing to live like the depraved beasts in the Wood of Suicides.

I climbed the nest for the last time.

The Queen sat, slightly hunched, gazing at the clenched hands she wrung in her lap. A thing of sorrowful beauty, of lost hope. "I know why you've come," she said.

No smartassery on my part. I didn't have it in me.

"I'm sorry. I actually am. Nuts, right? I've…healed some, though. Thanks to you, a lot. But I've gotta get out of here for good. You taught me a thing with the kid—that no matter what my life is, it's mine. I want to live it. I have to make my life up there, try to matter as me, you know?"

The Queen surprised me with tears in her eyes.

"I've grown tired, Charity," she said gently. I didn't remark on the use of my actual name this time. It was a defeat she was willing to accept, a white flag.

"I bet. You've been Queen of Hell for as long as I've known you, anyway."

She smiled sadly. "I believe I was tired long before that."

"Yeah."

Not-awkward silence. A world of things never needed to be said between the Harpies; between all the hurt women of both worlds. We all had the same vibe, a light in the darkness that takes so many forms, growing and weakening within us. When we find each other, that light burns brighter—a smothered ember transforming to a flame, strengthened by one of its own. Fire spreads.

Like a disease, when it comes to the Harpies.

"You're tired as well," the Queen said, breaking the silence.

"In more ways than one," I muttered.

Rose's final words haunted my sleep until I'd leaped from the unicorn blankets in the dark, cold sweat layering me like a second skin, splashing cold water on my face, avoiding the mirror.

"Get out before I give you something to plead for."

I might have let Rose go…but she wouldn't let me go. She didn't have it in her to leave something together that was already falling apart.

The Queen caught me wincing, tilting my head as if I could shy away from the needling words. "What is it?" she asked.

"Rose. She'll be like thirty, twenty…I can't do math but she'll exist in my timeline." My voice cracked when I said, "She's gonna come looking for me."

The Queen chuckled, as if she found me endearing. Maybe she did. "Are you looking for a loophole, or for protection?"

"If you'd asked me a couple of days ago, I'd have said a loophole."

"And now you fear her."

Admit it. Do the human thing. "Yes," I croaked.

With a sad little laugh, Queenie said, "I could offer you greater power, darling. To fight her off."

"You know I can't take it."

That elegant head dipped, her crown tipping toward me as if offering me one last chance to take it. It didn't last more than a second and the Queen resumed her poise. "She'll be there, looking for you. Rose…the child never stops searching," she said, shaking her head with this wistful quirk in her lips. "But she will only see you from the wrong side of one-way mirrors and through frosted glass. You'll share a world—but not the same world. Gradient shades of the same existence, ever-so-slightly intersecting but never given the chance to join."

My heart broke a little more as I thought, *safe.* I loved Rose. And I'd never known safety in my life.

I couldn't stop nodding in understanding like some idiot, and she broke the awkwardness for me.

"Have you heard of rose-tinted spectacles, Charity?"

"Huh?"

"Farmers used rose-tinted glasses on chickens in the early twentieth century, as the color disguised the shade of blood. The muddled color prevented the chickens from cannibalizing the injured of their flock."

"So wait, they put these…glasses…on chickens. Like, actual chickens."

"Yes," she answered through warm laughter. "The beacon of weakness was unrecognizable." She leaned in, voice thick with intent, pleading for me to understand. "But the aggression was still there, Charity. Waiting for the time the glasses came off." A warning, then. Never truly safe.

A cacophony of Harpy screeches assaulted my ears after that, and I shivered in the Hell-heat, closing my eyes against it. I cleared my throat. "So, I need you to take. These broken wings. And learn to f—"

"Stop," she said with a grin that I was glad to see. It didn't hide the despair, but it was enough. "Charity, there's no great de-winging ceremony. I don't need to take what you're giving away. After all, I never gave them to you to begin with, did I? They explode from in here." She laid a black-taloned hand on her heart, then pointed to mine. As if tied together, my hand went to my own human heart.

Human.

Shaking my head, I said, "Yeah okay, I get it. The power was in me all along and now I just have to click my heels three times, right?"

The Queen's brows furrowed, eyes narrowed; a wince. If I

didn't know better, I'd have thought she was going to miss me. "I'm afraid so," she said.

I didn't take one last glance around, didn't search out familiar inhuman faces, didn't commit the stench of blood and carcasses to memory. "Okay," I said. "But you have to do one thing for me."

"What is that?"

"Close the portal behind me. Seal it. Never come for me again."

She blinked lazily. "Well, if I knew how to do that, my dear..."

The vortex ripped me from the Wood like a hole punched in a space shuttle, sucking me out in a breath-stealing cyclone of noise and cold.

The Queen never finished her sentence.

ROSE

wo years and six days.

That's how long it took me to...*train.* To take the tests, the experiments, the increasingly difficult challenges that the Facility managed to create for me. That's how long it took for me to see the very fabric of reality.

Only a fool thinks they know everything there is to know because the world has labeled them misunderstood. Genius, savant, monster, all words used to describe those of us that defy other titles.

I was sure others were out there.

It didn't stop me from feeling utterly alone.

In two years, while girls my age on TV got gushy-eyed over boyfriends and fought with siblings over inconsequential things, I'd taken apart everything from cancers to bombs. And I'd waited. Waited. For the time when I could take apart the one thing that held me back:

Time.

Time, I'd explained to Mr. Cleary, is merely a concept. Made by men, taken too far and too much to heart by women. A rule in a lawless world that humanity scarcely understood.

He'd nodded enthusiastically, but the fear in his eyes didn't require any dissecting to see.

One thing I had not found a way to dissect was how exactly Charity, Jen, the Queen, how they all had *become* Harpies to begin with. It defied science. It defied logic. A physical transformation, a dimensional migration, based on…what?

Despite how much I'd grown, the difference between the child I was then and now at fourteen, one thing never changed.

I despised having questions.

I finally had to just *stop.* Stop doing the challenges the doctors and Mr. Cleary had created for me. The careful identification and extraction of a single wire from a bomb without direction. The disassembling of out-of-commission army tanks without moving my hands. The taking apart of handwriting to determine exactly what type of person had written it, then taking apart the very words themselves until I could see just where that writer was, near or far. The simpler stuff of examining the minds of silent subjects to determine their plans—some blindfolded, others having been interrogated for an untold period of time already, some on drugs, some merely begging for what I didn't know—all had to stop.

And then later, the slow burning of a mix of chemicals with the sheer heat of my stare through a window, causing eruptions and gases and new creations. Sometimes someone else was on the other side of the window with the formulas— but not for long.

It was after one such experiment that I sprang upon Mr. Cleary how disturbed I was during our afternoon tea.

We had tea together every day. He never took a day off.

Some days I only saw him for tea—other days he was by my side when I woke up and when I went to sleep, but never a day passed without him. His stamina was nothing short of inspiring. His dedication to me…I never wanted to mistake it for something it wasn't, but I couldn't stop.

"Mr. Cleary," I started, not wanting to admit I was afraid to disappoint him, "I need rest."

He cocked his head at me, brows knitting. "Are you feeling all right, Rose? Need a nap, perhaps?"

"No, I mean a longer break. A few days. Maybe longer."

He took a sip of his tea—real china cups from England—raising his eyebrows again as though I'd introduced an idea he'd never heard of before. "You've never asked for such a thing," he said.

"And I'm not asking now. I need a break. The chemicals…" I gulped, thinking of the gas filling up the room, a new chemical that *I* created, managed to bind. Of the rats I killed. Of the people.

Mr. Cleary clinked his delicate china cup onto the saucer. Pink, this one, with blue and purple flowers. Pansies.

Annie.

I shook my head, brain knocking around in there to rid my thoughts of my old friend.

"I understand, Rose," he said. "That's fine."

"Not asking."

"No, of course not. You call the shots. It stands to reason that you'd be exhausted. Troubled. You're doing some very grown-up things."

My heart pounded when he said that, the acknowledgement that I was still only a child, really. As much as I hated being thought of as just that, I annoyed myself with the longing for its simplicity as well. And for the kind words that a child got. That I'd once gotten from my mother. From Annie. Even from *her.*

I stiffened my spine. "I'm doing things no *grown-up* has ever done, and I need rest. I hope that doesn't disappoint you."

His eyes, his demeanor, his insides spoke truth to me when he said, "You could never, ever disappoint me, Rose Preston."

Dropping my head, letting my fingers squeeze the teacup handle, I murmured, "Thank you."

~

For the next four days I barely got out of bed. I'd intended on using my rest period to concentrate entirely on *time*, what it was, how it worked, to achieve my goal. But instead I drifted in and out of fitful sleep, dreaming of melting into the same numbing state I did as a little girl in Manomet. Trodden by loneliness, bludgeoned under the overwhelming *difference* about me, overcome by feelings and responsibilities and fears.

Now, so many years later, I'd been through a hundred thousand changes, but I hadn't really changed. Nothing was different when I took it all apart and looked. Evolving, but staying the same.

I'd gotten my period with no one to tell except a nurse.

I'd had a crush on one of the other patients that I'd occasionally seen in the garden when I walked with Mr. Cleary. A tall, shy boy, always dipping his head when he smiled at me across the flowers, blond hair glinting in the sun. I never spoke to him. I'd been too nervous, could never tell him what I was doing there. And then he didn't come back to the garden after a while. I had no one to tell that I was sad about that.

I'd gotten my first bra from Mr. Cleary. I hadn't had the sense to be horrified.

I hadn't worn anything *new*, from a mall or a store, since my birthday last year when Mr. Cleary took me out shopping as a surprise. The lights, the crowds, the horrible, all-consuming noise had caused me to fall to the ground, clutching my knees to my chest, sobbing, crying over that one fateful day in Boston when I opened the window... Mr. Cleary had held me close and rocked me, right there against the glass railing on the second floor as people passed, pointing and giggling, and he told me it would be okay. Him. A scientist.

Not my friends, not a boyfriend, not my mother, not Charity Blake. A scientist.

"I have to get out of here," I muttered to myself.

My door wasn't locked—they couldn't contain me if they tried. No prison held me besides my own mind. I raced through the halls in my pajamas, past nurses who swung around, calling after me.

I'd never remembered one of their names. Not one.

I slammed through swinging doors, the Facility zipping by me, surreal. Images of my home on the beach interfaced with a series of disconnected snapshots of the Facility, nothing cohesive or logical. Memories of the glass railing at the mall became memories of the window, the heckling shoppers becoming the people with the chemicals, screaming, skin bubbling and peeling off. I raced past locked rooms with barely a window to pass food through, rooms that were wide open with children playing inside, rooms like ICU units with beeping machines and monitors.

Annie.

On my knees suddenly, the image of her attached to machines just like those, ripping through me.

I climbed to my feet as footsteps rushed down the tile floor behind me, yelling for help. Nurses or scientists or doctors or officers, they all were one.

Running now, and the flickers kept coming. *The apartment in Boston, its stark, white walls; the beach; the seagull; my mother, smiling like sunshine; Annie at her little table; Sean Singh.*

My skirt around my knees.

His spit on my face.

The flush running through my whole body, a heat of humiliation and fear and despair.

And more, more, more pictures I couldn't see but only *understand*, that they were horrible things opening holes in my brain, forcing me to see them. New things. Hidden memories.

I don't remember when the screaming started. I only remember the piercing sound of it, my throat raw with it, the clumps of hair clutched in my fists as I curled up on the cold floor.

Four hands gently, but firmly, took my arms, pulled me to my feet. As if I were seeing myself from somewhere else where there were no Sean Singhs or anyone that could hurt me, I saw how I snarled at the nurses, who reeled back. They still held me but I squealed at them like some wild pig, and thrashed until they let me go, one crying out and clutching her hands—they were bright red and blistering. Another reached for me, snarling right back.

When she fell back, four of her fingers were burned clean off.

Growling, I slammed against the double doors, but they didn't budge. A number panel was on the wall beside them. I tried to disassemble the keypad in my mind, a thoughtless maneuver for me, but was interrupted by a streak of white-hot memory.

"I'll undo you, take you apart."

While the nurses screamed behind me in chaos and more feet plodded down the hall, I cried out at the knife of icy pain in my brain that arose with another memory.

My brain is dying. Being killed by memories.

I stared, tried to focus on the double door handles, but my brain was numb. I brought that heat up from my belly instead, channeled it through me. The heat full of desperation and anger.

Cody Reese.

Sean Singh.

Charity Blake.

I put all the rage into the door handles. But the handles didn't move.

Instead, the doors themselves shook, trembled hard, screeching metal, and a giant, flaming hole *like the one burrowing into my brain* tore through the doors. And then I just stepped through, cries of my name ringing through the hall behind me.

~

I'd only intended on going to the garden. The garden, where he'd leave me alone. Mr. Cleary knew where to look for me, though he rarely did. The scientist respected that I needed a place of my own, where I wasn't the wildest thing growing.

But when I stepped through that hole in the door, it wasn't to the garden. No, I'd become Alice, falling down the rabbit hole into Hell.

The first word I heard when I landed in the Wood of Suicides was, "No."

An exasperated, sing-song voice from over my head, cutting through the din of animalistic human howls and beastly bird screeches. "No," she said again. I knew that voice, a thing of dreams and nightmares, a thing of elegance and anger.

I put my hands flat on the ground, let the red-tinged hay

stick up through my fingers, took in the dry hush of it as I pushed it down. I got to my feet, blood squelching under my pink satin slippers adorned with big red roses—a gift from Mr. Cleary. Slippers that both spoke to a princess of a little girl and a passionate growing woman.

I crushed the remnants of a purple organ underneath, twisted my foot to bury it, right along with my toe, soaking the red rose and turning it black. The visual of it, seeing the layers of gore that created it down to the tiniest sinew, filled me with pride and strength that made me feel weightless inside. The feeling flowed out of me. Flames licked around my feet, raising me off the ground, holding me in the hot red air like a feather in my garden's water fountain.

"Hello, my Queen," I said, my words billowing out in black smoke that even took me aback. So it was done then.

I took one last breath as Rose Preston, human girl, an abomination among people—but a miracle amongst monsters.

When I looked up at the Queen, tears traced lines down her cheeks, dribbled onto her lips. I didn't look deeper to understand why.

"Don't be afraid," I said. And the laugh from deep in my belly rose like lava, searing me inside and out, burning up the soft thing I used to be.

The Queen and I walked, me as giddy as she was solemn. The Harpies blinked big, bloodshot eyes at me, some cooing little words my way, some saying "the girl" in disbelief. My power rumbled through them with every one of my footsteps, creating tremors in their bones—but their eyes, their hearts, still saw a little girl. I didn't mind. They deserved to have a child among them, breathe life back into them.

This place…for as ugly as its existence was, here I was *both* child and miracle, and now, visionary. A way to relive their childhood the way they wanted it to be, a new hope to believe in. A leader that they didn't know they needed.

"I promised Charity that I wouldn't find you again, you know," the Queen said sadly.

"You didn't."

"No. I didn't." She snickered once, under her breath. "I sensed you, *reaching* for us. Trying to find a way in. Now that you're here, do you know how?"

I swallowed, not entirely sure of my answer. "I was very, very emotional. Out of control. Memories…"

I got the feeling of having failed a test with her next words. "You're not a Harpy yet, not until you've taken apart completely where your violence comes from. I hope for your sake, you never figure it out."

"You can't hide anything from me! Tell me right now, how did I end up here? What made that hole open up?"

She tilted her head at me, all calmness on the outside, but her heart was trembling, I could see it plain as day. "Finally, she has questions. Seems you don't know everything just yet, do you? Our poor, darling Rose. You'll never have all the answers, my child…and you'll never stop tearing the world apart until you find them." She leaned in close, her whisper more penetrating than every scream in the Wood to my ears. "I will *not* be bullied, darling, and I will not help you."

Fury clouded everything. To be denied this, another abandonment, another underestimation, more *undoing.*

My turn to undo.

The Queen's dark silhouette twisted, mangled, turning in on itself like a puppet on strings being tied in knots. Her eyes the wide and glassy things of a doll, her joints disconnected and connected again with a series of pops and cracks, limbs elongating and contracting as I rearranged her, until I found what I wanted deep underneath the strata of mythic queen and power-hungry child and hurt woman.

I found what she knew, what she wanted to hide. And it changed everything.

"No." The word a billow of black smoke, dark as the truth. I fell back to the ground, the flames holding me aloft extinguished, the fire inside me, extinguished.

The Queen, hunched, panting, hands on her knees in the elegant black gown, now in tatters and burning fragments on her body, couldn't catch her breath between sobs.

"You really were protecting me," I muttered, tears blurring the crimson sky to pink.

"Of course," she said, her voice hoarse. She cleared her throat, stood straight again. The blood vessels in one eye had burst, the white now a deadly red.

I'd seen what the Queen knew. It was a dirty gem of knowing, a spark of knowledge that ate at her. She'd learned it while I was in Room 6, while she filled my head with the memories my mother had stolen from me.

The Facility had saved me.

My mother hadn't brought me there and left me, hadn't given up on trying to take care of the shameful secret I was.

I saw the memory in the Queen's mind and took it from her. One memory she hadn't wanted to show me.

The cottage. I'd come out of my bedroom, pink and white night-gown, bare feet, sun streaming in, went straight to my mother at the stove. "Good morning!" she said.

Stone-faced, I jerkily put both hands on her hips and spun her around. She cried out in shock but laughed—until I grabbed her shoulders, shoved her onto her knees, putting her at eye level with me as she'd always done, always making me feel like her equal before I was better than her. The fury I'd awoken with channeled through my body, coarse streams of energy that made my eyes glow and reflect in hers. She cried, lip trembling, spittle dripping in her terror of me. Me, a little, little girl.

"I dreamed of it," I said.

I grabbed both sides of her head, put my forehead on hers as she sobbed, our eyeballs centimeters apart, mine glowing, like embers. "Give it to me," I hissed, exhaling black smoke. I dug my fingers into her temples, she screamed like a wounded animal (knife of memory, squirrel, pressing on his chest, mole, squeezing him hard, gull, dismembered, undone), *blood dripping down her cheeks, the words and pictures and knowing poured from her head, through the black smoke, and I saw it all. Saw it in pieces and chunks, the guts of what she knew, the viscera of what she'd hidden from me, its bones and pink tissue and red blood had happened to* me.

The past rained on me in vomitous torrents of gore.

No. Not the past.

My mother.

I had ripped my mother apart.

Flayed her like a fish, gutted her until I could see the tendons and nerves and blood like she'd been turned inside out and flash frozen, suspended in that permanent state of torture. And still, I screamed in her ravaged face that I wanted answers, every answer.

She burst into a million tiny pieces on me, pink and red bits dripping from the ceiling and walls of my childhood home.

At daybreak, I killed my mother. The Facility came for me when the clock struck noon. The police didn't know, the ambulances hadn't come, there was no one to call and say that something was wrong at the Preston house. But the Facility knew. They'd always been watching.

"Thank you," I said to the Queen, wanting to share with her how it felt to *know.*

And I pulled her apart in just the same way.

~

I'd had my first real *dream* in the Facility. Of the garden outside, the birds and squirrels and deer coming to rest against me, snoozing as ladybugs tickled our toes. It began to rain, and the trees overhead curled to shelter us, drawing the animals and I closer together, the scent of their woodsy musk still heavy in my nose even now.

I never pulled these animals apart, searching their bones for marrow, searching their blood just to see how deep I could go. I never pulled their limbs apart with my mind. And Cody Reese never invaded that copse, never invaded *me* in that hypnotic sleep. It was then, age twelve, that I realized I'd had nightmares every night of my life, even when I thought I was happiest.

My happiest moments had been plagued by nightmares.

But this…

This surreal state was no nightmare. It was far, far worse.

I murdered the Queen of the Wood of Suicides.

The evil deed had me convulsing on the ground, every twist of my body wrapping me in more gore, mummifying me as a murderer, showing me how much blood I was covered in, chunks of flesh clinging to my arms, my legs, sticking to my cheeks. For every second my eyes lingered on the skinned remnants of the Queen, bones crumpled in a heap mere feet away, a hole opened up in my brain. Then another.

I could *see* them. Cigarette burns in my mind, watching from the inside.

Holes that would empty me.

It was so clear now.

Harpies hovered over me, trying to determine if I was fresh meat or something *else*, the screams of the suicides permeating every inch of my soul—what was left of it.

And from the holes in my brain emerged pictures.

Every last detail of killing the seagull.

Every millisecond of my defamation at Sean Singh's hands.

The obliterating noise of the traffic outside my window in Boston, reaching into me until I could only think of becoming a part of it, climbing to the window, working to get out onto the ledge, to let the memories of Cody Reese become one with the noise and the ground far below.

But worst of all, memories of my mother.

Of baking Christmas cookies with her as the wind

howled outside our little cottage, rattling the windows that should be boarded up this time of year. Monopoly at our old kitchen table, her telling me stories of my dad—not about a murderer, but about a man that loved me more than his own life. Mommy planting a garden in the backyard while I ran through the sprinkler, the *tick-tick-tick* of its movement a rhythm in time with the birdsong overhead.

I remembered the fear in her eyes every time she told me I was special. Different.

She'd believed I was a precious, vital organ with a spark of magic nestled inside, but underneath, that spark had burned out and I'd turned hard.

My body jolted upright, a ragdoll yanked to attention, suspended in the crimson air.

"Murderer!" a cacophony of hellish voices hissed around me. An enormous one, an Amazon warrior of a Harpy, held me up by the back of the neck, her claws digging in. An army of the women surrounded me, ready to attack.

"You destroyed our Queen," the Amazon growled. *"You. A child."*

A Harpy crouched near the ground leaped at me, kicked me square in the stomach with both of her heavy back claws. I doubled over, only to be torn back up by the Amazon. Then another came at me, raking my face as another unseen one clawed at my hair. One by one they got their hits in while I dangled, unable to lift my head or cry out any longer.

Until my leg snapped.

I let out a nasty howl through a puff of black smoke and sparks, stars flashing behind my eyelids.

The holes in my brain flared like cigarette butts, ash-tinged images of every time I'd been too supple in an unkind world, again and again.

Words poured from my mouth in a blaze, Harpies screeching to see the dead air we breathed taken apart in their wake into appearing and disappearing cubes of atoms, of nothing, of gases as I screamed, *"Not. Soft. ANYMORE."*

Glass shards sliced through my shoulder blades in a single, harrowing second. My bones cracked like eggshells, blood poured in a thick heatwave down my back from the giant wounds, puddled at my toes where they scarcely touched the ground.

My screams were a creature of their own, birthed from a pain so excruciating I welcomed the death they'd bring.

But as fast as the torture ensued, it dissipated, leaving me with towering wings of steel, feathers like razor blades, the cold of them soothing to the gashes on my back. They glinted, reflecting in the wide eyes of the Harpies as they backed away.

Strong and sharp as my wings were, they moved with me as easily as my arms, each feather like fingers.

I didn't need protecting anymore. There was no hiding now.

With a great beat of the new appendages, I rose higher. Sparks flickered when my wings brushed each other—an embodiment of the spark I'd had as a child, the one that nearly everyone I ever met worked at burning out of me.

No. That spark had only simmered, gathered its power, become a fire in my belly.

The heat I forever felt in my chest, my gut, now made my skin glow an unearthly orange-red, heated my body like desert sun. Still blazing, it burst out of my mouth in a stream of fire, igniting the wretches below me that sought to destroy the last bit of a little girl with the softness of an angel, but held fury like a dragon.

Held aloft by my gunmetal wings, poised in Hell's sky over the burning beasts below, I addressed the mob of remaining Harpies.

"Your queen is gone!" I shouted in a voice that was not quite

my own. *"I've seen inside every one of you in a way she never could. Your lives have been chosen for you—I know how that feels. You cower here, torturing the tortured, and you suffer worse than any of them! Forever treated as underlings, wallowing in filth, when legend created you and evolution favored you. You, my friends, have suffered enough!"*

Cries of support heralded me from below. Enchanted faces, adoring me like my mother once had, lips parted, features softened. Despite their incinerated sisters, my words spoke true to them. These women were no strangers to agony, to sacrifice, and they were accustomed to birth by fire.

The fear in their eyes had mostly evaporated now. These creatures of myth ached for change and didn't even know it.

And I, a child from above, would raise up these martyrs from below to see the world once again.

To make it theirs.

"Here you go, shorty, that'll be a fiver. Two fivers if you're nasty."

The old guy was nice enough and didn't leer at me like most of The Full Sail's high-class patrons. He slipped me a ten and I gave him no change.

"You're all right, Chuck."

"My name's Terry," he said with a grin.

"I'll be sure to remember that," I said and winked.

The other bartender, Tony, had worked there since the place opened, he said. I think The Full Sail only opened like a year ago, but whatever. Sick of the testosterone party, he'd hired me when I went in for a hundred beers one night, needing some way, any way at all to occupy myself now that I was Harpy-free, three months strong.

"Terry likes you," Tony said, wiping a glass with a dishtowel.

"His name's Marty, and yeah, of course he does. I'm supremely likeable."

Tony laughed, loud and boisterous, smiling nicely. He had a *nice* smile. He was a nice guy all around. "No," he said through his laugh, "it's Terry, and I'd like to thank you once again for sharing your tips with me."

"I don't *share,* it's been our arrangement the whole time. It's not like I want to give you money."

"Please," he joked. "You could pocket the tips and I'd probably never know."

"Shut up," I mumbled, popping the top off another beer that was partially frozen and handing it to some gross regular who I hated. I'd caught him one night drunkenly putting his hands on the eternally drunk lady who lived in a tent behind Cordage Park. I'd kindly popped my body between both of theirs, the lady stumbling away, unaware of her surroundings as usual. The heat-seeking missile that was my Harpy-Spidey sense hadn't glowed… It was leaving me. And that pissed me off more than the gross regular had. So I wrapped my fingers around his throat, spit in his face and kneed him in the crotch, hissing in his ear that if I wanted to I could needle out his intestines with one fingernail and devour them while he watched.

And I really did want to. Jesus, did I want to.

When I brought out the bar trash that night to the alleyway, I'd craved blood so badly that I tackled a raccoon with residual Harpy speed and sunk my teeth into its neck like a fucking vampire.

Finished with his glasses, Tony came closer, leaned his elbow on the bar, but not in a sleazy way. "Seriously, I never got tips before you got here unless the guys were too drunk to count. They like a pretty girl who'll give them a hard time. These guys…they don't probably have super exciting lives outside of here, you know?"

"Yeah. Yeah, I know," I said more grudgingly than I wanted to. I did *not* want Tony asking me about my personal life, or what the long face was for. I didn't want any friends, I just wanted to get through the next night and the next and the next until…

Until my heartache for Robbie was a thing of the past.

Until the Harpy wasn't part of my present.

But that meant, for the time being, that the greatest excitement in my life came from finding a new neighbor to "borrow" laundry detergent from, in the event I bothered with clean clothes. In the beginning, I could actually *taste* the acid in my heart every time I swallowed, the bile that rose up when I thought of Robbie never coming back. I'd thought the Wood of Suicides was surreal…no. No, life, alone in the apartment without the one person who'd believed in me, *that* was surreal. Drifting through late afternoons into ugly nights, wanting blood, wanting a reason, having nothing but booze and television and fucking unicorns. I smashed so many of them, left them on the floor, my feet cut up every time I got out of bed, my soul cut up when I went into it.

I realized I had nothing to live for outside of an image a man had of me.

No, I wouldn't go out that way. How withering, to depend on what any man, as good as Robbie or not, thought of me. I deserved better.

I actually thought that. *I deserve better*. Even in this condition, it still wasn't my worst. I could get better in fits and starts.

But the way I'd wanted to go back and fix everything—the suicides' lives, my abuse, taking Rose out of her time, fixing what I'd done with Evan, what I'd done to Turner, didn't only show me that I wanted to be good.

It also showed me that I was still making bad choices every single day.

The nightmare I'd survived, continuously survived, became an excuse to be an impulsive dick. I hadn't had the proper role models, one might say, but I had to do better than eviscerating and belittling and beating myself down. Had to close that door.

One day I *started.* Doing *things.* Tried to budget out a couple of meals until I realized I'd rather just drink than cook. I vacuumed, tried to repair the cabinets I'd broken, boxed up Robbie's things and left them for him at the door. He'd texted me that he wanted to come when I wasn't home, so I broke my introvert phase and went out to The Full Sail, where I could afford a terrible beer. When I pulled a handful of ones out of my jeans pocket, that's when Tony asked me in full-on bartender mode if I was down on my luck. I couldn't be bothered to lie, so I said luck was a land of make-believe, and that I sure as fuck was.

Easiest job interview ever.

I handed out a few more beers to the early crowd. It was eightish and the non-regulars filtered in to slum it. The speed of the night crowd was actually a little exciting. The rush and bustle with Tony—we had a flow, and it worked.

Then came the bump in the road.

"Hi, Charity."

I'd gone a long time without much interaction aside from Tony, and I wanted to keep it that way. When I looked up, not wanting to recognize the voice, my stomach plummeted.

"Hey, Jen," I said. "Messin' around above ground?"

"We need to talk."

"We really don't."

Tony glanced at me, juggling a few beer bottles.

"I'm a little busy, right? I can't do this. Not now, not ever, Jen." I turned to get another Bud out of the crappy cooler for one of the regulars.

"Charity, it's Rose."

My blood went as cold as the beer in my hand. I banged it down in front of the customer. I spun on Jen, leaned across the bar, and snarled every word in hopes that I'd convince both of us that I no longer cared.

"I never want to hear her name again. That kid needs to stay clear of me which should be really fucking simple. I'm not a Harpy, she's not in this timeline," I said, waving my arms around.

"She was never meant for a normal life, Charity, you know it. You brought her back to her own time, but she…she came to the Wood. A little older—"

"Dude, it's been like, a few months."

"No. Not for her."

I fucking hated that Jen was here, interrupting the life I made, getting in the way of the good thing I had at this job.

"Fine," I spat. "Come back at two."

Leave it to a Harpy to not care if it was the "middle of the night." She nodded. "I'll be here."

That was exactly what I was afraid of.

~

Two in the morning. Bar was acceptably clean, Tony was tired, and my night was just starting. Just when I'd gotten out of the routine of having a night life.

"Night, Tony. See you tomorrow."

Tony panned back and forth between me and Jen. He didn't like it, either. Perceptive dude.

"Yeah, see you tomorrow, Charity." As Jen pushed open the door and I turned to leave, he put a hand on my shoulder. "Be careful, huh? That girl's trouble."

"Wow, first time I've heard that about someone else."

"Seriously." He glanced over my head, catching Jen's eye and leaving me in the center of the awkward. "There's something about your friend."

"We're not friends." I smiled at him, realizing that he and I were. "I'll see you tomorrow and I'll be cool. Promise." With a nod, he let me go.

Jen and I walked up to the cemetery instead of going to my place. I was in no mood to let her think she was welcome in my home, despite the fact that she hadn't done much to deserve such an attitude. I was comfortable in the cemetery anyway, went up there a lot during the day to get out of the house. It was up on a hill behind the apartment building, which was also on a hill, ancient and totally shrouded in trees. The graves there were really old, so no visitors. Just me.

I plunked down on the bench at the top of the stone stairs. "Okay, first things first. I'm sorry I took off on you, but shit happened. I had to go. I'm not a Harpy anymore, I don't want to be and that means I have to leave every part of that world behind me. It's not you, it's me. Though you did 'walk of shame' it that morning, yourself."

She sighed. She was so much different than when she was just a person. Black skinny jeans showed how bony she'd become, a plain white t-shirt and black heels instead of flowery blouses and flats. The Harpy fashion show, I guess. She sat down beside me, laughed that inappropriate laugh she'd always had. I dropped my head, wishing she was still Mom-Jeans Jen.

I would have done things a lot differently. Like never talking to her.

"I'll cut right to it," Jen said. Also unlike her. She'd always been one for small talk. "Rose is in the Wood. She…a couple of years have passed for her. She's older. I don't know how."

"The kid always had weird talent."

"Yeah. And a chip on her shoulder. And a hell of a lot of power. Charity, she killed the Queen."

She told me this with a hand on my knee, comforting me

for the words I wasn't able to absorb. The Queen…*dead*? But was she ever, really?

"Rose is one of us now."

"One of *you*, you mean."

"She's powerful, sharp. She killed dozens of Harpies—"

I sucked in a breath. "Loretta?"

"No. Only the ones who…beat her up. After she killed the Queen." Jen gulped, waiting for my reaction.

A rush of dizziness overcame me. I clutched the edge of the bench under my knees, reliving the words again. "The Queen can't die. I killed her once before." But this felt different. Rose didn't think like me, didn't act like me. What she did was thought through, executed, had motive.

The Queen was dead. Dead.

"I've never seen anything like Rose before. Her wings are *metal*. And she…she breathes fire, Charity."

My mouth could have caught flies. "Whoa."

"She's got plans." Jen turned her body to me, squeezed my hands. "She wants to give the Harpies the strength to go above ground. She makes them feel like they aren't bottom-feeders. She said she'll give the Harpies a chance they deserve —and take chances from those who don't."

I searched her face for…I don't know what. A hint of what *Jen* wanted underneath the propaganda. I found myself shaking my head at her. "Jen, those aren't your words. What does that mean, that she's taking chances—"

But I knew. I knew exactly what that meant because I'd had a very similar state of mind before I attacked Turner Reese—for her. To give her a chance and take his away. Turned out I had the wrong predator-in-the-making.

Jen broke me out of my frozen state by saying, "She'll be coming for you."

"Well, good luck to our princess Rose," I sneered, my automatic defensive reaction to any and all threats.

"Rose thinks you abandoned her, just like everyone else has."

"I did what was right."

"That's what they all say," Jen answered, and Rose would have said exactly that.

Fuck. Of course, Jen was right.

I'd thought for a hot minute that Rose could help me take the Wood apart, the ultimate redemption, two sisters rising up from the trenches. So much for the good intentions of giving her *the life she deserved* in her own time. What the Queen and I hadn't thought of was, what if Red used her childhood like a tool, taking it apart like a machine to get the end she wanted?

To become a villain?

"Guess I'm on the run again," I said coldly. I'd been forced onto the wrong path, veered to the right one semi-willingly. "It's not fucking fair."

"Running isn't your only choice, Charity."

I curled my lips in until it hurt and was probably really ugly. "What's my other choice? Fight Rosemary's Baby using what, a broken beer bottle, my wit and charm? Not fucking likely. Oh, wait, I know what you mean! You want me to go with you to the Wood, be a Harpy and save the day, right? What fun we'll have! Me, giving up everything to save you and the Harpies—to be clear, fucking *monsters* who eternally eat people in Hell—and become the ruler that our artist formerly known as the Queen would be proud of? Thanks, but no thanks. That world isn't mine. It shouldn't be anyone's." My stomach churned, my heart palpitated, tears welled. "Rose should *not* be there. She's too good for that fucking place." Fucking hell, look what I'd done to the kid.

Jen put a hand on my shoulder, but I shrugged it off. "Charity," she sighed, "You don't always have to fight."

Fuck this patronizing smile of hers, who the fuck was she to talk down to me?

"Actually, I pretty much have had to fight every second of my life, so…"

"Not the Harpies. Come with me, we want you there! Why try so hard to make a life up here, working another crappy job?"

Because I was no bright and shiny, path-of-the-righteous sort no matter what, I had to agree. The Wood always did welcome me. The Harpies, even the ones who fought me, had been my people from the second I saw them. The ugly ones, the human-ish ones, the Queen…

The Queen. Dead.

I waited too long to answer, and Jen took it to heart. "I see how it is," she said, venom in her voice. "You like to screw up other people's lives, then keep going forward, like it's *your* loss." She stuck a finger into her chest with the next words, snarling. "But it's *us,* the ones you *cared about* that have to live with it. You clean house of people you pretend matter to you, but nobody matters to you! You're selfish, cruel. I loved you, Rose loved you. The Harpies…you can't abandon the Wood of Suicides like you do everything else, Charity. It's yours whether you like it or not. The Queen saw it, I see it, Rose sees it." She shook her head, a new anger emerging. "You were never my friend. You don't know how to care about a person. I hope Robbie got away before he noticed."

When she stood up, she burst into her Harpy form. My heart lurched at the sight. Goddammit if I didn't want my wings like a junkie wanted that next high, knowing it would destroy them. No matter how long I was away, the power was always close.

"Goodbye, Charity," she said. Her lip still dipped to the side when she spoke. The last remnant of the friend I'd loved.

~

I paced the cemetery in the dark, muttering, "Fuck, fuck, fuck." A few giggling, swearing teenagers came in through the gate with beer, stolen or bought by some of-age loser. They froze when they caught me in full-on crazy.

"Stop staring or I'll take your shitty beer."

They scattered like I was the cops. Then I realized the cops would be sweeping soon enough and I left, too.

The apartment was too bright after the cemetery. Keegan chirped incessantly, caged like me, the TV was too active to be background, I could've ripped my hair out from the fucking roots, uncomfortable anywhere in this world. Except now I got tips from townies and it was the greatest acceptance I'd received since—

Robbie.

I rolled my eyes. *Saint Robbie,* I thought, in one grand fucking gesture of not deserving him ever.

"Shit!"

The realization hit me hard. Rose wouldn't come for me first—she'd go to the boarding house. Because Turner was still alive.

And who would be there to defend the boy, but Robbie.

I couldn't go near that place ever again. For the first time in I don't know how long, I took my phone out of my pocket and actually contacted someone. Someone who might know what to do.

~

*"G*ood to see you, Charity."

"Yeah, good to see you too, Psychiatrist." I fell into my usual spot, breathing out just as the cushion did the same. Tried to relax but my foot wouldn't stop tapping. Any other psychiatrist would think I was strung out on something but Mortimer knew me too well. I'd gotten him called in as an emergency—those secretaries knew I wasn't about to let up. Every second I waited was one for Red to file down her plan to the most effective version.

Jesus fuck, it had only been a minute since human time moved for me again now that I wasn't a Harpy, and just like that, time hung over me like the grim goddamn reaper.

"What's happened, Charity?"

This is it. Time to be completely honest, because you have no fucking idea what you're doing.

I told him the whole story. About time travel—to which he cocked his head—and Rose. About what we did to Turner, which made him steamed for not being notified by the authorities. And about the Facility, Jen, the danger they were all in, every last one of them. A danger with me smack in the middle when I just wanted to move on.

Now, Psychiatrist always pretended not to believe me, treated my Harpy stories as metaphors. But as fucked-up as this latest story was, it was also very well-oiled to roll off the tongue as a figment of my imagination. And—call me crazy, often—I saw something spark there in his eyes.

Recognition.

"This girl, Rose, you say?"

I nodded.

"You mentioned a Facility…"

"You're missing the point, Psychiatrist."

"Tell me the year again, Charity. What year was it?"

"1987. You're looking a little crazier than me right about now, just sayin'."

"Tell me about Rose, Charity." He kept saying my name the way he always did, but it wasn't in the same *I'm listening* mannerism as usual—he was pleading with me.

"Rose Preston. She was twelve when I took her out of the Facility. She'd lived in Boston—like I did as a kid. And she was raped—like I was as a kid. By one boy, some dick named Cody Reese."

Dr. Mortimer blanched white. "My God," he sputtered.

And he passed out cold.

Secretaries tittered over Dr. Mortimer, about how he didn't drink enough water as they bumbled over calling 911. Appointment over. I was on my own again, and I was wasting time.

I knew where I had to be.

~

Only a few blocks away, Robbie lived at the boarding house. For three months I'd missed him. Three months I'd avoided "finding" something of his in the apartment so I could beg him to come over. No drunk texting him, no showing up when I just couldn't take it anymore, or when I wanted to tell him I was torture-clean, wanted another go. Three months of not telling him how sorry I was. Three months of him avoiding me, too. Three months that he'd been in the clear, moving on just like he should be doing.

All it took was a threat from Hell to bring me closer.

Jeans, t-shirt, combat boots, no makeup, I showed up at the door, hating myself for half-hoping he wasn't there. I hadn't had a moment to hope Turner wasn't the one to answer the door.

"Turner."

"You?"

"Hey, um…"

"I'll stop you right there. Robbie!" Turner backed away from the door, shouted over his shoulder again, never blinking. I wouldn't have either—too much can happen in the blink of an eye. I'd proven that to him once.

The kitchen had changed since I'd pretty much destroyed it a few months before. I touristed around it anxiously. One more yell for him from Turner, and Robbie came bounding down the stairs like a kid on Christmas.

"Hey, what's up?" Robbie called out as his feet pounded the old wood stairs. Then he spotted me. Of course he said my name like everyone says when the worst person shows up unexpectedly. "Charity?"

"The one and only. Unless you found my body double. Bitch always takes my socks."

"You don't wear socks."

"You look good, Robbie."

"What are you doing here?" he said with that sideways shake of his head that said he felt bad for me and wished I was somewhere else.

"You're in danger." I glanced at Turner, decided I'd rather spare his life than his feelings. "You both are."

Robbie came down the rest of the stairs, got close to me. He smelled like cedar. "New…new cologne."

He ran his fingers through his hair, and my chest constricted. "Tell me about the *danger*. From who?"

I swallowed, couldn't stop risking glances at Turner, so I just faced him full-on. "Rose."

Robbie's face went through a short series of: *that's ridiculous; that's not a name I expected to hear again; how is she here*, and finally, *oh shit, she scares you*. But it ended on an accusatory glare that totally did not say, *thank you for reopening old wounds to help us, I really loved you all along; I miss you and want to come home*, or *Charity Blake, you're my hero*.

I didn't have time to get openly annoyed about that—and trust me, I was. I'd agonized over my former, current, and future fucking life choices and ended up with a resolve to do everything the hard way. Not to mention facing over-whelming guilt over both Rob and Turner, and yeah, a little fucking betrayal at the whole *I'll love you no matter what and you're beautiful in any form* thing. I kinda expected the universe to cut me some emotional slack here. For him to do the same.

But I did get a surge of who I used to be—the Charity who didn't care about not having a "normal" future, who didn't give a fuck what anyone thought no matter how they felt about her. And most of all, the Charity who thought feelings were something that stood in the way.

I was stronger than feelings.

I could have them now, but they'd never control me.

"Save your unending praise for later, Rob. Right now it's time to call in some of those good-boy favors you have with the cops and get some protection. Like, a cop entourage."

His lips turned down, eyebrows raised with humbled surprise. "You mean…you're not…"

My upper lip wrinkled, and I made my most ornery face, tongue sticking out, when I said, "*No,* I'm not—" and flapped my arms.

His unwitting little nod of approval pissed me off at being-a-nickel-short-and-the-convenience-store-dude-not-letting-it-slide level. "Turner, go get some clothes and your toothbrush, some money, you can use my duffel bag." *Jesus Christ what a martyr.* "Thanks, Charity. I'll um…text you when we get—"

Nope, he wouldn't.

And too late.

A ball of flames burst through the front door I'd so politely knocked on, sending planks of wood flying into the room, chairs spiraling, knocking down that shelf of mugs that never stood a chance. Sharp stuff everywhere, the sharpest of which was a *shing* of metal blades.

Rose, surrounded in an orange glow like some *Mortal Kombat* character.

Robbie got knocked to his side on the floor, tried to scramble up, but Rose put one black-clawed foot on his hip.

"I'm not here for you," she said. And her pretty face turned toward me at haunted doll speed. "Not even for you. Not yet."

"Good to see you too, Red."

Fury licked at her eyes—like seriously, I watched orange heat crawl up her body from the center of her exposed chest to her cheeks and ears and then tinge her eyes the color of the rising sun. "Traitor," she spat.

Sigh. "Red—"

"Stop calling me that."

"Yeah, okay, Red. What? That's what I call you, it's like an endearing thing." She started to get ragey again. *Keep it cool, Charity.* "Fine, chill. Rose. I made some mistakes—well, not *mistakes,* really, but I've had a change of heart."

She snickered. Ugly on her sweet face surrounded by golden waves of hair. First time I'd seen it unbraided. "I bet you have," she said, and curled her metal wings around herself, the sound of a hundred swords being slowly drawn, until they hovered around her like Medusa's snakes, ready for orders.

"I'm not afraid of you," I said reflexively. "I mean, yeah, I kinda am because holy shit, Rose. Horseman of the Apocalypse much? But that's not why I changed my mind." She dug her claw into Robbie's side harder, making him grunt. I put up a hand, silently asking her to stop. "You're right. Re—Rose, you're right. I left you right back where you started after being so fucking convinced I needed to get you out of there, and maybe it was a bad place and maybe it wasn't...but either way I...I said you were my sister and I left you."

Her puffy pink lips pursed, her eyes softened and the

whites came back instead of that fireball orange. "You're only saying that. You don't mean it."

"I do." Gulp. "Take me apart, kid. Look as deep as you want and see if you find any doubt in there that I should be part of your life, helping you along, no matter *what* you need help with. Go ahead." Deep breath. But she just blinked rapidly, nothing more. "I may not be good for much, but I'm committed, that's for sure. Nobody could accuse me of being half-assed, right Robbie?" Like Rose, he was silent, and managed to wiggle out from under the kid's talons. The discarded doorknob rolled toward him, slow-motion, a cartoonish mishap that I was a spectator for. Robbie stumbled, his injured hip buckling. He slipped on the knob, and fell again.

Onto Rose.

Every sound halted. The shifting of broken wood with our slightest movements. The formerly ignored frantic voices from the top of the stairs. The sirens getting closer. Every sound except a sticky *shlunk*.

Bent in half, Robbie reached for something to grab onto, pulled back when he found only more razors that sliced his fingers. He didn't wince. The pain of that was nothing, couldn't be anything when the longest of Rose's metal feathers had skewered his stomach, holding him while his arms flopped around, the only movement he could make to try...just try. There would be no freeing himself. The blank glimmer in his eyes showed it before he knew it himself. He shifted, a sucking sound breaking the silence, making way for a sob from Rose. A choked scream from me. The sirens wailed.

Rose threw herself back, the blade tearing out of him in one rough motion. I got to him before he hit the floor, grabbed him as he cried out. A tide of blood spurted from his mouth and he clung to me as we sank to the ground.

Rose screamed in the distance. The kids screamed from the stairs. I heard them, far away, but nothing mattered aside from that man I loved, in my arms, bleeding more than I thought anything could bleed, his eyes fluttering. I ran my hand over his dark waves, thought of a thousand times he'd put his fingers through it and smiled shyly at some crass thing I'd said, kissed his forehead over and over, rocking him, knowing I held him too tightly but he held me back, one arm around my waist, burrowing his face into my side. I blubbered how much I loved him over and over through sobs, and he tried to say something back, tried, but could only squeal, wheeze. He moved me off him a little with that arm around me. His doe-brown eyes slowly searched mine. His tongue peeked out as it pressed against his teeth, trying to form a word that I hoped so deeply was "love."

"I love you," I moaned, not blubbered, but *said* it, said it so he knew I meant it.

He smiled.

Raised one hand to my cheek.

It didn't get there before it fell with a *thunk* to the floor.

I howled, long, hard. "No, no, no! Robbie!" More screams. I heard every sound I made as vividly as the sound of that blade piercing his flesh, sinking in, driving him away from me, from life with or without me. A crash behind me as Rose fell into the wall, a *swoooooosh* as she slid down. No metal sounds. No clacking of talons on the floor. Just the wails of a little girl who'd done too much.

Turner pulled Robbie from me hurriedly, put a dish towel on the wound, instantly soaking it in red. The white turned pink, red, redder, redder, spread until the white was gone. Turner crying, rocking Robbie. Robbie's body.

Red and blue lights reflected in Turner's eyes as we stared at each other over my lover's body. My eyes darted at Rose, back to Turner. He slowly shook his head.

There was no way out now. Not for any of us.

Rose took my hand. I let her, unable to make anything happen, just wait for the police to come and do something with me, her… I was too tired of fighting for *everything*, only for this shit life I'd earned.

I destroyed everyone I met.

When I thought she'd just wanted to hold my hand and wait for the police, I was wrong. Very, very wrong.

With her free, blood-coated hand, she made movements through the air, tracing lines to open the portal.

"No," I mumbled, as if half in a coma, "no, don't go."

Rose took the air *apart*—didn't create a portal the way I used to, but *changed* the world, disassembled it. A chasm, emptier than I felt at that very moment, like it was the only place someone like me should be. My heart wanted to be there but instinct told me the thing was wrong.

"Ro…Rose." Police erupted through the broken door, guns drawn, screaming at us to get down. But when they saw her, they fell back fast. The second line of cops never even made it to the door before either catching sight of Rose or feeling the chasm reaching into the ugliest parts of them, pulling them closer. The emptiness reached and reached out, reaching for the police, the kids, for all of us. The portal to the Wood of Suicides was like a living thing that she'd created. A puppet of her most volatile parts.

I was frozen, numb, hoped that this was how death felt.

Rose took my chin in her hand, turning me to her roughly. "We aren't part of this. If you're with me, you're with me."

Poor kid, I thought reflexively. She sounded so sure of herself, but her terror rummaged inside of me, digging for a place that understood her. I didn't turn away from her *looking*, wanted her to see that I knew, I knew she didn't mean it, that I was there for her. And I couldn't explore the bloodshed and the living hole she'd created. The kid was being taken apart, too. *She's just a child, all alone.*

My throat was a desert from gawking at Robbie, the cops, the chasm, Rose, the blood. I couldn't speak, didn't know what to say. Robbie was *dead.* Murder. Prison. Funeral. Gone. I'd do anything for her, she was all I had, I was all she had— but we couldn't just disappear.

I shook my head at her, mouth working, no sound.

The paramedics had managed to get over the scene, scrabbling to Robbie underneath the chasm, barely able to focus on him as they threw glances over their shoulders at the calling darkness, working with shaking hands to get him on a bed.

It was no use.

Some of the police snapped out of it when they saw the paramedics in action and yelled at us to get down. I dropped to my knees, thankful for the rest. Rose didn't.

"Stay back!" she yelled, her voice a myriad of dark things, not Rose's real voice. The cops turned their guns on her. And the weapons fell to pieces on the trashed floor, taken apart by a flick of her hand. *"I won't hurt you,"* she told the cops. *"I'm helping you before anything goes wrong."* Goddamn cops froze up again, sneaking glances at each other, hands empty of anything but flashlights.

I got a *really* bad feeling in the split second of quiet right then.

Rose turned her back on the cops and focused on Turner.

Head shaking, throat lumped up, I tried to tell her to stop. I grabbed her hand. She said in her own Rose voice, "If you're with me, you're with me."

"Rose…"

She looked away from me and back at him and I could only watch as Turner Reese *changed.* His face went from his own to someone else's. *Cody,* I realized. Their faces mixed and he moaned as his features warred with each other, taking each other apart to become Cody's or Turner's, a severe and horrendous mix of both.

When Rose was finished taking one apart and mixing him with the other, she had a grand finale planned.

With one dramatic twist of her hips, her shoulder pointed toward the floor, and one wing had fanned out in a wide, stunning arc.

Splitting Turner Reese into a dozen sections like an egg slicer had gone right through him.

The pieces remained suspended there, hovering like the worst magic, until with a slippery *shluck,* same sound that had killed Robbie, the boy fell into pieces.

Vomiting went around the room, catching like a yawn, snapping me out of my numb and dumb state. Complete panic overtook every officer and medic, all the kids screaming from the stairs, nobody was immune. Rose spun slowly, metal feathers dripping blood and gore, and addressed her audience.

"What you've just seen," she began in that booming, authoritative voice of Harpy Rose, *"is only a sliver of the pain his father caused me as a child a third of his age. And that boy,"* she pointed at the quivering chunks that had been human seconds before, *"would before long become the same monster his father was. I've seen it, ingrained in his DNA, a layer of him. It's where he comes from, and it was his future. I merely eliminated the threat."*

Sobs broke out amid the vomiting and screaming. Robbie's body was still so close to me, too close. I brushed pieces of Turner Reese off of him frantically.

But the chasm beckoned me, looked deep inside me just like Rose could, and found the part that thirsted for the blood of the wicked men of the world. Fucking hell, the Harpy desired dirty blood.

Rose tiptoed through the nightmare she'd created, stopping, gaping, whimpering here and there. *She's scared of what she's done,* I thought. *She's not lost yet.* When she got to the chasm, the thick gray owlish feathers on her lower half now dripping with the blood she'd waded through, she looked to me. Not expectant, but questioning. Waiting for me to say something, to pony up and take the lead.

"I can't condone this, kid," I said, finding my voice.

"You nearly *did* this," she said sadly. "You do worse all the time."

"You're right. Nearly. What you're doing...I know you're raising an army. Is this what you want the world to look like, Rose?"

She cast her eyes around to the mayhem of the room, and she sobbed once before saying, "This is what I've always seen."

Then she gave into the chasm, disappearing into the Wood.

~

*T*he boarding house closed down. All those kids that Robbie tried to keep clean, or keep safe, or do both, had to go to foster families or other boarding houses. Hopefully none ended up in juvie or on the street for the first, second, or third time.

I wandered a lot after being questioned. Got picked up the next night for public drunkenness when they found me screaming incoherently at people outside 7-11. Spent that night in lockup, more because they didn't know what else to do with me. Nobody ever did, even though everyone had ideas. I was never much for a plan. I was like the Joker in that way. What was it he said...something about being like a dog chasing a car, but not knowing what to do if he caught one.

She never laid a hand on him, but everyone saw Rose kill Turner Reese. The cops who'd been there all made the same statement—at least the ones able to make a statement from their hospital beds. I'd be seeing those guys at Psychiatrist's office after Rose's stunt. Nobody alive saw what happened to Robbie, but the consensus was that Rose did that, too. After all—they knew me around the station, but not as a murderer.

"Thanks, Brinkley."

"That's *Officer* Brinkley, Charity," he said as he walked me out. The cops walked me out of the station now, like every time was a date. If that were the case, I should have a ring by now. When we got to the door, he stopped me, took me by the shoulders. The dad face he gave me made me want to hug him, for him to hug me until I fell asleep. "Take it easy. Lay low, get to that psychiatrist of yours." He put a hand on the side of my head, cupping it. "Take care of *you*. You've had it rough, kiddo." He gulped, furrowed his eyebrows, glanced around at the other officers nearby. "We're all sorry about Robbie. He was a good man."

I couldn't say thanks or anything, just give this really sad nod that got me the offer of a ride home, which I took.

~

*P*sychiatrist took a personal leave.

What. In the actual. Fuck.

I was in a total crisis mode, and fucking "reached out" the way he always told me I needed to, and here he was, boating off Lake Douchebag somewhere? The good news was that my anger issues resurfaced at this, momentarily replacing my grief, and I was good ol' jerk Charity again, which was like stepping into a hot shower after being covered in blood.

Cleary. That was the scientist, the guy she missed from the Facility. I mean, she didn't *say* she missed him, but it was obvious the way she talked about him like he wasn't a weirdo in a secret lab. If that was in 1987, how old would the guy be now? Christ, I hated math.

Yup, focus on the pain Rose is in, and you won't want to gouge her eyes out with her own morbid-ass razor blade feathers and make her eat them.

I shook the thought off. Tried to. But fucking hell, that little bitch killed Robbie. It didn't matter that it was an "accident." There are no goddamn accidents when you show up ready to murder people, only casualties.

There is nothing *fucking casual about my Robbie.*

I whipped an ugly coffee mug full of pens and pencils across the room, gritting my teeth so hard I wished they'd break off. That fucking child, a *child*, stole what chance I had left at something good. Stole *Robbie's* chance, all of his chances. He deserved to live out his life more than any one of us, even Rose. He was the only one doing the right thing, everything good, his entire life, and that little fucker destroyed all the good he would have done. She took every chance the kids who hadn't met him yet would have had. Their lives couldn't possibly be as strong as they would have been without Robbie there to believe in them, sticking by them every moment their weaknesses showed up to devour them. This selfish little fuck destroyed actual generations. Not to mention killing that kid—brutally killing that kid—who didn't deserve to die.

Who was next? What would she do now?

Holy shit, leave it to me to find a kid more of a nightmare than I ever was. She needed help, she needed a friend, and she needed to be stopped.

Getting to Rose without being a Harpy would require like, Nancy Drew-ish tactics. Then I just had to convince her not to rip my guts out.

Refreshed from an actual morning shower, not just a

metaphorical one, I threw on a skirt and a t-shirt—conservative as fuck, just like me these days—pulled my hair into a ponytail which was a new thing also and surprisingly comfortable despite being pedestrian, and grabbed my keys. Hand on the doorknob, I wondered where in hell I thought I was going. I had ideas, but that was it. Contact Psychiatrist and find out how he knew Rose, why he'd taken off so suddenly after having a little fit over the mention of her name, or find Cleary—which meant going to the Facility. Plus getting there, in Boston, a forty minute drive away with no gas money, if regular cars could even access it. Someone had gone to a lot of trouble to make sure the Facility looked abandoned, blending in with all the other wrecks around it. I'd seen no signs of life outside it when I'd been there before. The staff probably had some underground garage, or they lived in the tunnels like Disney employees... Being able to fly overhead had its perks. I wanted to do something, but *how?*

"Keegan, tell me what to do," I muttered, door still open, hand gripping the knob. He was no help.

I had to talk to somebody. Somebody who wasn't a Harpy.

Frustrated out of my mind, I slammed my fist into the door frame, making Keegan flutter in his cage. I muttered a sorry and wished to fuck I could just do something *right* to undo all this ugliness. But the only way I knew how to help was by drawing blood.

Blood.

The word brought a rumbling in the pit of my stomach, a sweep of hunger that went deeper than my gut.

"I gotta go, Keegan," I said under my breath and he chirped back. Not for the first time, I wished someone would close the cage door on me, but let me die slowly and pleasantly inside.

~

*B*lood. It was out here, I knew it.

My head whirled around in the bright sun, and my body spun with it when I found nothing, frantically searching, early morning walkers and joggers glaring at me. The Harpy billowed up like a ghost inside me, but no heat came with her, alerting me that someone needed killing. *And it's daytime. Never in daytime.*

The smell made my hands shake, the tips of my toes burn, waiting to split open and let the talons emerge. My arms tingled with growth from wrist to shoulder as the feathers tried to needle their way through, and I couldn't breathe that scent for one more second. Roller-coaster-drop of the stomach mixed with the refreshed hunger for meat had me double over, but I forced myself upright, afraid of anyone coming close to see if I was okay. I didn't trust myself near anything with flesh and blood, and then an unpleasant thought invaded.

If Rose ever feels like this, she won't even try to stop herself.

The realization had me run for the closest bushes, and the measly contents of my stomach came up in a flash of heat. Heat that clung to my forehead, made me dizzy and tip over onto my side, the world spinning fast.

I crawled under a hedge in someone's neglected front yard, inches from those incessant fucking joggers and still in range of the blood scent, now mixed with vomit. The thought of Rose ever needing the blood as much as I did, of the constant question of her worth, of her thinking she was nothing more than death, of wanting a life less than being a murderer... If ever I wished I could die, it was this moment, slumming it like that homeless guy, the one Robbie's drummer said bore striking resemblance to Meatloaf. And as nasty as I felt, the word *meat* made my stomach rumble. I moaned helplessly, unable to see any way to ever recover, to ever get myself to stand and walk again. I'd die under this hedge, sweating and sick, finally done in by myself in the most pathetic way ever.

There was no new blood scent, nothing more than my own addiction curling up like devil horns and trying to have their way. A coping mechanism that made decisions easy. Want. Need. Hunger.

This is what the Harpy had done to me.

"No," I choke-growled. The puking was a disgusting fucking metaphor for…something. But that winged bitch was out of my life, had to be.

I dragged myself to my feet, head spinning, and goddammit if the rich blood scent didn't come my way again. I shook it off, righted my day-old stinky clothes—and then I saw it.

The butcher shop.

"Fine," I huffed out loud to the beast. "You want some action? This is the last you'll get of it."

I stormed across the street and up a block to the butcher shop, hating to admit to myself that I was a fucking idiot for never visiting before. I mean, a love of meat isn't a crime, and if raw meat each day keeps the bird bitch away…

The doorbell clanged annoyingly behind me, and the intoxicating scent of fresh meat accosted me, like entering a bar after being dry too long, making me heady and swoony. I breathed it in deep, hard, with that sucking sound and everything. I definitely freaked out the butcher, and that's gotta be some kind of world record. I brushed hair off my sweaty face, and smiled charmingly. Though judging by the butcher's face, maybe I was laying on the charm too thick.

"Hi, Butcher Boy, I'd love twenty bucks worth of your bloodiest whatever. No, make it fifteen, I need coffee money."

Fluorescent light glinted off his mostly bald head, and he put his hands on his oddly-comforting-to-look-upon round belly under his bloody apron. "We're not open, lady."

"Door's open," I said, bug-eyed and pointing.

"We. Aren't. Open," he spelled out.

I rolled my eyes. "I need meat, you need money. Does it really fucking matter?"

"It's not TIME."

"Fine, holy hell. Thanks for nothing."

I slammed the door the best I could behind me but it didn't really work because it was one of those really light glass doors. Now I was totally restless, feeling sick and hungry, the Harpy buzzing at me, and still full of *thoughts* and *feelings,* topped off by being slighted my meat. I walked around the butcher shop, circling it like a shark, intent on waiting him out while trying not to envision the soft crinkle of the butcher paper, the pink stains inside when I unwrapped it. It would have to wait. *I* would have to wait.

My aggravated muttering was interrupted by a loud splash and that delicious smell again. I found myself staring at a Butcher Boy Minion who was dumping, probably illegally, a bucket of blood out back. I walked right at him, and he was staring at me with narrowed eyes, blood dripping on his shoes from the bucket he held. The boy had those cute pimples, you know the ones that aren't nasty, but it means he's really just a kid. His blond hair was kinda messy, not on purpose, and he was rail-thin. Pretty brown eyes. *This kid coulda been friends with Turner Reese.*

"Ma…ma'am?" he stuttered. I was about six inches from him, after all, and just searching him, and all around him.

"Yeah, hey buddy," I said. God, he was covered in little meaty bits and blood ran in a river toward a drain. "Whatcha doin' with that?" I said, pointing at a second bucket of meat.

"I just throw it away, ma—"

"Call me 'ma'am' again and you'll be the one in the bucket." To his credit, the kid didn't run screaming. "You gonna eat that?" I reached for the bucket and he moved aside. I sat on the tiny stone wall separating the shop from the next yard and took a deep whiff of the unused parts.

"Miss?" the boy said in a hush. But that was it. He glanced at the shop's back door, indicating he had work to do.

"Kid, it's like, balls early. The boss doesn't need you. You're working with a customer." He nodded, blinking like a sonofabitch. I held out my twenty and winked at him. He took it. "Mind if I eat this here?" I picked a hunk of red-laced light pink parts out and tore into it before he could answer. When I opened my eyes after the soul-satisfying cold flesh left its flavor in my mouth, the kid was lab-rat-white and gaping. "Save you a piece?" He shook his head so fast I thought it would fly off. *Mmmm, neck muscle blood.*

I crossed my legs, leaning an elbow on my knee, and studied the kid as I gnawed on a bone. "Here's the thing…"

"Matt."

"Here's the thing, Matt." Crunch, crunch, crunch. "I have a lot of shit," whirling my free hand around my head, "up here, you know? And if I ever want to move forward, I gotta unload it. I gotta unload it on someone who's got no stake in it. You get what I mean?"

"Yes."

"Good. 'Cuz Psychiatrist is MIA, my boyfriend's dead, my —little sister—is into some serious shit, and I'm trying to get *out* of that serious shit. I need someone to listen. I also need meat, Matt. Lots of meat."

He cleared his throat, the color back in his face. The sun was burning brighter and I needed real sleep.

"Um," he said, "I empty the stuff at seven every morning? I could…I could come earlier? Before my dad gets here?"

"Whoa-oah, that's your dad? He's super fun, right?"

That got a shy laugh from him. And a smile from me.

"I'll be here tomorrow morning at 6:30, okay?" he asked.

"Be there or be square, Meat Matt."

He turned toward the door, then back to me for a second. "Could you…not call me that?"

"What, you like Blood Bucket Boy?"

"Just Matt," he called back.

"The Winnards with the Innards."

"Matt will be great," he said. He had a shiny little sideways smile that reminded me of Jen's once upon a time. I shoved a gristly wing with feathers still on it into my mouth.

"You got it, Matt. You bring the meat, I'll bring the mouth."

ROSE

THE WOOD OF SUICIDES, NO YEAR

"*R*ose, I can't help you if you don't speak to me."

I wanted Jen to go away but I had no willpower to speak.

"You've been like this for days. Curled up in a ball, shaking. I don't know what you're saying…" She trailed off and as soon as her voice was gone the images came back.

Sean Singh.

Turner Reese, sliced like a can of cranberry sauce on Thanksgiving.

The window opening, the din outside assaulting me.

Squeezing my eyes shut under the covers, Mommy calling me weakly, blackness inside and out.

And so many other things I didn't understand, didn't remember. Bloody, screaming faces, claws digging slowly into veins, pools of intestines, howling laughter, more violence than I knew existed.

And I'd seen so much.

The holes.

The holes were opening in my brain again.

I was going to die.

"Rose, let me take you home, for help."

That incessant voice, annoying, whining woman. But she could help me. I needed help.

"I know you need help, Rose, that's good, that's good, keep talking."

I'd said that out loud?

"Cleary."

"What? Say it again, Rose."

"Cleary." Louder, stronger.

"Cleary. Cleary. Where?"

Frustration blossomed in my chest, that she couldn't just *take it apart* in my mind and know what I needed, it was all right there and she was too dense to reach for it.

I snapped out of the ball I'd become in a single jerking movement, my bones cracking. I grabbed Jen, her face a vision of fear that sent a jolt of fear right back through me. *I'm scary, just like Sean Singh, just like Cody.* I didn't want to be scary.

"Come," I pleaded with the blue-eyed woman. She bobbed her head, and with a thrust of my arm, I opened a doorway to the Facility.

ROSE

THE FACILITY, 1989

"She's here!"
"Oh my God."
"What's happened to her?"
"What *is* she?"
"Don't touch her!"
"Get me out of here!"
"Demon!"
"Check her vitals."
"Miss—"
"Jen."
"Miss Jen, you need to wait outside."
"No."

"Everybody, quiet!" I shouted, my own voice frightening me. I searched the crowd of nurses—some shaking, others crying, one clawing at the door handle to get out. "Please, Mr. Cleary. Just you. Just you."

He nodded and everyone else ran for their lives.

Mr. Cleary bent to pick me up off the floor where I'd landed in the clatter of scrap metal that were my wings. Fine lines of blood rose to the surface, scattered razor slices on my arms, legs. A warm trickle down my nose, my forehead, my cheek. "Don't touch me!" I cried, but carefully avoiding my wings, my claws, he reached under my arms and lifted me with a grunt, got me to the bed.

"Can you make the wings go away?" Mr. Cleary asked me gently, smiling a little.

I was exhausted, but I imagined taking the wings apart a little at a time, envisioning it, until finally the weight of them disappeared. And they were heavy—not an extension, like Charity's or the Queen's were, or even Jen's humble ones. My wings were a burden, a test of my strength.

"I was so sure I could do this," I whimpered to Mr. Cleary as he sat at the foot of my bed, the sheets torn from my blades, streaks of red left behind.

"Do what? Rose, where have you been?"

Focusing my blurry eyes on him, Jen in the background, I confessed in a tiny voice. "The Wood of Suicides."

He pursed his lips the way Daddy used to when I'd eaten all the Halloween candy without asking, blinked long and slow, then took my wrist to get my pulse. All was forgiven, I understood. "You'll tell me what's happened, won't you, Rose?" he asked, but it wasn't a question. He was a scientist, after all. "How you've become this."

"I'll try," I murmured.

He trained his eyes on me, satisfied with my pulse. "You've never *tried* anything in your life, Rose Preston," he said, bopping me on the nose with one finger. I sobbed at the kindness. "You'll tell me where you've disappeared to, who you've been with, who *that* is," he snapped, pointing at a complacent Jen, "and how you've changed into another form of being." His voice was low and dangerous, angry like Mallory Keaton's dad when he caught her smoking marijuana. "You owe me that," he said, and his voice cracked. He smirked, like he found the emotion funny.

"You love me," I said, my voice flat.

He clenched his jaw, stood up. "Get some rest, Rose. I need to talk to your friend."

"I don't need rest. I've been...catatonic. Trapped in my mind."

"Depressive episode?" he asked.

"More than that." My throat tightened, my heart constricted. I wanted to take the walls of my room in the Facility apart by every brick, the mortar, the paint, but I focused and forced myself to say what I knew was true. "My memory is making holes in my brain. If you don't help me, I'll die."

With a deep breath, he put his hands on his hips, scrunching up his lab coat. He looked at the floor, as if he, too, wanted to take something apart but he of course could not. "You healed your brain once before, Rose. You're stronger now. Evolved, a...a..." he waved his hands at me in disbelief, "a higher being. You have the power to take apart a tumor like *that*," he said, snapping his fingers.

Gulping, I said, "That's just the thing. It's not a tumor this time. They're *holes*. I can't take them apart. They don't exist."

Nodding, he wiped a hand down his face. "What happens when you remember everything?"

"Then...then I disappear, too."

～

I'd been given a short opportunity to make something of my life. My life would not be long, but my reign could be. The leader I'd become in the Wood of Suicides would be a legacy long after my memories obliterated me as a human.

My mother always said I was meant to become someone who mattered because I already did matter. Mr. Cleary told me I had the power to change the world under everyone's noses. Charity Blake said there was no one in the universe as powerful as Rose Preston—not Rose the prodigy, just *me*. But something stronger always comes along.

My time was limited.

I had much to do. No time for depression, self-doubt, fear, trauma, childish coping mechanisms. There was only time to leave my mark. I knew enough fairy tales to understand that happy endings didn't happen for the short-lived characters.

In my short time, I could provide so many with the happy endings they deserved. For the Harpies. For so many girls and women who would know great violence.

I could change the world. And I would.

Saying goodbye to Mr. Cleary wasn't an option. Abandonment was a language that I spoke fluently, and Mr. Cleary would never, could never leave me. The *only* person who'd never leave me. His deepest layer breathed a life of its own, a driving force to find greatness. Not only had he found the potential for limitless greatness with me, he'd found something he hadn't known he wanted: love. I saw his surprise at it whenever he was near me.

I couldn't survive without his support. I couldn't take on the responsibility I intended to without being able to *rest*, and I could only get that in the Facility. With Mr. Cleary. The only one who really loved me.

…who was still alive.

"The nurses are all afraid of me," I'd said to him.

He hung his head, his elbows on his knees as he leaned close to me, always intently poring over my words. He bobbed his head up and down before meeting my eyes again. "Yes."

"I'm still Rose."

"Yes," he repeated.

"But they weren't this afraid of me before, not even the ones I'd hurt."

He sighed. "You were a little girl before. It's a lot easier to be afraid of someone that isn't human."

I glanced at what was supposed to be the one-way glass mirror, saw the huddle of white coats on the other side of it.

"I don't want them here," I said. "Not now, not ever."

Mr. Cleary told me it wasn't that easy.

His shoulders went back, he leaned away when I turned my gaze on him, teeth gritted against threatening tears. *He can* never *say no to me,* I thought to myself. "I've done things…taken apart a man with the mere thought of it. You're telling me you can't get rid of people who change sheets and take a temperature and old men who carry clip boards." I gulped. "I want no one here who fears me more than they care about me."

The stillness of his face, the lack of his impressed smirk told me that he was afraid of me, too. But he would stay. For whatever his reasons were, he would stay.

With a single nod, he got up and left the room.

~

"*J*en should be here."

Mr. Cleary put down a stack of sheets on my desk.

"She's gone home," he said simply.

"The Wood."

"Yes," he answered, bustling about the room. He put a pack of Fruit Stripe gum on the end of my bed and I grabbed it up, grinning despite myself.

She'd left me.

She's still Charity's friend. She can't be trusted.

"I would like to see Dr. Mortimer," I said.

Mr. Cleary stopped moving. "Dr. Mortimer is no longer available, Rose. You're no longer his patient. You haven't seen him in a very, very long time."

"And he won't come back."

"No."

"He won't help me with my memories, the parts I can't fill in. Even though they're making holes in my brain. He won't come back even if he can save my life." He was still board-stiff, and I looked harder into him, right through, and saw exactly what I didn't want to. I gasped, horrified, and ashamed. "He won't come back *because* he could save my life," I whispered. I'd seen it like a play that hadn't been written, tasted the vomitous resignation straight through Cleary from Dr. Mortimer's depths. He would kill himself before he ever spoke with me again.

No scientist was there when Mr. Cleary's eyes settled on mine, only deep regret and fear. "I'll find a way to save you myself," he breathed, brows furrowed.

Head shaking like mad, I cried, "You don't know every-thing that happened to me, what I'm missing! He's the only one." Never mind my brain, my heart deteriorated with the understanding. I would die.

There was no choice for me but to be a Harpy. Humanity would kill me.

But choice was something I refused to sacrifice. No, sacrifice was something best left to those terrors-in-waiting who would destroy another's life without thinking. Sacrifice was snipping off potential at its greenest to prevent the toxic flower from blooming. Its sweet, fresh petals, though deserving of one more minute in the sun, must be crushed early, because every second it's permitted to bask and ripen is one stolen from a younger, innocent life. My *choice* was to shear the carnivorous, poisonous beauties before the allure of their scent turned deadly. I would do the deed despite losing moments of its purity because I, alone, saw what lurked within.

Potential is opportunity, but fate is a gaping jaw. Open, poised, waiting to consume innocence because it was the one who planted the seed.

I had a duty. To save the truly innocent from the ones who were temporarily so. I would grow into my fate the way the unwittingly doomed rapists and torturers would grow into their gene pools. Those whose destinies were predetermined for them, I would stop it. *Their* choices were the ones to be smothered. Their choices carried too much weight. My choice was to sharpen my skill, take them apart before fate's jaws closed and made them monsters. Fate and choice wound together like vines—me, the healthy one strangling the weeds like Turner Reese. It all built in my mind in a simple construct more important than anything Charity Blake could do.

Mr. Cleary bit his lip, a new thing for him.

"He's not the only one."

"I'm sorry, what?"

"Dr. Mortimer isn't the only one who knows the depths of your past. There's someone else, Rose."

My body positively bubbled with giddiness, a sensation I only got after eating a lot of raw meat, and my brain was moving too fast trying to come up with simple solutions. Manic, I swung by Psychiatrist's office after guzzling a gallon of coffee basically out of the pot. Chased it with a couple of shots to soothe my skin, which felt like lightning in this mood.

"Hey, looking for Psychiatrist, got one?"

The lady at the desk hated me. All of them did, they were all the same person. This one wrinkled her nose as if she could smell the shooter from behind the glass.

"If you mean Dr. Mortimer, he's still not in the office, Miss Blake." She gave me a once-over again. "You don't seem well. You should go to the emergency room."

"It's not that kind of emergency." *Deep breath, don't scream at her, you'll get dragged out of here.* "I really need to discuss personal business with him that affects *him*."

"That sounded like a threat, Miss Blake."

You don't want me to threaten you, lady. "It's not a threat, goddammit, it's important. About him, his past. It's critical. Crucial." Those were secretary words.

"I can refer you to—"

"No! No 'referrals to.' It's not about some other guy's past, is it? No, it's about Psychiatrist's. So get him on the horn or I'll find another way to get to him and who will be to blame for that, when I show up on his hidey-hole doorstep, hmm? Do it the easy way, Florence. Call the doctor." I smiled a little to see which button on the phone she was reaching for so quickly. "Na uh, not security—Mortimer. I'll be waiting." I flashed a distinctly frightening grin, Harpy-reminiscent, the kind that stuck a finger of fear into everyone.

I plopped my skinny ass into an uncomfortable chair, thought of picking up a magazine to show I was ready to hang around, but decided making every other lunatic in the waiting room antsy would get me results faster. I smiled at them all, sickening smiles as they gaped at me or hid their eyes behind their phones. "Hey, buddy," I said to a guy in all tan a few seats away, "you've got pyro written all over you. Tell me 'bout your last fire."

His eyes lit up but he glanced at the secretary, who clenched her jaw and puffed up her nostrils like a bull. Good, it was working then.

Winking at a lady dressed too well to be actually nuts, I leaned over a little closer and asked if she wanted to see my boobs in the bathroom. She grumbled, moved to another seat. "Anyone want to keep me company?" I called out to the rest of the busy waiting room. "I'm saving this seat especially for you," I said, pointing to the hairiest man I could find.

The secretary slapped her hands on the desk, stood up, and knocked on the window separating her from the common folk. "Miss Blake, if you would please—"

"I'll approach the bench, Your Honor." *Accidentally* kicking over a few handbags on the floor as I made my way for extra measure, I said, "Yes, how can you help me?"

Her eyes burned with fury, it was great. "I will contact Dr. Mortimer, if you'll just leave please. I won't bother with security again this time."

"Yeah, those guys are nice. I don't think they like you much, Florence."

"Patricia."

"No, I'm Charity. So yeah, I'll just wait right outside these doors," I said, sweeping an arm to indicate the hallway, "until I hear from you in a few short minutes. Because you're definitely going to arrange for me to talk to him. No running to security. We all know that running from your problems just lands you in Psychiatrist's office. And whaddya know! Here we are already! So don't try and pull one over on me, Carla, because I might be trash, but I'm not stupid. Capiche?"

"Patricia..." another librarian-ish secretary or whatever said from deeper in the office.

"I'm fine," Carla-Florence barked. "Wait outside. I'll be with you in a minute."

"See, was that so hard?" I popped a piece of Rose's gum in my mouth and with a mass goodbye to the waiting room, took my spot just outside. It wasn't five minutes before Secretary met me out there, post-it in hand.

"Here," she said, thrusting it into my palm. "I know where you'll be, and I have the police on speed dial."

"Everyone does, jackass, it's called 911."

With a red face and a barely-stifled scream, she slammed back through the door, leaving me to read the note scrawled in obviously secretary bubble writing: *Outside in 15 minutes.*

~

"This is fucking weird, Psychiatrist."

Psychiatrist hadn't said a word or even looked at me since I got into the passenger seat of his Volvo. *He seriously cracked up,* I thought. Like, his thinning hair disheveled, glasses askew, eyes red-rimmed, but wearing a button-down shirt and decent pants like that would hide the crazy.

"Can I bring you to my home?" he asked quietly.

"I'll stray away from any buy-me-dinner-first jokes for now, but yeah, sure." I liked how Florence told me she knew where we'd be when *I* was the one going to *his* house. "You haven't gone totally off-rail, right? You're not a serial killer now? Or am I the start of it?"

He didn't answer. I had to shake my head to clear memories of Evan's house, everything that started weird and ended worse.

"Don't offer me anything to eat, okay?" I blurted out breathlessly, then squeezed my eyes shut at my idiocy. But Psychiatrist was too wrapped up in his own weirdness to notice.

I sat at his normal kitchen table in his normal house, and it was nothing like Evan's. I was certain there was no Chinese food in his fridge to bond over. Pictures of children were framed on the walls. I never once thought of him having children. I never once thought of him as a person at all, I guess. Fucking hell, I was selfish. It hit me in more ways every minute since Robbie…

Dr. Mortimer put a glass of water on the table in front of me and sat down, staring at me like we were in an interrogation room. The hackles on my neck rose.

"You passed out that day because I told you about Rose." I started right in. The meat-eater adrenaline hadn't subsided and every second I was more anxious.

"Rose Preston was my patient," he said, clearly not

wanting to dwell. He brushed a sweaty palm through his mess of wispy hair, making it stand up straight in spots. "Your timeline works with the timeframe when I was treating her."

"For her rape."

He nodded.

"That's normal stuff for you, though. What made you freak out, faint, take off from work—"

"I stopped seeing Rose when it became obvious she had abilities that weren't human, not normal. When she began to remember her past, the abilities became stronger, and Rose became…" He trailed off, eyes glazing over, lip curling up in a momentary wince.

"Psychiatrist?"

"More than I could handle alone. She had this *fire* in her…"

"Fire. Actual fire, right?" No answer. "Well, it is now," I said. "And she has wings, she's a Harpy, Psychiatrist, she has wings made of metal. She…she killed Robbie—by accident but she still did it, and she killed a boy—"

"My God."

"Yup. She killed a kid, like, in a way even I'll have nightmares about. His dad was the one who raped her when they were kids."

Psychiatrist was always one step ahead, didn't question me, only gave me more answers, knew what I was driving at right away, saw the high I was on underneath it. "But that's not where Rose's troubles ended. She was bullied terribly at school, and harassed by another boy."

It clicked together fast, too fast, like a puzzle exploding in my brain.

She'd gun for everyone who ever hurt her.

Rose felt wronged by almost everyone.

And Rose was a mastermind with crazy powers who'd murdered an *ancient queen.* The Harpies loved her, a child of their own. They would follow her. She had an army and she'd know exactly how to motivate them.

Dr. Mortimer continued, "Certainly she'll hunt down this boy who terrorized her in elementary school—this man now —Sean Singh."

I found my head bobbing in agreement, but the brain inside was whirling even faster. "Turner was Cody's son. She has Cody in the Wood of Suicides." I cringed to think of the thoughts of suicide Rose could plant in a person's brain, far more powerful than anything the Queen had done to keep her place fully stocked. Rose had a more personal, crueler agenda. I trained my eyes on Mortimer's, trying with every inch of me to brand the words into him, make him understand. "She won't stop with this Singh guy. She'll find his family. She'll destroy anyone she decides is bound to be a predator because of what's in their genes or whatever. And the kid, she can *see* their genes." I gulped. "Dr. Mortimer. Have *you* done anything to upset Rose?"

The horror flickered across his face with a trembling lower lip. "She wouldn't," he whispered.

I glanced at the wall of framed photos. "She's so alone… The kid's been hurt by everybody—or at least she thinks so. And she knows she's special, she wants to change it, make things better, get rid of future generations of predators, assholes, people with bad intentions. Problem is, she's starting to think *everyone* has bad intentions." Psychiatrist was a good man, his kids would be good kids. He'd never *hurt* her. But in Rose's warped, aching mind… "No one is safe."

Psychiatrist was babbling to himself. Great.

"Hey!" I snapped my fingers in front of him. "We have to stop her. You know this Mr. Cleary. You can get to him in the Facility."

He sat back in his chair, fiddling with the button on his shirt.

"You can't get out of this. You're not safe, your kids aren't safe. Help me."

"Charity, couldn't you convince her as the Harpy that—"

"Whoa, whoa, what the *fuck?* I realize you're going fucking crazy with guilt or whatever over how things ended with Rose—and I still don't know why—and that you've thrown your Psychiatrist persona right the hell out the window, taking a patient home and all, but you cannot be fucking serious if you think all that time spent convincing me *not* to be a monster is just gone now because it *works for you?* Are you fucking kidding me?" I was ready to jump across the table and slap him. What a fucking betrayal. Constantly fucking betrayed.

Shit, if Rose feels an ounce of the anger I feel right now at him...

Fuck it, I did indeed jump across the table and grab him by the shirt, popping a few buttons, making him yelp. "Here we go, up close and personal," I said through gritted teeth. "You want to get this close to Rose Preston?" He shook his head madly. "Smart." I let him go, sat back down, wished I had a cup of coffee. "I'm not gonna Harpy it up to conveniently protect you, but I will help you. You've always helped me. Red needs to be understood, we have to help her let go of the past or she'll be trapped as a Harpy forever, in actual Hell." I dropped him from my grip.

"Red?"

"Yeah, like the—"

"Tea, yes." He took a deep breath, straightened his shirt. "You've become quite the psychiatrist yourself," he kidded, and we both relaxed. "You love the girl, don't you?"

"Yeah, well." *I just can't throw her away.*

He leaned across the table, glint of excitement in his eyes. "This is a monumental breakthrough for you, Charity! Understanding someone else's needs, selflessly wanting the best for her, and reaching out of your comfort zone to ask for help!"

I felt myself blush, for fuck's sake. "Guess I've kicked myself out of the nest a bit." Nervous laugh, just like Jen's. *Christ almighty.*

He was all bright now, happy to do his work, and I was kinda proud of myself for being the one to inspire him, try as I might to not give a fuck. "Charity—"

"Psychiatrist."

"Tethering yourself to others is a different kind of freedom, I hope you see that."

That hit me, caught me by surprise, the words ringing in my belly. I sneered to draw attention away from the well of tears in my eyes. "Yeah, thanks, sure." Back to business. "Enough about me. First time you've ever heard me say that, right? You know as well as I do—Red can't suffer in silence with these memories of hers. Kid can take the Earth apart one rock at a goddamn time. She'll take the world down with her."

His lip trembled. *What did you see in her, Psychiatrist?*

"Her mind is a machine, Charity. She was a scientist before she knew the word, disassembling nature to see what made it tick, and she'll do the same to anyone she suspects is a threat. Now she's fortified with experience and more power. And anger." His jaw went slack when he said, "No human or monster stands a chance."

I gulped, the inevitable truth slapping me harder than any of my mother's boyfriends could have. "You're wrong," I whispered, my boiling blood freezing inside me. The first time I bothered to look forward, and this was the future I was faced with? "She won't execute *everyone* she condemns. They'll beg for their lives, and Red, she's persuasive as fuck, vulnerable but so goddamn smart." I couldn't help smiling at her brilliance. "She'll find the dark that haunts them—she did it with me—" She was my sister, the thing I needed most in the world. "She'll show them the light and they'll follow her *anywhere.* Rose is a natural leader, and the Wood of Suicides needs a leader, Mortimer." My head swam, my heart hurt, throat tight and squeezing harder.

His eyes rolled around like he was looking for some way out of this nightmare. Just like all of Rose's victims would do.

"*I* had victims," I muttered. "Rose doesn't think that way."

"She's the hero of her story," Mortimer murmured.

"She's always thinking a step ahead, a big picture person, way smarter than me. She won't be out just killing bad guys —she'll make them *hers.* When she's done with them they'll all drink the Kool-Aid."

"What do you mean?"

I could hardly contain my frustration at his slowness. "Think about it. Sweet-faced angel of death shows up, tells him the worst about himself, shows him a way out—before you know it, he's in the Wood of Suicides. The ones she shows 'mercy' will worship her, like that bug-eating dude from *Dracula.*"

Mortimer's lip trembled.

"No wibbling. Get me to Cleary," I said. "He's the place to start. The only one who can help us stop her." *Or save her.*

Psychiatrist was analyzing me—I knew the look too well. Something snapped him out of his mortal terror that scared him more. "What?" I asked him. Didn't want the answer.

"The brain can only survive so much. The spirit has limits, too. Charity, she won't come out of this one."

"She will. She's better than the rest of us."

"And worse, goddammit!" he shrieked. "Stronger isn't better. She must be eradicated before she ends us all! There's no helping her anymore! Only stopping her. She's inhuman, Charity. Incurable."

"She's a *kid.* You're so proud of my evolution into regular human being?" I managed to say through my desire to just lie down and die, to not be a part of the future Rose could create, to not witness the multiple things she'd think of that I didn't, and yet I'd do anything to save her from herself. "Don't stop helping me now. Follow me. You don't get to just *quit.* There's no quitting this life, you taught me that. If you don't let me lead you through bringing her back, you've proven that Hell is already on Earth, Mortimer. Be better. Be like me."

The deepest sigh from him, a loosening of his being. "The student becomes the teacher," he quipped.

Relief, and a sort of foreign joy crashed through me in gorgeous violence. A certainty that I was facing my end and my purpose at once. "Your brain," I said, "and my *heart,*" the word a punch to my gut, I clutched my chest to hold it in as it ached and soldiered on, "were meant to come together from the very beginning." We were one big circulatory system. Mortimer, me, Rose, Turner and Cody, Maggie, Painter, everyone. Fleshy pinkness and throbbing red, organs like I'd consumed and saved, the decayed and the fresh, twisted together in a cage of bones. "Between us, we can save everything that matters."

ACKNOWLEDGMENTS

My deepest thanks to Jill and Sanjana at WME for believing that the Harpy needs to be seen and heard, for going out on a limb and trusting their guts.

Thank you to my team at Audible who keep asking for more. You helped build this dream.

Thank you, everyone at Inked Entertainment who've come together to make these books the best they can be.

And my greatest gratitude to Debbie and David Purse, pinnacles of kindness, generosity and support. Their vision has made me bring The Harpy from one book to a Harpy-verse. Without their hearts and brains, none of this would have come to life, and I'm constantly amazed by what they can accomplish. They're limitless. David, you inspire me and support me in a way I never thought possible. I love you, my friend. Thank you for creating this world with me.

Thank you for reading THE HARPY 2: EVOLUTION! If you enjoyed the book, I would greatly appreciate it if you could consider adding a review on your online bookstore of choice.

Reviews make a huge difference to the success or failure of a book, especially for newer writers like myself. The more reviews a book has, the more people are likely to take a shot on picking it up. The review need only be a line or two, and it really would make the world of difference for me if you could spare the three minutes it takes to leave one.

With all my thanks,

Julie Hutchings

RUNNING HOME
BOOK 1 IN THE VAMPIRES OF FATE SERIES
BY JULIE HUTCHINGS

Death seems to follow Ellie Morgan. Now someone's out for blood.

Tucked away in rural New Hampshire, awkward booklover Ellie lives a simple life, keeping herself detached from others. With just a single friend in a world that has taken her family from her, a part of Ellie longs for something more than nights on the couch and dull days working in a gift shop.

Enter Nicholas French.

Something about the new guy in town sparks a burning desire within Ellie, something more than his rugged good looks and piercing gaze that can see into her lonely soul. Fate has led him to Ellie's small town, and Nicholas' interest in her is more than undeniable attraction.

As Ellie learns more about Nicholas' dark yet noble nature, she discovers a part of herself she never knew existed, and why the threads of her destiny feel intertwined with his. But Ellie's chance at a new life comes at a cost, and in the end, fate may be the one to decide if she'll live or die.

RUNNING HOME is the first book in the dangerously passionate and deeply romantic Vampires of Fate series where not all monsters are evil, and love comes with a bite.

Get your copy of RUNNING HOME today and delve into the new and seductive paranormal romance series everyone is talking about.

THE WIND BETWEEN WORLDS
BOOK 1 IN THE FIVE POISONS SERIES
BY JULIE HUTCHINGS

Celeste is the Witch of Stars, but the future of her coven is far from bright...

Something is stirring in The Gone, the dark realm where demons reign supreme and plot to break through the chains which bind them. Sworn to protect the world from those evil forces, sixteen-year-old Celeste's greatest powers are chewing anxiety pills and stress-eating.

As the head of her generation of witches known as the Five Poisons, Celeste struggles to lead the wild and reckless girls who are supposed to be her sisters-in-magic. Where they are free and uninhibited by their powers, Celeste keeps hers buried inside, afraid to use her magic which weakens her mother every time she dares use it.

When a demon manages to slip into their world in the form of a troubled boy with a destiny as big as her own, Celeste must confront her fears head-on and take charge. As Celeste tries to reunite her estranged sisters to come together as one to fulfill their purpose, a hidden truth unearthed from the depths of the covens' history is revealed. A secret which threatens to burn both the human and demon worlds to ash, and the only thing standing in its way are five dangerous and dysfunctional girls.

**THE WIND BETWEEN WORLDS is the first book in the wickedly dark and spellbinding Five Poisons series where not all demons are evil, and magic comes at a price.
COMING SPRING 2021!**

www.ingramcontent.com/pod-product-compliance
Lightning Source LLC
Chambersburg PA
CBHW050749190726
48285CB00005B/1588